"There are other ways to cope with stressors in life."

"You sound like a shrink," Reza murmured. But then he glanced up. Surprised to find her watching him, her eyes dark, her cheeks flushed. What would she do if he touched her? He reached out, cupping her calf, still slick with sweat.

Emily stilled, her eyes going wide as he slid his hand down her smooth skin. Her lips parted. But she didn't pull away.

"You can't be serious?" she whispered. "We're outside. In broad daylight." And chasing those words was arousal, hot and pulsing through her veins to settle between her thighs.

"You've never gotten naked outside before?" His voice was thick.

"Not next to an army airfield," she whispered. She felt foolish. There wasn't anyone around for miles.

"Trees overhead." He inched his hand higher up the back of her leg. "I hear it's great stress relief."

"Getting naked or getting caught?" She gasped as his thumb stroked the inside of her knee. Such a simple touch. Electric and erotic. "I have to go back to work."

He shifted then to crawl between her thighs. He captured her between his body and the truck. "You don't need anyone's permission for this," he whispered against her mouth. "Be wild for once."

JESSICA SCOTT

All for You

FOREVER

NEW YORK   BOSTON

Copyright © 2014 by Jessica Dawson
Excerpt from *It's Always Been You* copyright © 2014 by Jessica Dawson

Forever
Hachette Book Group
1290 Avenue of the Americas
New York, NY 10104

www.HachetteBookGroup.com

Printed in the United States of America

Originally published as an ebook

First mass-market edition: November 2014
10 9 8 7 6 5 4 3 2 1

OPM

Forever is an imprint of Grand Central Publishing.
The Forever name and logo are trademarks of Hachette Book Group, Inc.

The Hachette Speakers Bureau provides a wide range of authors for speaking events. To find out more, go to www.hachettespeakersbureau.com or call (866) 376-6591.

The publisher is not responsible for websites (or their content) that are not owned by the publisher.

To Shawntelle
For lifting me up

Acknowledgments

I have to thank Shawntelle Madison for standing with me, for making me laugh, for being my strength when I wondered why we keep doing all of this madness. Elisabeth Barrett for making me laugh and being the inspiration for the scene where Emily tries to put together her gear. My agent, Donna Bagdasarian, thank you for your continued hard work and dedication. And finally, my talented editor Michele Bidelspach: Thank you for falling in love with Reza and for letting me write him the way that he deserved to be written. My work is stronger with your guidance. Thank you for giving me back the joy in writing.

All for You

Prologue

Camp Taji, Iraq

2007

Sergeant First Class Reza Iaconelli had seen better days. He closed his eyes, wishing he was anywhere but curled up on the latrine floor in the middle of some dirty, shitty desert. The cold linoleum caressed his cheek, soothing the sensation of a billion spiders creeping over his skin. He had to get up, to get back to his platoon before someone came looking for him. Running patrols through the middle of Sadr City was so much better than being balled up on the bathroom floor, puking his guts out.

He'd sacrificed his dignity at the altar of the porcelain god two days ago when they'd arrived in northern Baghdad. It was going to be a rough deployment; that was for damn sure. Dear Lord, he'd give anything for a drink. Anything to stop the madness of detox. Why the fuck was he doing this to himself? Why did he pick up that godforsaken bottle every single time he made it home from this goddamned war?

The walls of the latrine echoed as someone pounded on the door. It felt like a mallet on the inside of a kettle drum inside his skull. "Sarn't Ike!"

Reza groaned and pushed up to his hands and knees. He couldn't let Foster see him like this. Couldn't let any of his guys see him like this. "You about ready? The patrol is gearing up to roll."

Holy hell. He dry heaved again, unable to breathe until the sensation of ripping his guts out through his throat passed. After a moment, he pushed himself upright and rinsed out his mouth. He'd definitely seen better days.

He wet his brown-black hair down and tucked the gray Army combat t-shirt into his uniform pants. Satisfied that no one would know he'd just been reduced to a quivering ball of misery a few moments before, he headed out to formation, a five- to seven-hour patrol through the shit hole known as Sadr City in his immediate future.

He was a goddamned sergeant first class and he had troops rolling into combat. They counted on him to do more than show up. They counted on him to lead them. Every single day.

Maybe by the time he reached thirty days in-country, he'd stop heaving his guts up every morning. But sick or not, he was going out on patrol with his boys.

The best he could hope for was that he wouldn't puke in the tank.

Chapter One

Fort Hood, Texas

Spring 2009

Where the hell is Wisniak?" Reza hooked his thumbs in his belt loops and glared at Foster.

Sergeant Dean Foster rolled his eyes and spat into the dirt, unfazed by Reza's glare. Foster had the lean, wiry body of a runner and the weathered lines of an infantryman carved into his face, though at twenty-five he was still a puppy. To Reza, he'd always be that skinny private who'd had his cherry popped on that first run up to Baghdad. "Sarn't Ike, I already told you. I tried calling him this morning but he's not answering. His phone is going straight to voice mail."

Reza sighed and rocked back on his heels, trying to rein in his temper. They'd managed to be home from the war for more than a year and somehow, soldiers like Wisniak were taking up the bulk of Reza's time. "Have you checked the R&R Center?"

"Nope. But I bet you're right." Foster pulled out his phone before Reza finished his sentence and started walking a short distance away to make the call.

"I know I am. He's been twitchy all week," he mumbled, more to himself than to Foster. Reza glanced at his watch. The commander was going to have kittens if Reza didn't have his personnel report turned in soon, because herding cats was all noncommissioned officers were good for in the eyes of Captain James T. Marshall the Third, resident pain in Reza's ass.

Foster turned away, holding up a finger as he started arguing with whoever just answered the phone. Reza swore quietly, then again when the company commander started walking toward him from the opposite end of the formation. Reza straightened and saluted.

It was mostly sincere.

"Sarn't Iaconelli, do you have accountability of your troops?"

"Sir, one hundred and thirty assigned, one hundred and twenty-four present. Three on appointment, one failure to report, and one at the R&R Center. One in rehab."

"When is that shitbird Sloban going to get out of rehab?" Captain Marshall glanced down at his notepad.

"Sloban isn't a shitbird," Reza said quietly, daring Marshall to argue. "Sir."

Marshall looked like he wanted to slap Reza but as was normally the way with cowards and blowhards, he simply snapped his mouth shut. "Who's gone to the funny farm today?"

The Rest and Resiliency Center was supposed to be a place that helped combat veterans heal from the mental wounds of war. Instead, it had become the new generation's stress card, a place to go when their sergeant was making them work too hard. Guys like Wisniak who had never deployed but who for some reason couldn't manage to wipe their own asses without someone holding their hands abused the system, taking up valuable resources from the warriors who needed it. But to say that out loud would mean agreeing with Captain Marshall. Reza would drop dead before that ever happened.

Luckily Captain Ben Teague approached, saving Reza the need to punch the commander in the face. The sergeant major would not be happy with him if that happened. Reza was already on thin ice as it was and there was no reason to give the sergeant major an extra excuse to dig into his fourth point of contact.

He was doing just fine. One day at a time, and all that.

Too bad guys like Marshall tested his willpower on a daily basis.

"So you don't have accountability of the entire company?" Marshall asked. Behind him Teague made a crude motion with his hand.

Reza rubbed his hand over his mouth, smothering a grin. "Sir, I know where everyone is. I'm heading to the R&R Center after formation to verify that Wisniak is there and see about getting a status update from the docs."

Marshall sighed heavily and the sound was laced with blame, as though Wisniak being at the R&R Center was Reza's personal failing. Behind him Teague mimed riding a horse and slapping it. Reza coughed into his hand as Marshall turned an alarming shade of puce. "I'm getting tired of someone always being unaccounted for, Sergeant."

"That makes two of us." Reza breathed deeply. "Sir."

"What are you planning on doing about it?"

He raised both eyebrows, his temper lashing at its frayed restraints. His mouth would be the death of him someday. That or his temper.

Right then, he didn't really care.

He started ticking off items on his fingers. "Well, sir, since you asked, first, I'm going to stop by the shoppette for coffee, then take a ride around post to break in my new truck. I'll probably stop out at Engineer Lake and smoke a cigar and consider whether or not to come back to work at all. Around noon, I'm going to swing into the R&R Center to make sure that Wisniak actually showed up and was seen. Then I'll spend the rest of the day hunting said sorry excuse for—"

"That's enough, Sergeant," Marshall snapped and Teague mimed him behind his back. "I don't appreciate your insubordinate attitude. Accountability is the most important thing we do."

"I thought kicking in doors and killing bad guys was the most important thing we did?" Reza asked, doing his damnedest not to smirk. Damn but the man tried his patience and made him want to crack open a cold one and kick his boots up on his desk.

Except that he'd given up drinking. Again. And this time, it had to stick. At least, it had to if he wanted to take his boys downrange again.

The sergeant major had left him no wiggle room. No more drinking. Period.

"Sergeant—"

"Sir, I got it. I'll head to the R&R Center right after formation. I'll text you…" He glanced at Foster, who gave him a thumbs-up. Whatever the hell that was supposed to mean. Wisniak was at the R&R Center, Reza supposed?

"You'll call. I don't know when texting became the army's preferred technique for communications between seniors and subordinates. I don't text."

Reza saluted sharply. It was effectively a fuck off but Marshall was either too stupid or too arrogant to grasp the difference. "Roger, sir."

"Ben," Marshall mumbled.

"Jimmy." Which earned him a snarl from Marshall as he stalked off. Teague grinned. "He hates being called Jimmy."

"Which is why you've called him that every day since Infantry Officer Basic Course?"

"Of course," Teague said solemnly. "It is my sacred duty to screw with him whenever I can. He was potty trained at gunpoint."

"Considering he's a fifth generation army officer, probably," Reza mumbled. Foster walked back up, shaking his head and mumbling creative profanity beneath his breath. "They won't even tell you if Wisniak has checked in?"

"I practically gave the lady on the phone a hand job to get her to tell me anything and she pretty much told me to kiss her ass. Damn HIPAA laws. How is it protecting the patient's privacy when all I'm asking is if the jackass is there or not?"

Reza sighed. "I'll go find out if he's there. I need you to make sure the weapons training is good to go." Still swearing, Foster nodded and limped off. Too bad Foster wasn't a better ass kisser; he'd have already made staff sergeant.

But Marshall didn't like him and had denied his promotion for the last three months because Foster was nursing a bum leg. Granted, he'd jammed it up playing sports, but the commander was being a total prick about it. It would have been better if Foster had been shot.

"Damn civilians," Reza mumbled, glancing at Teague. "I get that the docs are only supposed to talk to commanders but they make my life so damn difficult sometimes."

"They talk to you," Teague said, pushing his sunglasses up on his nose and shoving his hands into his pockets.

"That's because they're afraid of me. I look like every stereotype jihadi they can think of. All I have to do is say *drka drka Mohammed jihad* and I get whatever I want out of them."

"A Team America: World Police reference at six-fifteen a.m.? My day is complete." Teague laughed. "That's so fucking wrong. Just because you're brown?"

Reza shrugged. Growing up with a name like Reza Iaconelli had taught him how to fight. Young. With more than just the asshole kids on the street. He'd learned the hard way that little kids needed a whole lot more than attitude when standing up to a grown man.

"What can I say? No one knows what to think of the brown guy. Half the time, people think I'm Mexican." He started to walk off, still irritated by Marshall and the unrelenting douche baggery of the officer corps today. They cared more about stats than soldiers. It was total bullshit. The war wasn't even over yet and it was already all the way back to the garrison army bullshit that had gotten their asses handed to them from 2003 on.

"Where are you heading?" Teague asked.

"R&R. Need to check up on the resident crazy kid and make sure he's not going to off himself." He palmed his keys from his front pocket. Reza slammed the door of his truck and took a sip of his coffee, wishing it had a hell of a lot more in it than straight caffeine.

He ground his teeth. Things would have been different for Sloban if they'd gotten things right. If *he'd* gotten sober sooner. But no. He'd dropped the ball and Slo had paid the price.

He'd rather have his balls crushed with a ball peen hammer than deal with the R&R Center. He hated the psych docs. They were worse than the bleeding heart officers he seemed to find himself surrounded with these days. Just how he wanted to start off his seventy-fourth day sober: arguing with the shrinks.

Good times.

"I don't really think you understand the gravity of the situation, Captain."

Captain Emily Lindberg bristled at the use of her rank. The fact that a fellow captain used it to intimidate her only irritated her further.

Add in that he was standing in front of—no, he was leaning over—her desk trying to back up his words with a little threat of physical intimidation and Emily's temper snapped. Captain Jenkowski was built like a snake—tall and solid and mean—and he was clearly used to bullying his way through docs to get what he wanted.

Well not today.

She inhaled a calming breath through her nose and spoke softly, deliberately attempting to keep her composure. "I'm sorry, Captain, but I'm afraid you're the one who doesn't understand. Your soldier has experienced significant trauma since joining the military and his recurrent nightmares, excessive use of alcohol to self-medicate, and inability to effectively manage his stress are all indicators of serious psychological illness. He needs your compassion, not your wrath."

"Specialist Henderson needs my size ten boot in his ass. He sat on the damned base last deployment and we only got mortared a few times. He's a candy pants wuss who has a serious case of *I do what I want-itis* and now he's come crying to you, expecting you to bail his sorry ass out of a drug charge." Emily could practically see smoke coming out of the big captain's ears.

Once upon a time she would have flinched away from his anger and done anything to placate him. It was abusive jerks like this who thought the army was all about their ability to accomplish their mission. The mouth breather in front of her didn't care about his soldiers.

It was up to folks like Emily to hold the line and keep the army from ruining yet another life. There had already been more than fifty suicides in the army this year and it was only April. "What Henderson needs, Captain Jenkowski, is a break from you pressuring him to perform day in and day out. My duty-limiting profile is not going to change. He gets eight hours of sleep a night to give the Ambien a chance to work. And if you don't like it, file a complaint with my boss. He's the officer in charge of the hospital."

"You fucking bitch," he said. His voice was low and threatening. "I'm trying to throw this little motherfucker out of the army for smoking spice and you're making sure that we're stuck babysitting his sorry ass. Way to take care of the real soldiers who have to waste their time on this little weasel instead of training."

The door slammed behind him with a bang and Emily sank into her chair. It wasn't even nine a.m. and she'd already had her first go round with a commander. Good times.

A quick rap on her door pulled her out of her momentary shock. "You okay?"

She looked into the face of her first friend here at Fort Hood, Major Olivia Hale. "Yeah, sure. I just..."

"You get used to it after a while, you know," Olivia said, brushing her bangs out of her eyes.

"The rampant hostility or the incessant chest beating?" Emily tried to keep the frustration out of her voice and failed.

"Both?"

Emily smiled grimly. "Well that's helpful."

Moments like this made her seriously reconsider her life in the army. Of course, her parents would be more than happy for her to take the rank off her chest and return home to their Cape Cod family practice. The last thing she wanted to do was run home to a therapy session in waiting. Who wanted to work for parents who ran a business together but had gotten divorced fifteen years ago? At least here she was making a difference, instead of listening to spoiled rich kids complain about how hard their lives were or beg her for a prescription for Adderall so they could stay up for two days and prepare for their next exam.

Here she could make a difference. Do something that mattered.

Her family wouldn't understand.

Then again, they never had.

"Can I just say that I never imagined that I'd be going toe-to-toe with men who had egos the size of pro football linebackers? Where does the army find these guys?"

"Some of them aren't raging asshats," Olivia said. "There are a lot of commanders who actually care about their soldiers."

An Outlook reminder chimed, notifying her that she had two minutes. Emily frowned then clicked it off. "It must be something special about this office then that attracts all the ones who don't care."

She'd recently moved to Fort Hood because it was the place deemed most in need of psychiatric services. They had the unit with the highest active-duty suicide rate in the army. She was trying her damnedest to make a difference but the tidal wave of soldiers needing care was relentless.

Add in her administrative duties on mental health evaluations and sometimes, she didn't know which day of the week it was.

"Does it ever end?" she whispered, suddenly feeling overwhelmed at the stack of files on her desk. Each one represented a person. A soldier. A life under pressure.

Lives she did everything she could to save.

Olivia shrugged. "Not really." She glanced at her watch. "I've got a nine o'clock legal brief with the boss. You okay?"

She offered a weak smile. "Yeah. Have to be, right?"

Olivia didn't look convinced but didn't have time to dig in further. In the brief moment she had alone, Emily covered her face with her hands.

Every single day, Emily's faith in the system she'd wanted to help weakened. When officers like Jenkowski were threatening kids who just needed to take a break and pull themselves together to find some way of dealing with the trauma in their lives, it crushed part of her spirit. She'd never imagined that confrontation would be a daily part of her life as an army doc. She'd signed up to help people. She wasn't a commander, not a leader of soldiers. She was here to provide medical services. She'd barely stepped outside her office so all she knew was the inside of the clinic's walls.

She'd had no idea how much of a fight she'd have on a daily basis. Three months in and she was still shocked. Every single day brought something new.

She wasn't used to it. She doubted she would ever get used to it. It drained her.

But every day she got up and put on her boots to do it all over again.

She was here to make a difference.

A sharp knock on her door had her looking up. Her breath caught in her throat at the sight of the single most beautiful man she'd ever seen. His skin was deep bronze, his features carved perfection. There was a harshness around the edge of his wide full mouth that could have been from laughing too much or yelling too often. Maybe both.

And his shoulders filled the doorway. Dear Lord, men actually came put together like this? She'd never met a man who embodied the fantasy man in uniform like this one. The real military man was just as likely to be a pimply-faced nineteen-year-old as he was to be this...this warrior god.

A god who looked ready for battle. It took Emily all of six-tenths of a second to realize that this man was not here for her phone number or to strip her naked and have his way with her. Well, he might want to have his way with her but she imagined it was in a strictly professional way. Not a hot and sweaty way, the thought of which made her insides clench and tighten.

She stood. This man looked like he was itching for a fight and darn it, if that's what he wanted, then Emily would give it to him.

It was just another day at the office, after all.

"Can I help you, Sergeant?"

Reza glanced at the little captain, who looked braced for battle. She was cute in a Reese Witherspoon kind of way, complete with dimples and except for her rich dark hair and silver blue eyes. If Reza hadn't been nursing one hell of a bad attitude and a serious case of the ass, he would've considered flirting with her.

Except that the sergeant major's warning of *don't fuck up* beat a cadence in his brain, so he wouldn't be flirting anytime soon. Besides, something about the stubborn set of her jaw warned him that she wasn't someone to tangle with. She didn't look tough enough to crumble a cookie, and yet she'd squared off with him like she might just try to knock him down a peg or two. This ought to at least make the day interesting.

Reza straightened. She was the enemy for leaders like him, who were doing their damnedest to put bad troops out of the army. People like her ignored the warning signs from warriors like Sloban and let spineless cowards like Wisniak piss on her leg about how his mommy didn't love him enough.

This wasn't about Sloban. He couldn't help him now and that fact burned on a fundamental level. He released a deep breath. Then sucked in another one. "I need to know if Sergeant Chuck Wisniak signed in to the clinic."

"I'm sorry but unless you're the first sergeant or the commander, I can't tell you that."

Reza breathed hard through his nose. "I'm the first sergeant."

Her gaze flicked to the sergeant first class rank on his

chest. He wasn't wearing the rank of the first sergeant, so his insignia was missing the rocker and the diamond that distinguished first sergeants from the soldiers that they led. Sergeants First Class were first sergeants all the time, though.

Her eyes narrowed. "Do you have orders?"

Reza's gaze dropped to the pen in her hand and the rhythmic way she flicked the cap on and off. He swallowed, pulling his gaze away from the distracting sound, and struggled to hold on to his patience.

"First sergeants are not commanders. We don't have assumption of command orders." He pinched the bridge of his nose and sighed. "Ma'am, I just need to know if he's here. Why is this such a big deal?"

"Because Sergeant Wisniak has told this clinic on multiple occasions that his chain of command is targeting him, looking for an excuse to take his rank."

"Well, maybe if he was at work once in a while he wouldn't feel so persecuted."

The small captain lifted her chin. "Sergeant, do you have any idea what it feels like to be looked at like you're suspect every time you walk into a room?"

Something cold slithered across Reza's skin, sidling up to his heart and squeezing tightly. "Do you have any idea what it feels like to send soldiers back to combat knowing they lost training days chasing after a sissy-ass soldier who can't get to work on time?"

A shadow flickered across her pretty face but then it was gone, replaced by steel. "My job is to keep soldiers from killing themselves."

"And my job is to keep soldiers from dying in combat."

"They're not mutually exclusive."

Silence hung between them, battle lines drawn.

"I'm not leaving here without a status on Sarn't Wisniak," Reza said.

Captain Lindberg folded her arms over her chest. A flicker in her eyes, nothing more, then she spoke. "Sergeant Wisniak is in triage."

"I need to speak with him."

Lindberg shook her head. "No. I'm not letting anyone see him until he's stable. He's probably going to be admitted to the fifth floor. He's extremely high risk. And you're part of his problem, Sergeant."

Reza's temper snapped, breaking free before he could lash it back. "Don't put that on me, sweetheart. That trooper came in the army weak. I had nothing to do with his lack of a backbone." Reza turned to go before he lost his military bearing and started swearing. She'd already elevated his blood pressure to need-a-drink levels and it wasn't even nine a.m.

He could do this. He breathed deeply, running through creative profanity in his mind to keep the urge to drink at bay.

Her words stopped him at the door, slicing at his soul.

"How can you call yourself a leader? You're supposed to care about all your soldiers," she said, so softly he almost didn't hear her.

He turned slowly. Studied her, standing straight and stiff and pissed. "How can I call myself a leader? Honey, until you've bled in combat, don't talk to me about leadership. But go ahead. Keep protecting this shitbird and tie up all the counselors so that warriors who genuinely need help can't get it. He doesn't belong in the army." He swept his gaze down her body deliberately. Trying to provoke her. Her face flushed as he met her eyes coldly. "Neither do you."

Emily sucked in a sharp breath at Iaconelli's verbal slap. In one sentence, he'd struck her at the heart of her deepest fear.

It took everything she had to keep her hands from trembling.

Her boss Colonel Zavisca appeared in the doorway, saving her from embarrassing herself.

"Is there a problem, Sergeant?"

Sergeant Iaconelli turned and nearly collided with the full-bird colonel, who looked remarkably like an older version of Johnny Cash.

Sergeant Iaconelli straightened and his fists bunched at his sides. "You don't want me to answer that. Sir."

"I don't think I appreciate what you're insinuating."

"I don't really give a flying fuck what you think I'm insinuating. Maybe if your doctors did their jobs instead of actively trying to make my life more difficult, we wouldn't have this problem."

"What brigade are you in, Sergeant?" her boss demanded.

She watched the exchange, her breath locked in her throat. The big sergeant's hands clenched by his sides. "None of your damn business."

Colonel Zavisca might be a medical doctor but he was still the senior officer in charge of the hospital. Emily had never seen an enlisted man so flagrantly flout regulations.

"You can leave now, Sergeant. Don't come back on this property without your commander."

The big sergeant swore and stalked off.

Emily wondered if he'd obey the order. She suspected she already knew the answer.

Her boss turned to her. "Are you okay?" he asked. Colonel Zavisca's voice was deep and calming, the perfect voice for a psych doctor. It was more than his voice, though. His entire demeanor was something soothing, a balm on ragged wounds. His quiet power and authority stood in such stark contrast to Sergeant Iaconelli.

Men like Sergeant Iaconelli were energy and motion and hard angles. And he was rude. Colonel Zavisca was more like some of the men at her father's country club except without the stench of sophisticated asshole. He was familiar.

"I'm fine, sir. Rough morning, that's all."

Emily stood for a long moment, Sergeant Iaconelli's words still ringing in her ears. He had no idea how much his comment hurt. She didn't know him from Adam but his words had found her weakness and stabbed it viciously.

In one single sentence, he'd shredded every hope she'd held on to since joining the army. She'd wanted to belong. To be part of something. To make a difference. He'd struck dead on without even knowing it. Her family had told her she'd never fit into the military. She fought the urge to sink into her chair and cover her face with her hands. She just needed a few minutes. She could do this.

The big sergeant didn't know her. His opinion did not matter. Her parents' opinions did not matter.

If she kept repeating this often enough, it would be true.

Her boss glanced at the clock on her wall. "It's too early for this."

She smiled thinly. "I know. Shaping up to be one heck of a Monday. Is triage already booked?"

He nodded. "Yes. I need you in there to help screen patients. We need to clear out the folks who can wait for appointments and identify those who are at risk right now of harming themselves or others."

"Roger, sir. I can do that. I need to e-mail two company commanders and I'll be right out there."

"Okay. Don't forget we have the staff sync at lunch."

Even this early, the day showed no sign of slowing down and all she wanted to do was go home and take a steaming hot bath. She'd been trying to work out a knot behind her left shoulder blade for days now and things just kept piling up. She needed a good soak and a massage. Not that she dared schedule one. She'd probably end up cancelling it anyway.

"There's that smile. Relax. You're going to die of a heart attack before you're thirty. The army is a marathon, not a sprint."

"Roger, sir." She waited until he closed the door before she covered her face in her hands once more. She could do this. She just needed to find her battle rhythm. She'd get into the swing of things. She wasn't about to quit just because things got a little rough.

Her cell phone vibrated on her desk. Oh, perfect. Her mother was calling. Not that she was about to answer that phone call. She couldn't deal with the passive-aggressive jabs her mother was so skilled at. Besides, she was probably just going to press Emily to give up on—as she put it—slumming in the army and come home.

She'd worked too hard to get where she was and she damn sure wasn't about to go limping home. How could she? Her parents had looked at her like she was an alien when she'd told them about Bentley. As though she had somehow been in the wrong for her fiancé's betrayal. As though, if she'd been woman enough, he never would have strayed.

If she ever went home again, and that was a really big if, she would do it on her own terms. She'd walked away from everything in her life that had been hollow and empty.

She was rebuilding, doing something that mattered for the first time in her life. Every day that she avoided calling home or being the person her father and his friends wanted her to be was a victory. No one in her family had supported her when she'd needed them. She might not have found her place yet in the army but just being here was a start. It was something new and she wasn't about to give up, no matter how much Monday threw at her.

Tuesday really needed to hurry up and get here though, because as Mondays went, this one was already shot all to hell.

Chapter Two

The text message of doom vibrated on Reza's phone as he pulled into his company ops parking lot. Reza was wanted in the sergeant major's office.

He did his best to avoid the brigade headquarters. There were too many names memorialized on the walls. Too many ghosts that walked the halls, overshadowing everything they did. Demanding that Reza do better. Train harder. Do more to bring their boys home.

He swallowed, gripping the steering wheel as his phone vibrated in his lap again.

He supposed he couldn't avoid the sergeant major forever.

Maybe today the ghosts would leave him be.

He walked down the long hallway of the Reaper Brigade headquarters, fear choking him as the memories of lost friends hung like empty, cold spaces in the sterile, buffed hallway. He wanted to keep walking but his boots slowed, stopping in front of the memorial for their fallen brothers and sisters. Smiling faces. Easy grins.

They'd had no clue that the photos on the wall would be how they were memorialized for all eternity. His gaze landed on his old first sarn't and his throat tightened. Story's loss was still fresh enough to hurt.

Reza scrubbed his hand over his mouth, swallowing, trying to push the lump down.

"Ornery bastard," he muttered, staring at Story's pic. Story hadn't smiled in his picture. He'd never smiled, that Reza could recall. But that had done nothing to dampen Reza's loyalty to his friend. He clenched his fists by his sides.

Funny how he'd gotten so used to seeing "private" or "sergeant" as the rank of the dead. First Sergeant...

He'd served with Story as a drill sergeant back at Sand Hill eons ago, when they'd both been more motivated, less cynical. Before the war had chipped away at their humanity.

His eyes burned and he blinked rapidly. Shit, he couldn't go into the sergeant major's office all misty-eyed. He'd never hear the end of it.

Reza didn't have time for long chats. He had men to train. They were about nine months out from another deployment—Reaper's 4th tour into Iraq—and that meant that there simply weren't enough hours in the day to get everything done. He hoped Foster had moved on with the weapons training without him. It was better to suffer during training than bleed in war.

The sergeant major knew that. So why was he wasting Reza's time with an office call? Probably some spouse complaining about Tricare again or something else that the military couldn't fix for them.

Reza was of the mind-set that if the army had wanted you to have a family, it would have issued you one. He stayed single for exactly that reason. There was no end to the number of soldiers he had to pick up at the R&R Center because they'd married the first girl they'd lost their virginity to and that girl had turned out to have the heart of a pit viper.

Reza walked into the command group. A skinny private

who looked like he needed to report to the dermatologist motioned for him to head straight in. Sucking in a deep breath and shoving away the sadness that always shadowed him when he was in the headquarters, he rapped on the door frame.

Sarn't Major Giles glared up from his computer. "Get your ass in here, Ike."

Sarn't Major Giles was not a friendly man. There was no teddy bear hiding beneath his tough, sandpapery exterior. As far as Reza knew, the man didn't have a heart and his veins were filled with pure meanness. He'd told Reza once that all that kept him going was training his troopers. That would explain why he was on marriage number four but hey, Reza wasn't there to judge.

But no matter how much Reza liked to avoid him, there was no one more effective at taking a scared nineteen-year-old private and giving him the confidence to be the first man in the stack to kick in a door. Giles might not be nice but he was effective.

"Iaconelli," Sarn't Major said, kicking his feet up on his desk. "What happened at the R&R Center today?"

Reza frowned. "Nothing significant to report." It was his way of trying to brush off answering the old man. He really didn't feel like rehashing the entire conversation with the doc and then her boss. Sergeant majors tended to get cranky when sergeants stepped out of line—something Reza was prone to do more often than not.

Giles chomped on the cigar in his mouth, his eyes pitiless and cold. "I'll give you one more chance," he said quietly. "Explain to me why I've got a full-bird colonel calling over here, pissing on the boss's leg about you."

Ah, hell. Reza clenched his fists at the small of his back. "I got into it with one of the docs over there. She wouldn't confirm whether one of my dudes was there or not."

"So you cussed out her boss?" Deadly, quiet words.

A chill slithered up Reza's spine and settled around his shoulders.

"I may have uttered a creative turn of phrase, Sarn't Major." He'd made it his life's work to try and get the sarn't major to crack a grin. He'd never once succeeded. Not once.

A slow flush crawled up Sarn't Major Giles's weathered neck. Today was not that day, either.

"Shut the goddamned door," Giles growled. Reza toed it shut and it slammed with the finality of a crypt vault. "The hospital commander called directly to Colonel Horace. He skipped all the levels of the chain of command and went right to my boss."

"Glad to see the phone books are up to date," Reza said. His skin prickled with awareness that the man in front of him was about to unleash the fury.

A man that Reza owed his loyalty to. And the remains of his career. Reza was under no illusions—he should have been forced to pack his bags after the Colorado fiasco a few months ago.

He still had a job. But given the look on Giles's face, he wasn't sure how much longer he could count on that.

God, but life was so much simpler when he was drinking. The temptation to reach for the bottle hissed in his ear. Seductive. Warm. Comforting.

He swallowed and straightened. He could take an ass chewing.

He'd done it before. He could do it again.

All the old man could do was yell at him, right?

Apparently, it was Reza's day to be wrong. Again.

Giles moved with a speed that should have been impossible for an old infantry sergeant major, but his elbow was against Reza's throat before Reza had even registered he'd moved.

Pictures rattled as Reza's body slammed into the concrete wall. A memory, harsh and raw, scraped against the threat blocking his lungs. Another elbow. Another time.

Fear, both old and new, mixed in his veins, and he was once again sixteen years old. Fighting a man who was twice his age and size.

Reza struggled to breathe and keep his composure but his mind couldn't grasp that the man with his elbow to his throat wasn't the man who'd put his mother in the hospital all those years ago.

The memories twisted and writhed. Reza focused on Giles's face. Facing the anger right in front of him. Ignoring the ghosts.

He forced himself to react, shutting down the muscle memory that had his own hands curling into the sergeant major's shirt collar. Releasing his grip, he relaxed, pushing down the ingrained urge to fight.

Giles's breath was hot on his face.

Silence hung in the air.

Another moment and the sergeant major released him. "I don't appreciate your smart-ass comments," Giles said with a snarl, shoving him away. "I can't protect you from this."

Reza breathed deeply through his nose to calm the adrenaline running through his veins, more than sick of dealing with the sergeant major's PTSD and whatever other psychosis he carried around with him. "I didn't ask you to."

Giles rounded on him, shoving his cigar into Reza's face. "You're one ungrateful son of a bitch, you know that, Ike? Colonel Richter had to pull some major strings to keep your ass out of a sling after the Colorado fiasco and now you're home, swearing at senior officers? How fucking stupid are you?"

Reza wisely chose not to answer.

"Are you drinking again?"

His temper flared, bright and hot inside him. He didn't get a chance to argue.

"The only right answer is 'No, Sarn't Major.'"

"No, Sarn't Major," Reza mimicked. A truth, for once. No matter how hard it was, he hadn't had a drink since the accident in Colorado had nearly cost his best friend her career.

He didn't care about how his drinking fucked up his own life. But when it came to his friends? Yeah, that was too far. Funny though, how no one—not Claire, the little sister he'd never had, and not Sarn't Major Giles—believed him when he said he wasn't drinking.

He'd failed at not drinking often enough. He couldn't really blame them for not believing him. But it had to stick this time. It had to.

The problem was, if he started drinking again, he could be out of the army by the end of the month—thrown out on his ass as a rehab failure. And the army was the only good thing he had in his life.

"Ike, you need to dial it back. You can't go around swearing at the hospital commander and expecting to get away with it. That chest full of medals won't do you a damn bit of good at a court-martial."

"I haven't done anything worthy of a court-martial." At least, nothing he'd been caught for.

"Yet." Giles stalked to his desk. "I got the colonel to agree to let me handle this."

"And by 'handle this' you mean choking me out?"

The cigar was back, an inch from the tip of Reza's nose. "Don't push your luck." Giles was a full head shorter than Reza but Reza knew better than to tangle with him. Reza might have been all-army combatives champion a few years ago but that didn't mean he could beat the sergeant major in pure meanness.

The sergeant major's drivers wouldn't even wake him up

in the field. They flat-out refused because he woke up swinging every time.

"Don't come back in here again," Giles said, sitting down at his desk. He thrust a sheet of paper at him. "Wisniak is being admitted to the hospital. Here's the list of shit he needs."

Reza accepted the paper, barely managing to avoid swearing under his breath.

Dismissed, Reza stepped into the hallway and headed for the door. It was only when he was in the quiet cab of his truck that he rested his head on the steering wheel and released a shuddering breath.

The flask he kept in the glove box whispered his name. Calling him. Just one sip.

He breathed deeply. He'd never thrown the flask out. He'd wanted to believe that he was strong enough to do this on his own. That he could be around the alcohol without drinking.

It was a daily test.

He knew what it would taste like: bitter and sharp, and it would burn the whole way down.

And the numbness would follow. A comfortable numbness would spread through his veins. The pressure on his chest would be gone.

He'd be able to focus. To relax.

Instead he sat there, breathing in. Out. Slowly.

Struggling to hold on to the sobriety that was his only chance of remaining a soldier.

It was a long time before he drove back to the company ops.

The flask remained unopened.

Emily knocked on the door, waiting for the soldier inside to answer. A muffled sound was the only response, so she pushed it open gently. Slowly.

Sergeant Wisniak wasn't a skinny kid but he wasn't fat, either. He was just kind of puffy. Soft, maybe, might be the best description for him. She'd been seeing him for about a month now and the thing that struck her most about the soldier sitting quietly in the sterile room was the utter emptiness in his eyes.

A week ago, he'd been excited. Motivated that the fog in his head was starting to lift.

Eager to be the leader of men that he'd always wanted to be.

Today, that eagerness was gone. Left in its place was an empty shell.

"Sergeant Wisniak?"

He blinked up at her.

"We're going to admit you," she said quietly.

Blink. Blink.

"Do you think you can tell me what happened?"

He looked away.

Her heartbeat was the only sound. She stood there a moment longer, hoping he would answer. Hoping he would confide in her.

Hoping he would give her some way to help him.

But he said nothing and the silence grew too heavy.

She left, wondering how she was going to find the strength to make it through the rest of the day.

Reza walked into the first sergeant's office and closed the door. It still didn't feel like his space. He wondered if it ever would. Maybe if he wore the rank it would feel real. Right now, it felt temporary. Transient.

But that didn't take away a single iota of the responsibility he had. He might not be getting paid for the job but he damn sure would give it everything he had.

He stared at his computer screen, his lungs tight with frustration.

He sent Foster a text message, telling him to round up Wisniak's stuff and get it up to the hospital.

He was just glad that Marshall was out of the office. Maybe Reza could get some work done without his commander dumping more shit on his desk.

He glanced up as Sloban walked into his office. The young specialist should have looked rested and recovered from his month-long stint in rehab. Instead, he looked harried and stressed out.

Sloban had changed so much since the last deployment. The kid with a steady trigger finger and bright, laughing eyes was long gone, buried from too many head injuries and no time off from the war.

Sloban had done three tours. Three tours that had taken a vital piece of his soul and left this shattered man in his place.

Guilt slithered up and threatened to choke him.

Reza hadn't been able to protect Sloban. Not from the chain of command. Not from the nightmares that haunted his sleep.

Sloban's body might have survived but the war had broken him anyway.

It was breaking all of them.

"Doesn't look like your vacation did any good," Reza said lightly. Hoping the kid would crack a joke. Hoping he'd see a flicker of the warrior he'd known.

Sloban twisted a cigarette in his hands. New nervous habit. "It sucks, Sarn't Ike, let me tell you. Rehab totally fucking sucks."

"I thought you weren't due back for another week."

Sloban's smile was bitter. "I was but Captain Dick Face pulled me back because he said my medical board was almost complete and since I wasn't going to stay a soldier any longer, I didn't need any more treatment."

A warning crawled up Reza's spine. Why hadn't Marshall

told him he was pulling Sloban out of rehab? As the first sergeant, that was something he should have been told about. "Who went and picked you up?"

"Sarn't Song and Sarn't Pete."

Reza nodded slowly. Song and Pete were two of Marshall's boys that had come with him from First Brigade. He'd never liked either one of them. Thought of them as bullies. Marshall thought they were great soldiers, though, and they got away with damn near anything they pleased.

"You don't look like you're doing too good," Reza said.

"I'm not using," Sloban said. "But it's not as easy as it sounds." He scrubbed his hands over his face. Reza wished he didn't notice how they shook. "Marshall said the docs aren't giving me a good rating for disability." There was panic in Sloban's voice. "I can't work like this, Sarn't Ike. If I could, you know I'd be fighting to stay in. The docs...if Marshall's right..."

Reza ground his teeth. He knew exactly who to call to find out what was going on with Sloban's packet. "Let me talk to Marshall and make some calls. I'll find out what's going on. Just stay clean, okay?" He breathed deeply. "And I haven't seen your packet yet so don't give up on me. Let me see if I can fix this."

A flicker of something flashed across Sloban's face. Reza wished it was the rock solid kid he'd known. "Sure, Sarn't Ike. Whatever you say." Sloban pushed out of his chair, pausing near the door. "I'm sorry to be such a pain in the ass. I know you've got other things you need to be doing."

"You're not being a pain in the ass, Slo. You're a fucking warrior." Reza drummed his fingers on the desk, itching to pick up the phone. He hadn't been able to see Sloban's slow spiral into addiction but damn it, if he could help the kid now, he was going to. He'd move the fucking planets to make sure he got the right ratings. Slo had given the army everything he had. The least the army could do was take care of him now that they'd broken him. "I'll fix this."

A promise he didn't know if he could keep.

He made it anyway.

Relief washed over Sloban's face and stabbed Reza with the expectation he saw there. "Thanks, Sarn't Ike. It means a lot to me that you don't treat me like shit because I fucked up."

"You didn't screw up, Slo." *I did, for not catching your problem sooner.* But he didn't say that out loud. Maybe if Reza hadn't been drowning his own demons in the bottle, he'd have seen what was happening with Sloban.

But he hadn't.

Sloban left, leaving Reza wallowing in the morass of his own hypocrisy. Sloban had deployed and gone through some bad shit. He hadn't dealt with it well. Not at all. He'd turned to meth and Reza hadn't been able to help him. Because he hadn't seen.

But that didn't mean Reza would turn his back on him now. Sloban had been one of his and Reza protected his own.

He picked up the office phone, calling the R&R Center to see if he could hunt down the doc who had Sloban's packet.

It was a long shot. The medical separation process was an archaic, tangled mess that no one, not even the docs, fully understood. It took months to put a soldier out of the army for medical reasons.

Some guys, like Sloban, deserved to be taken care of the rest of their lives. They were heroes. They'd deployed, gone where the army had asked them, done what it had asked them.

He glanced down at his cell phone. Foster was heading to the hospital with Wisniak's stuff.

The psych doc's words haunted him. How was he supposed to have loyalty to a soldier who'd never deployed, never gone to war? How was he supposed to help someone who took resources away from the men and women who needed it? He had no loyalty to someone like Wisniak, who'd never sacrificed anything and couldn't cope with life, let alone the army.

There was no answer at the clinic. He shouldn't have been surprised. The only doc he could get after duty hours was in the emergency room.

He'd follow up on Sloban's packet first thing in the morning.

He wrote up the serious incident report about Wisniak's being admitted to the hospital and sent it to the commander, then tackled the hundred and twelve e-mails in his inbox.

The silence in the office was beautiful. He fell into the work until there were only a handful of e-mails that needed further action.

The day that had started with a bang ended with a whimper and Reza couldn't have been more relieved.

Shutting down his computer, he headed for the gym, needing the time with the weights to wear him down enough so that he could sleep without a drink.

Because tomorrow was a new day.

One more day sober.

By the end of the day, Emily didn't think she was going to have the stamina to do anything but curl up into a little ball of misery and die, but the weight pressing on her chest demanded she do something to ameliorate it. She'd long ago discovered the link between endorphins and her anxiety levels, and knew that if she didn't go for at least a little run she was going to have to drink to get through the rest of the week.

And Emily did not drink. At least not much.

She certainly wasn't going to fall into the same routine as

her father. A martini at lunch, another after work, all with top-shelf liquor, of course.

No, she didn't need that. There were other, better ways to cope.

She pulled into the parking lot at the gym, ignoring the chime of her cell phone. She couldn't deal with anything else from work today.

Wisniak had been admitted to the fifth floor psych ward earlier that morning. He hadn't said anything during the entire process.

Once, he'd told her that all he'd ever wanted to be was a soldier. A leader of men.

He'd built this ideal up in his head of what he was supposed to be. He'd never been good at anything. He'd thought he could be a good soldier.

But he wasn't living up to his own idealized image. He was so traumatized by his past and by his own perceived failure as a soldier that every day was a struggle.

What he did to himself was far worse than anything anyone in the unit could do to him. His sense of failure was staggering in its depth.

She simply counted her blessings that he'd come to her when the thoughts had gotten too dark this time.

It could have been so much worse.

Walking into the locker room, she changed quickly into an Under Armour t-shirt and running shorts. After stretching, she straddled the treadmill as she entered her weight and time. She wanted—no, she needed—to go hard and fast. Her family members worked out with trainers to maintain their appearance, and when that failed they went under the knife.

Emily worked out simply because she'd learned to love it.

Popping her ear buds in, she cranked up the hard core techno she'd learned to love before her sister had looked down her nose at it. Finding her rhythm, she focused on her breathing and just *ran*.

In. Out. Her breath was rhythmic and steady. Her arms swung and with the constant motion, the tension in her chest melted away. She glanced in the mirror to the gym behind her. There were several guys lifting weights. One man's expression was so intense and scrunched up it was almost comical. He was the kind of guy who would make very loud noises just to prove his own badassery on the weights.

He probably made that same face in bed when he was coming. She giggled despite herself and saw a couple of heads turn in her direction. She looked down, embarrassed that she'd drawn attention. She wasn't there to get stared at.

She clicked to the next song and then added incline. Her lungs protested the extra effort but she needed it. Needed the pain. Needed the pride that came in beating her previous standards. It was never good enough to simply show up. She had to do her best.

Soldiers were counting on her. Soldiers like Wisniak, who needed an advocate to stand strong for them.

She'd seen firsthand what happened to soldiers who lacked an advocate. It was why she'd joined the army in the first place. She'd lived a life of spoiled privilege.

Memories rose unbidden, taunting her with their relentless familiarity. Try though she might, she couldn't un-hear her father's biting words when she'd told him she had joined the army.

"Are you trying to embarrass me?" he'd asked.

"No, Father. I'm making this decision for me."

"For you? What about Bentley? What about Chloe?"

Bentley might have been her fiancé three hours before, but she was no longer bound by that loveless pledge. And Chloe?

Emily had walked the halls of the veteran's hospital and every word out of her best friend's mouth had shriveled a piece of Emily's soul. There was false compassion there. A need to be seen as caring or empathetic. But every word her best friend had uttered had dripped with a disdain, a simpering pity, a desire to be somewhere else.

For Emily, every patient they'd visited had been a different kind of need. A need to find some way to help. Listening to spoiled sons and daughters of privilege whine about their lives had suddenly seemed so...trivial.

"I'm sure Bentley and Chloe will be just fine without me." She didn't mention that she'd caught her best friend with her mouth on her fiancé's erection in the pool house earlier that afternoon.

When she'd been looking for a new start, she'd chosen a place where she could make a difference and put all that East Coast Ivy League education to good use.

She glanced over as the door to the workout floor swung open.

Sergeant First Class Iaconelli filled it, his gaze sweeping the room.

It had only been eight hours since the confrontation in the office but she'd forgotten how big he was.

He no longer wore his uniform. Instead, his body was on full display in a long-sleeved t-shirt that hugged his arms and accented his broad chest. The outline of his dog tags pressed against the black fabric. It was strange that he wore the long-sleeved shirt in the warmth of the gym and in the heat outside.

She was amazed by the sheer power of the man. He did not simply fill the doorway. He owned the space.

She looked away, focusing on the rhythm of her legs, hoping he wouldn't notice her. His being here completely defeated the reason for her workout. She'd needed a run to escape the harsh slap of his words—that she did not belong. She refused to let him get to her.

But instead, she'd run right to him. How had she never seen him there before? Gym rats were creatures of habit. Same machine. Same time. Same routine. She stared straight ahead but the specter of Iaconelli moved into her field of vision. He stood behind her, his reflection blocking out a large part of the workout floor.

She could pretend he wasn't there and continue her run or she could face him and pray there would not be another confrontation. She might be a novice at Conflict Management 101 but she was getting better at it every day. She refused to be bullied by this man or anyone else. She glanced down at her time. She'd only gone about two miles in fifteen minutes. She'd wanted to go another half hour at least.

Iaconelli simply stood behind her. Waiting. Solid. Stoic.

She ignored him and kept running.

She even reached forward and pushed the speed faster. Her legs pumped, her lungs threatened to explode.

Still she ran, refusing to let the big man intimidate her.

She ignored him when he climbed onto the treadmill next to hers. Standing beside her, she felt the heat from him merely standing there. His was an oppressive presence.

He seemed determined to interrupt her run.

But she was determined to finish. No matter how much he silently demanded that she stop.

He was a beautiful man. She wished he wasn't. Somehow it was easier to get into pissing contests with these testosterone-driven men when she wasn't thinking about them naked.

And it was so, so easy to.imagine this man naked. The long-sleeved t-shirt hugged his skin, leaving little to the imagination. Was his body as hard as it looked?

Sweat beaded on her forehead as she ran. She could practically feel the irritation coming from him.

Of course, Iaconelli would be the first man she'd actually

thought about that way in a long, long time. A man who looked like he'd rather throttle her than talk to her.

That way? Oh Lord. What was she, twelve? She shuddered and shook off her thoughts. She was no longer the girl who couldn't say the word "penis" without turning fifty shades of red. No, she'd gotten over any inhibitions the day she'd found her fiancé with his dick where it didn't belong.

She was a soldier now and soldiers didn't blush when they said the word "dick" or "penis" or any other creative turns of phrase.

If she thought Iaconelli was a beautiful man, she wasn't going to apologize for that.

She glanced down at the timer. Deciding she'd proven her point, she slowed down to a jog.

When her breathing had slowed enough that she wasn't gasping, she hit the emergency stop button and turned to face him.

Her body glistened with sweat. It formed a light sheen against the cream of her skin. Her eyes, pale blue earlier, sparkled now like a far-off ocean he remembered from a distant dream. They were darker from her exertion.

He hadn't expected that she'd be at the gym. He'd been planning to ask her about Sloban's packet tomorrow. During duty hours. But seeing her at the gym gave him the opportunity to do something now and now was always better than tomorrow, when a hundred other things would demand his attention.

Reza looked up at the cute doc who looked so different out of uniform. She wiped the sweat from her forehead then draped the towel over her shoulder. "Can I help you, Sergeant?"

Reza blew out a hard breath. "Do you have a separation packet on a Specialist Neal Sloban?"

Her nostrils flared slightly. "I have forty-two packets on my desk on any given day. I'd have to check and get back to you," she said.

He nodded gruffly. "And what's going on with Wisniak?"

She tipped her chin at him. "Are we really going to have a conversation about a soldier's private medical issues in the middle of the gym?"

Reza ground his teeth. "It's a simple question."

"It is," she agreed. "But it's not one we should have here."

"Where would you like to have it?" He didn't raise his voice. He didn't have to. The reaction on her face was enough to let him know he'd made his point.

He didn't really care where they had the conversation but it needed to happen. He wasn't going to let this doc brush him off. Too many of his peers would let the docs do just that. Soldiers suffered.

"Give me a sec." He watched her as she wiped down the treadmill and tried not to stare flagrantly at her ass. It was a really great ass and the way she moved was pure grace. Satin layered over steel. He took a step backward and followed her out of the gym. He walked with her silently, enjoying the relative quiet of the end of day at Fort Hood. Oh, there was traffic and the constant hum of life around them but the crush of soldiers swearing at each other, the unending shouts, were gone. But compared to the incessant growl of generators broken up by the helicopters whirring overhead and bursts of machine gun fire from the test fire pit, an afternoon at Fort Hood was relatively quiet.

He followed her around the Greywolf gym and down a gentle slope toward the parking lot. "I don't usually see you in here," he commented. A deliberate attempt to lighten up the hostility between them.

"I usually run out by the airfield. There's a trail by Engineer Lake I like."

"You're not afraid to run by yourself?" he asked.

"I don't believe the media reports that all of you guys in uniform are closet rapists. I'll take my chances," she said dryly.

Well, how about that. Kitty had claws. He was mildly impressed.

She folded her arms over her chest. "Look, Wisniak is having a really hard time. Without going into too many details, he had an incredibly hard life growing up. He joined the army to be better than what he came from. And in his mind, he's failed."

He studied her as she spoke. There was no hint of the attitude that drove him batshit crazy about the head docs. No need to protect the poor soldier from the evil chain of command. No desire to save the world.

Just genuine concern for his trooper. Something Reza should have felt. He searched for a name for the misfit emotion swirling inside him. It was unfamiliar and fleeting. Flittering like a hummingbird against his heart before wrapping a cold wet blanket around him. Then he knew it. An old, long forgotten emotion.

Shame. It shamed him, deeply, that he could not feel empathy for Wisniak. "He doesn't need to stay in the army," Reza said softly.

"It's all he's ever wanted," Emily countered.

"He can want it all day long. Some people simply aren't meant to be soldiers." She flinched. He hadn't meant to slap at her but he saw he'd struck home nonetheless. He cleared his throat roughly. "Why is it so hard for you to understand that some people really don't belong in the army?"

"And why is it so difficult for you to understand that some people just need a little more help fitting into the life we lead?" She lifted her chin. "The failure of not being a good soldier is killing him."

The echo of her words pushed aside any hint of compassion, the shame replaced by the familiar burn of rage beneath his skin.

"It's killing him?" Reza said softly. "Like, literally killing him? Stabbing him with a bayonet killing him? Close quarters killing him? Or is he getting shot at three hundred yards?"

Her mouth opened but no sound came out as horror filled her pale blue eyes. "I didn't mean it like that," she whispered.

"How did you mean it, doc?" Reza swallowed the bitterness in his throat, fighting the urge to shout at her that she had no fucking idea about killing.

"It's just a figure of speech."

Reza smiled coldly. "See, that's where you're wrong. Killing is very much not a figure of speech where I'm from. Killing is a hot, bloody, screaming reality. A reality I'm supposed to be training our boys for. It pisses me off that I've had boys on the range that I couldn't go teach how to shoot because I've been running around after this kid."

"Then why are you even talking to me?" she asked, lifting her chin.

"Because I have to. Because Wisniak is in my company and that means I'm responsible for him."

"That's a stunning lack of loyalty," she said, her voice filling with challenge as she found her courage. "How can you lead someone you feel no loyalty toward?"

"Loyalty is earned."

"See, here's where you and I differ. You should have loyalty to all your soldiers."

Reza shifted and folded his arms over his chest, mirroring her own stance. "There are some who aren't meant to be soldiers."

"This again?"

"Why is that so hard for you to hear?" he asked suddenly.

"What is it about you docs that makes you feel like every broken, battered kid can be the next commanding general?"

"We have to try. Everyone deserves a chance."

"But what's the cost, doc? Every day I spend running around after this kid who wants to kill himself or that kid who can't take it because his sergeant yelled at him is a day I don't spend training soldiers for war. Which, by the way, in case you missed it, isn't over yet."

Her skin blanched, tightening over her cheeks. "I know that," she whispered.

He remembered the right shoulder of her uniform. No combat patch. He could have driven his point home then. Could have pressed his advantage, reminding her that he'd seen a side of war that would leave her trembling from the raw terror of it.

But he didn't. Something about the fear in her eyes reminded him of something he tried very hard to forget.

He lowered his arms as an old memory tickled the base of his neck. Fear, primitive and dark, looked back at him. Reminding him that he'd been young once. Young but never innocent. Never that.

But younger. Before the war had twisted everything up inside him. Before it killed anything good he'd managed to salvage from home.

He closed his mouth, swallowing roughly. "What are the visiting hours on the fifth floor?" he asked.

She shifted, brushing her hair out of her face. "He's not ready for visitors." A familiar gauntlet thrown between them.

"When will he be?"

"The attending physician will make that assessment."

Reza bit back a snarl of frustration and turned to go before he laid into her for the second time that day.

"What would it take for you to realize we can't all be strong all the time?"

Her words whispered across his skin, taunting him. If he closed his eyes, he would see their faces. The men who'd died on his watch. The men he'd destroyed because they'd dared to defend their homes. Men who looked like his mother's family.

He turned slowly to face her. She didn't back down, didn't step away from the rage grinding between his teeth. "I know all about weakness, honey. And that is not a position I will defend."

He stalked back into the gym, the need for a drink snapping at his heels. Taunting him.

Demanding he slake the thirst. Just a little bit. Just one drink.

What could it hurt?

He headed for the weights. He could do this. He could walk away from the anger and the rage and the hate.

It was a long time before he was calm enough to leave.

Chapter Three

Reza padded to the front door, the carpet soft beneath his bare feet. Someone was pounding on his door like the damn house was on fire and he felt a strong urge to whip someone's ass.

It had been a shit week as shit weeks went. The last thing he felt like doing was socializing.

He swung the door wide to see Ben Teague standing outside, sporting his Stetson and holding a Heineken in one hand.

"Get your shit. We're outside."

He hitched the towel around his waist and frowned. "Shit, I forgot."

Ben Teague was a captain who specialized in avoiding responsibility. He was one of the more senior guys but as far as Reza knew, he'd never been offered command. Which was a damn shame because Teague was a hell of an ally in a firefight. Teague wasn't the guy Reza wanted watching his six—he was the guy who wanted to be the first man in the stack, kicking in doors.

He couldn't seem to wrap his head around the fact that Reza had quit drinking.

"How could you forget about mandatory fun night? Grab your Stetson and let's go."

He didn't make a big deal out of it but nights like this where they were expected to socialize at one of the local bars challenged Reza's restraint. He was the first sergeant, though, so he had to be seen. The sergeant major would notice if he wasn't there.

But he *was* going, if only to prove that he could handle it.

"Give me five minutes."

"Cool. Hurry up."

Reza shut the door in Teague's face and padded back to the bedroom. He dropped his towel onto the bed and pulled on a pair of jeans and tugged a long-sleeved t-shirt over his head, keeping his back to the mirror. He didn't need the visual reminder of what he'd done to his body over the years tonight.

Tonight there were too many memories circling. There was no reason for the ghosts to be haunting him. Some nights were just worse than others.

Grabbing a bottle of water, he stuffed his wallet into his pocket and palmed his cell phone. He pulled his Stetson out of his truck and climbed into Ben's passenger seat, hoping tonight would be uneventful. Reza wanted to unwind tonight, if only to prove to himself that he could handle it.

His phone vibrated in his pocket and he pulled it out.

Leaving for NTC tomorrow. Stay out of trouble. He grinned at his phone. Claire had an uncanny ability to contact him when he was about to tip over the line. But he wasn't. Not tonight. Not tomorrow night.

He had this.

Ever since that mission in Colorado, when she'd laid it on the line and forced him to confront the fact that he had a problem, he'd refused to fail her again.

He slammed the door shut.

"What took you so long?" Teague asked.

"I was doing my makeup," Reza said with a grin he did not feel.

"You look pretty, honey. Try to leave some of the girls for us tonight."

Reza leaned his head back against the seat as Teague turned up the radio. Marilyn Manson blasted through the cab, the bass from "The Beautiful People" thumping in Reza's chest. It reminded him of the pulse of a fifty cal. A powerful comfort.

Abruptly, the music ended.

"What crawled up your ass?" Teague demanded.

Reza sighed. "Just first sergeant bullshit. Docs busting my balls at the office. Marshall being a pain in the ass. Same shit, different day."

Teague turned off the highway, heading toward Belton Lake. "Sometimes I think it's easier being deployed."

"We're heading to the MOUT site next week. Ought to break up the monotony." Reza took a sip from the water bottle, unable to avoid the reaction inside him that wished it was something stronger.

Excitement burned through him. He couldn't wait to head out to the Elijah MOUT site, the mock-up city where they practiced urban operations. He loved running the boys through kicking in doors and fighting house to house. He got a charge out of it.

It was the only place that felt like everything fit. Everything else was just a pause until he could get back to training or better, to war. Training soldiers for war was what he did. It was what he was good at.

He wasn't supposed to be some expert at mental health and suicide prevention.

The damn doc was wrong. Everyone couldn't be a soldier. He knew that truth down into the marrow of his bones.

He had the scars on his body to prove just how wrong she was. The army needed soldiers and no amount of time on the head doc's couch could turn a spineless weakling into a warrior.

He'd dealt with far too many so-called leaders of men who'd refused to leave a bunker when the mortars started falling. Far too many grown men who'd frozen the first time their convoy had gotten blown up and refused to ever leave the base again.

He didn't blame them for the fear. But he didn't respect them either.

Terror was part of combat. A heady marriage of fear and adrenaline and death. It was the most potent of drugs, he thought, twisting the cap on the water bottle. Combat rewired the brain like nothing else. And his blood was now hardwired to needing the fix.

He glared at the bottle, wishing he was strong enough to control the urge and have just one drink.

But he knew he wasn't.

Combat was his only addiction now. He needed it.

It was just a matter of time before he got back to it.

Emily walked into *Talarico's*, burned out and exhausted from the week. She'd processed nearly a hundred medical packets on top of her regular patient load. She'd put in five eighteen-hour days and she'd barely scratched the surface. There was so much to do, so little time.

She didn't want to be here tonight but she'd promised Olivia she'd meet for drinks. *Talarico's* was out on Lake Belton, a beautiful old building that had been redesigned with a Tuscan flavor and feel. The floor was polished concrete, the walls beautiful mixtures of warm bronze, gold, and yellows. Outside, there was a wide deck, illuminated by an outdoor fire pit and low-hanging lights.

"You are looking far too serious with all these sexy Cav boys running around in their Stetsons."

Emily ordered her wine then glanced over at Olivia. "Sorry. Shitty week."

They'd crashed a Cavalry event and Emily couldn't help but wonder if Olivia had an ulterior motive for dragging her out to *Talarico's* on a Friday night. The men were lingering around the bar or outside on the deck, sporting their Stetsons, the traditional headgear of Army Cavalry units. There was something powerful about the men in that room.

Olivia was nursing something pink and green, toying with the end of her straw. "You're supposed to be having a good time."

Olivia's black hair shined in the candlelight of the bar. Behind her wire-rimmed glasses, her green eyes glittered with the brightness of a little too much to drink.

"I thought we were celebrating your latest case?" Emily asked.

"I thought so too until I saw you over here sulking at the bar." Olivia smiled. "I put another scumbag in jail today for life. I'm going to celebrate, damn it, and you're going to join me."

Emily raised her glass. "To putting away scumbags," she said with a smile.

Olivia tinked her glass against Emily's. "To putting away the bad guys."

Emily took a sip of her wine. "How do you know the difference?" she asked quietly.

"The difference between what?" Olivia asked.

"The good guys and the bad guys?"

Olivia toyed with her straw. "I guess there isn't a clear line," she said. "Some things there is. Like there's no one on the planet that could convince me someone who hurts a little kid sexually deserves a second chance. Other stuff? It's more gray." She took a sip of her drink. "Most of it's gray," she added.

Emily was learning that. Her job would be so much easier if the medical records that came before her were clear-cut and easy to decide. But every single one danced in the gray areas. She made the best decision she could, case by case, based on the army's guidelines.

Always, she tried to remember that there was a soldier on the other side of that file, counting on her to get it right.

She thought of Iaconelli's words from the gym earlier in the week. Weakness he wouldn't defend.

The soldiers' packets that came across her desk weren't weak. They were broken, and there was a distinct difference in her world.

They deserved her defense. They deserved someone to advocate for them but even then, sometimes, there were cases she simply couldn't adjudicate in favor of the soldier. Sometimes, though, their problems were self-inflicted and she simply couldn't just check the block.

"You know what you should try," Olivia said, interrupting her serious train of thought. "I should see if I can get one of these strapping Cavalry men to give you a ride home."

"I'll pass, thanks," Emily said with a laugh.

"I thought you were giving up on your stuck-up Northeastern Old Money ways, Em," Olivia said with a grin.

"I am, but that doesn't mean I'm going to run around screwing the first thing that winks my way. I'm trying to be more selective than a hamster in heat."

"A hamster in heat? Are you serious? Who has hamsters these days?" Olivia glanced over at a tall Cavalryman, her gaze going dark with longing and something else. A freedom that Emily envied. "There is something about that hat that does something to my insides," Olivia said, lifting her beer toward one of the captains near the bar.

Emily followed her gaze. The tall Cavalryman had shoulders for days and an easy, carefree grin that radiated confidence that bordered on arrogance. Yeah, that hat did do something to her insides. It was a symbol. Of tradition. Of pride. Of a lineage to which she didn't belong.

She wished she could be like Olivia. Free. Comfortable in her own skin. Confident enough to undress a man across the bar.

She thought about Sergeant Iaconelli. About how he'd radiated power at the gym, in her office.

What would he be like in a place like this? Would he relax? Or would he wear his rank like a shield?

She swirled her wine in her glass, his words about weakness echoing in her brain. God but she wished she could turn it off sometimes. She glanced over at Olivia.

"What's eating at you?" Olivia asked, managing to tear her eyes off the captain across the room.

"Nothing. It's just been a long week." The truth. "Go. Have fun."

Olivia glanced toward the captain, who was now watching her. "You sure you're okay?"

"I'm fine," Emily said. Olivia tipped back the rest of her drink and set it on the bar.

Emily watched her friend weave through the crowd of broad-shouldered Cavalrymen and toward the captain. Alone at the bar, Emily twirled her wine in the glass, staring into the swirling pale golden liquid.

She sipped her wine and glanced around the wide open space, feeling the warmth. She was comfortable in this place. A drink after work. A good friend. This was a good life. It was simple. It had purpose. So much better than the complicated mess she'd left behind.

She lifted her glass, savoring the freedom of her rebellion. She might not fit into her uniform just right but she fit here among these soldiers better than she'd ever fit back home.

She saw Olivia gyrating slowly with the captain across the dance floor. Her friend's movements were slow and sensual, a sultry undulation that spoke of power and of sex. She smiled at her friend's pleasure. It was enough that Emily could enjoy another's happiness. She'd come here tonight to relax, to help Olivia celebrate.

"You don't come here often, do you?"

Emily glanced at the man who'd appeared at her shoulder. He'd been standing with the group of captains that Olivia had just infiltrated.

"Not really," she said, sipping her drink. She thought about easing away, putting space between where their upper arms touched.

Personal space much? she thought.

"Are you here with friends?" he asked. She caught a heavy scent of beer from his direction, beer mixed with cigar smoke. It was not unpleasant.

She glanced over at Olivia. "Yeah."

"Not up for company?"

She smiled and finally glanced back at him. "Not really. Thank you though."

He brushed the tip of his hat with two fingers. "My pleasure, ma'am."

He swaggered off, leaving her alone at the bar. That had been nice. Too bad she wasn't interested. Once upon a time, she might have danced but there was something missing from the way he'd carried himself.

He was missing that power that Sergeant Iaconelli wore like it was second nature.

She shook her head and took a long sip of her wine. She'd done nothing but argue with the man but now she was thinking about him in a way that was purely unprofessional.

The heavy iron door swung open at that moment and Emily's breath caught in her throat.

"Speak of the devil," she muttered.

Reza Iaconelli stood in the doorway, his gaze scanning the room as though he was taking a headcount. What was it about the man that he was always walking through doors at the wrong time? And this time, his gaze swept the bar and landed directly on her.

His eyes lit up, his mouth flattened. Just a faint flicker, but it was enough to tell her he'd recognized her.

And the familiar hostility was gone.

Her mouth went dry and she took another sip. He wasn't going to come over. It was going to be fine.

They would keep the rampant hostility and no lines would be blurred.

It would be fine, right?

Except that he was now coming over. Weaving through the crowd, his Stetson adding to his height.

What the hell was she supposed to do about that? The closer he got, the more her stomach flipped beneath her ribs.

She was too tired to fight. And the alcohol would probably allow her to say something that she'd regret come Monday.

His clean white shirt accented his shoulders and made his skin look darker, more appealing. His face was shadowed by the brim of the Stetson.

He was there. A short space separated them. He radiated something—a power.

A rawness.

She was doomed.

It was fate. It had to be. A slow warmth unfurled inside him as the doctor he could not get out of his head looked up at him, her cheeks flushing pink.

She was all buttoned up at work. Tonight, she looked different. Looser. Unbound.

Compelling. That's what she was. Her fire at work. Her refusal to let him bully her. He'd admired her backbone before.

Tonight, he admired her in an entirely new light. Her hair framed her face in careless curls. He hadn't expected to see her outside of work. He damn sure hadn't expected to see her here. An old familiar need rose inside him. A need for touch, human and warm. A need to lose himself for an interlude in sweat and sex and stunning pleasure. He'd given up drinking but women had apparently fallen into that category as well.

It had been months since he'd felt a woman's hands on his body.

This woman was not someone he needed to be talking to at the bar tonight but he found himself walking toward her anyway.

After the week of confrontation they'd had, he'd be lucky if she didn't slap him the minute he approached her.

He could do this. He could talk to a woman without drinking. Right?

Emily met his gaze as he approached. He almost smiled.

"Not your usual scene?" he asked, leaning against the bar.

She shifted, putting a little space between them. That slight reclamation of power. He made a noise of approval in his throat. "I'm surprised you're talking to me."

"I'm surprised you're here. Shouldn't you be home reading medical journals or something?" Her cheeks flushed deep pink and he wondered how far down her body that color went.

She tipped her chin then and looked at him. "Have you been drinking?"

He looked down at the bottle in his hand. "I don't drink anymore," he said quietly. No reason to delve into his abusive history with alcohol. "You?"

"Glass of wine," she said.

Reza shrugged and leaned on the bar, taking another pull off his water and being careful not to lean too close. She looked like she'd bolt if he pushed her. "That would explain why you're talking to me. We haven't exactly been friendly."

Her hair reflected the fading sunlight that filled the room from the wide-open patio doors. He wanted to fist it between his fingers, watch her neck arch for his mouth.

She motioned toward his bottle with her glass. "'Anymore'?"

He simply took another pull off his water. He was going to be damn good and hydrated after tonight. He wondered what she'd do if he leaned a little closer. "Long story."

"One you're not keen on sharing?" she asked. She leaned her cheek on one palm. The sun glinted across her cheek.

"Let's just say alcohol and I aren't on speaking terms. Bad things happen when I drink." It was nothing to be ashamed of but there it was. Shame wound up his spine and squeezed the air from his lungs. He was just like his dad after all.

"You say that like giving up alcohol is a bad thing," Emily said quietly.

Reza snorted softly. He should have guessed she wouldn't let it alone. She had stubbornness that could last for days. "It's not something I'm proud of."

Her hand on his forearm startled him. Soft and strong, her fingers pressed into his skin. "But stopping is something to be proud of."

Reza stared down at her hand, pale against the dark shadows of his own skin. A long silence hung between them.

He lifted his gaze to hers.

"It takes a lot of strength to break with the past," she said softly.

"What are you doing?" Her eyes glittered in the setting sun and he thought he caught the sight of the tiniest edge of her lip curling.

Her fingers slipped from his skin. "Offering my professional support?"

His lips quirked. "Was that a joke?"

"Maybe," she said. "I'm working on developing a biting sense of humor. Defense mechanism against raging asshole commanders."

Reza barked out a laugh. "You look different out of uniform," he said lightly, pressing his advantage at this unexpected truce.

"So do you."

He angled his body toward hers. "You like my makeup?" he asked.

Her lips parted as she tried to figure out if he was kidding or not. Finally, she cracked the barest hint of a smile.

Something powerful woke inside him and he moved before he thought about it. He reached for her, brushing a strand of hair from her cheek. The simple gesture was crushing in its intimacy. Her lips froze in a partial gasp, as though her breath had caught in her throat.

"Sergeant Iaconelli," she said quietly, her voice husky. But she didn't move away. Didn't flinch from his touch.

"Reza." He swallowed the sharp bite of arousal in his blood, more powerful without the haze of alcohol that usually clouded his reactions. "My name is Reza."

"Reza."

His breath was locked in his lungs, the sound of his name on her lips triggering something dark and powerful and overwhelming.

He wanted this woman. The woman who'd stood in opposition to him this week. The woman who lifted her chin and stood steadfast between him and his soldiers.

There was strength in this woman. Strength and courage.

"I'm Emily." Her words a rushed breath.

He lowered his hand, unwilling to push any further than

he'd already gone. This was new territory for him. Unfamiliar and strange and filled with potential and fear.

"It was nice talking to you tonight, Emily," he said when he could speak.

He waited for her acknowledgment that she'd heard him. Some slight movement of her head or tip of her chin.

Instead her throat moved as she swallowed and she blinked quickly, shattering the spell between them.

He left her then because to push further would challenge the limits of his restraint. He wasn't ready to fall into bed with someone. No matter how compelling Emily might be.

He waited and he watched for the rest of the evening. Watched her slip out with her friend, leaving an empty space at the bar.

Leaving him alone with the fear that included the empty loneliness as well as the cold silence of sobriety.

His thoughts raced as he made sure his troopers all got home that night, and Teague crashed on his couch.

He fell into bed later, need and desire twisted up, filling the cold dead space left inside him by the lack of alcohol. A dead space he usually filled with work while deployed. Tonight, though, unfamiliar pleasure hunted his thoughts, whispering that he could still love a woman, that he didn't have to be drunk to climb into bed with someone.

But Emily wasn't a random someone.

And she was so far out of his league, it wasn't even funny. Even if there was some sexual attraction there, she wasn't likely to go slumming with a burned-out infantryman like him.

He lay there in the darkness, waiting, clinging to the single, simple pleasure of her touch, hoping that maybe tonight he could sleep, avoiding the nightmares that reminded him of the monster he'd become.

A beast who had lost his compassion somewhere on the road to Baghdad.

Chapter Four

I think I drank too much last night."

Reza grunted as Teague sank into the chair next to his in the battalion classroom. Reza was testing himself. Seeing how far he could push it and still stay in control. His battle with alcohol was one he would win. Because he didn't lose. They'd gone out every night that week and still Reza hadn't drank. "You always say that."

Reza glanced at his watch. He needed to run down what was going on with Sloban's packet. It had been over a week of playing phone tag with the doc and if Reza didn't know better, he'd think she was avoiding him.

He hadn't given her any reason to avoid him. Not at all.

He was getting pissed, though. He needed answers. Not for Marshall or any stupid briefings. He needed them for Sloban.

The kid was counting on him.

Beside him, Teague scrubbed his hands over his face. "Because it's always true," Teague said. "I think my liver went AWOL after the sixth shot of tequila. And you had to go run off and ruin the party because you had to go to bed early."

Reza scoffed quietly. Teague had no idea why Reza had been called away. Being the first sergeant meant his phone was always on. Last night, Reza had spent a good portion of the evening talking a kid and his wife into marriage counseling because if the kid ended up arrested one more time, he was going to get his ass thrown out of the army.

Luckily, they'd agreed.

More than a week had passed since the incident with Emily at *Talarico's*. A week that Reza had been chasing the hair of the dog, looking for a cure to rein in the untamed beast thrashing inside him, dancing with temptation, seeing how close he could get before the fire inside him burned.

He'd managed. A week, and temptation always just a single shot glass out of reach.

He'd keep managing if he wanted to keep his career. With the deployment looming, he couldn't afford to screw up again. Not if he planned on being on that plane.

He wasn't going to let his boys go downrange without him.

"I can't help it if your tolerance is as low as a baby Chihuahua's," Reza said with a grin.

Teague groaned and covered his face with both hands. "What are we doing here anyway?"

He motioned around them to the classroom slowly filling up with officers and enlisted from around the unit. Some he was friendly with. Others, well, they weren't exactly in his fan club. Reza tended to get cranky with the staff when they didn't play nice or tried to make decisions for his soldiers. That was Reza's job as the first sergeant and he'd be damned if any staff weenie was going to do his job for him.

Reza glanced over at Teague. "You didn't hear?"

"Obviously not," Teague said dryly.

"There were five suicides this weekend. The corps

commander has ordered a stand down. We're getting training from the shrinks."

Just saying the words sent a twinge through Reza's guts. He sat back in his chair, shifting uncomfortably. Fort Hood was a big post. It was inconceivable that he'd know any of the victims even though a couple of them had been in the brigade. And yet a nagging sense of unease stirred at the nape of his neck.

Teague mirrored Reza's stance. "Five suicides in a weekend? What the fuck is going on?"

Reza slowly shook his head, rubbing his hand over his bottom lip. "I don't know, man. It's pretty bad. Three were in our brigade."

Reza kept watching the sergeants and officers as they filtered into the classroom.

Reza's phone vibrated in his pocket and he pulled it out. A single picture from Claire.

A memorial. There were four of them in that picture, taken the day they were supposed to leave for Kuwait: Claire, Reza, Miles and Wacowski. Their first deployment had been in the bag. One more mission and they were going home.

God, but had they ever been that young? The Thunder Run to Baghdad felt like a lifetime ago.

Bitter resentment burned in him. He'd taken 'Ski to the docs and they'd told him to take a sleeping pill and get a good night's sleep.

Ski had never woken up.

And Miles had died because Reza hadn't been on that last mission. He'd been tied up, arguing with the docs.

He'd lost two men that day. This day, seven years before.

Claire never forgot.

And Reza's arms bore the tributes to his lost friends.

"You okay?" Teague's words cut through Reza's ragged thoughts.

Reza shifted, scanning the room, shoving the emotions aside. Stuffing them down as he started taking head count.

Wisniak walked in, laughing with one of his buddies. He'd gotten out of the hospital last week and had been doing, oddly enough, really well, at least as far as Reza could tell. The wonders of modern medicine apparently had worked their magic for him.

More than once, Reza had almost approached him. Asked him if he was doing okay. But the marks on his arms burned, the pain in his soul a raging inferno, reminding him that he'd spent days chasing Wisniak around before he'd been committed to the fifth floor.

Days that he should have been leading his boys through battle drills. He hadn't approached. Hadn't been able to get past how much time the kid had taken from Reza training his boys, just to make sure that Wisniak didn't kill himself.

He'd lost too many men to the war. He didn't trust the mental health docs to get it right. Not with Wisniak, not with anyone. The irritation smothered any concern over loyalty or lack thereof.

Emily's taunt burned in his ears. *That's a stunning lack of loyalty.*

He had loyalty. To the men he would take downrange again. It bugged the living hell out of him that he couldn't get Emily's taunt out of his head even after that moment at *Talarico's*. He didn't do stoic introspection and the fact that she'd poked at him pissed him off.

He cared about all of his soldiers. It was simply that Wisniak wasn't one of them. He took from the team; he wasn't part of it.

On the nights when he'd lain awake, his thoughts tumbling through time and space, chasing elusive sleep, he argued with her. Told her that some people needed more help than others. That "team" was something Emily didn't understand.

Couldn't. With her neat hands and proper hair, he'd be willing to bet she'd never gone a day without a shower, let alone held someone while they bled out.

His breath caught in his throat as the woman he spent many nights arguing with in his head walked into the front of the classroom.

Shit. He'd been told this was a sensing session—a group hug about everything the leadership thought was wrong.

This was going to be so much worse.

Clearing his throat, he slouched down in his chair in the back of the room and wondered if he could sneak out without the sergeant major seeing him. "Is the shoot house still on for tomorrow? I want to blow some shit up."

Teague shifted in his seat, slipping his cell phone into his jacket shoulder pocket. "As far as I know. Why?"

"Haven't you heard? Weapons are therapeutic."

Teague chuckled darkly. "Yeah, I think I learned that somewhere on the road between Baghdad and Mosul."

Sergeant Major Giles walked to the front of the room and some enterprising soul had the insight to call "At Ease." Everyone shot to their feet in a show of respect for the senior enlisted man. Reza shifted behind a skinny lieutenant, not wanting her to see him. Not sure what he'd say or do if she did. He wasn't hiding, per se, so much as he was simply using available terrain to conceal his position.

It wasn't like they'd slept together. They'd simply chatted at the bar.

"All right, listen up. Give Captain Lindberg your undivided attention. No cell phones. No leaving. No interrupting. You will listen to what she has to say and you will learn something if I have to shove it up your ass."

Emily's eyes widened but otherwise her expression remained neutral. There was that backbone again. Reza suppressed a chuckle at Emily's stoicism. She kept her face carefully blank as she listened to the sergeant major. Obviously, she was not used to crazy, steely-eyed killers in the clinic. He doubted there was enough medication in the entire Darnall pharmacy to shrink Giles's head. The man had what polite company called issues.

She didn't flinch when Giles told everyone to take their seats. But then she scanned the crowd and her gaze landed for a moment too long on him. He refused to look away, taking in the single lock of hair brushing her forehead. The indentation of her lip as she chewed it.

Behind her professionally bland expression, he saw a flash of uncertainty. This was new for her, he realized. She might go toe-to-toe with a disgruntled sergeant in her own clinic, but right then she was facing an entire room of them. It would be disconcerting to a seasoned veteran, let alone a freshly minted army doc. He wondered if this was her first time outside of the sanctity of the hospital walls. If she'd never been around knuckle draggers before, how could she possibly understand the world that Reza's soldiers were describing?

If she'd never smelled the burned sulfur of spent ammunition, how could she explain away a nightmare of burning cloth and charred flesh? If she'd never been blown up, how could she possibly understand the momentary flashback between the boom of the thunder and the crack of the lightning and the gut-clenching terror as you tried to figure out if the explosion was an imminent threat or not.

Her gaze flickered back to him. An instance of acknowledgment and then it was gone. But in that moment, Reza knew they were worlds apart and that nothing would ever span that distance. He knew war. He'd lived it.

She knew nothing but talk of war.

As she shifted her notes, a quiet revelation whispered across Reza's skin. She was innocent. She truly thought she could make a difference.

She wasn't slick-sleeved because she sought to avoid the war. She was running toward the conflict in her own way—trying to help the soldiers she admired and respected.

As she lifted her gaze and faced a room of roughneck infantry and armor officers and sergeants, he realized that she would never again be the same. Even as she sought to understand the war and what it had done to him, to his men, he knew she'd barely touched on their darkest memories and fears. Her innocence would be tainted today. Just by being around them, some of the war would leave a smudge on her innocence.

He should have felt some bitter satisfaction that she would no longer be as sanctimonious if she lived through the war he'd fought. That she would descend to his level, would no longer be unblemished. But watching her shuffle her papers, he felt something new sidle up against his heart. The unfamiliar urge to protect: the fleeting hope that she would never face the war as he'd lived it.

But she wasn't his. Not his to protect, not his to keep safe.

Reza was no white knight, charging into battle to defend his lady's honor. No, never that. But as he watched Emily lift her chin and square off with a group of roughneck infantrymen, he knew she would never be the same after today.

And neither would he.

Emily shifted her notes and grasped a pen in her right hand, flicking the cap on and off. It was a nervous habit that had driven her father insane but today of all days, she was allowed. The blatant hostility from the room full of men was . . . well, "disconcerting" was too light a word.

She was nervous. Nervous but not afraid. There was a difference. And after her weekend of pulling double shifts in the ER, hers was a no-fail mission.

Something was drastically wrong at Fort Hood and these

men were key to helping figure it out. They were the ones who knew their soldiers the best. They were the ones who could identify the soldiers on edge before she could.

They could save lives. But they had to trust that the system would work, and if her previous conversations with Reza were an indicator, there wasn't a lot of love lost between the men in the ranks and the docs in her office.

Having so many eyes on her at once was unsettling at best. And when you considered what she was there to talk to them about—yeah, she couldn't really count on a warm reception and an invitation to drinks afterward. She figured it was close to what a rabbit must feel like when facing a pack of wolves. She glanced around the room, seeing that every single right shoulder sported the giant combat patch of the First Cavalry Division, a patch that covered the entire space reserved to tell the world they'd been to war. Her own right shoulder felt conspicuously naked. She was a slick sleeve. She'd learned that term recently and it was not a term of endearment.

But she wasn't a rabbit and damn it, she was not going to back down from doing her job.

The war was far from over. She'd get her turn to deploy. She knew that but standing there, in front of a room full of combat veterans, her carefully prepared speech escaped her. The notes on her slides, which had been vetted by the hospital commander, seemed somehow . . . empty. Futile.

"I'm here . . ." She cleared her throat as her voice broke. "I'm here today to talk to you about behavioral health." Someone coughed in the back of the room and she didn't dare look up. She was afraid she would see Reza watching her again. Afraid she would look in his eyes and see something there that she wasn't ready to deal with.

There were demons hiding in the shadows of his eyes. She didn't have to be a psych doc to see it. There was something deeper, though, beneath the shadows and the sadness etched into the lines beneath his eyes. Something that called to her. That urged her out of her tight, protected box. Something that made her want to reach out and seize the risk.

To touch him. The truest part of him, not the harsh exterior he presented to the world.

Refusing to be cowed, she lifted her gaze to scan the room once more. A mistake. The hostility was not in her head. Arms were folded across chests. Jaws ground furiously at being cooped into a hot classroom. Several cheeks were packed with chewing tobacco, their owners' spit bottles close by.

She was not going to reach anyone here. It dawned on her in that moment that the hospital commanders had no idea what the attitudes were down here in a line unit. How was she ever going to reach these men when they didn't want to hear one word she had to say?

The interpersonal conflict in her office seemed somehow so trivial. So distant, despite recognizing at least two commanders she'd gone toe-to-toe with.

Swallowing, she set down her papers and folded her arms over her chest. She glanced in Reza's direction, wishing she had a translator to help her figure these rough men out.

An echo of the first argument she'd had with Reza danced at the edge of her memory. She was not going to reach anyone with carefully prepared PowerPoint sides.

She swallowed and took a deep breath, speaking before her common sense took over and talked her out of it.

"So how many of you think that behavioral health is for pussies?"

Half the room burst out with coughs attempting to cover laughter. The other half were busy picking their jaws up off the floor. It had been a reckless gamble, one that would have made her father cringe in shame, but one that worked because the tension snapped, fizzling a little bit. Granting her an opening she might not have had otherwise.

"Be honest." She glanced at the sergeant major, who looked ready to brain the first officer or sergeant that raised his hand. "Never mind, don't answer that." She shot a quick grin at the sergeant major and a few more chuckles drifted out of the crowd. "Look, we all know that I've got you held captive for an hour and we can stand here and stare at each other or maybe we can talk about what's going on that we've got so many soldiers willing to hurt themselves."

She made the mistake of looking in Reza's direction.

He was watching her, his dark gaze intense, his mouth flat. At least he wasn't glaring at her. That was progress, she supposed.

She gripped the pen in her hand and motioned toward the men before her. "So maybe we can put aside the canned slides and talk about why you hate the shrinks. And maybe I can explain what it is that we do. And maybe, if we work together, we can save a life."

The silence was back, a wet blanket settling over the room. She glanced around as the brief opening she'd attempted to walk through shriveled and shrank.

"I have a question." Reza raised his hand. His eyes glittered darkly. "Sergeant First Class Iaconelli, ma'am. My question is: Why do we have to spend so much time chasing after the shitbirds who are smoking spice or some other shit that's not meant for human consumption and then when we try to throw them out, you all stop the process and tell us they have PTSD?"

"Ike, your attitude is part of the damn problem." All eyes turned in the direction of a hard-looking sergeant first class. He had no hair and there was a hint of a black tattoo ringing his neck. Sergeant First Class Garrison was a big man. "Intimidating" was too light a word for him. And yet, on his left hand, a wedding ring shone bright gold. Someone had tamed this man. She found herself wondering at the woman who'd married him then pulled her thoughts sharply into focus. "You can't run around calling our soldiers shitbirds. They'll always do what you expect and if you expect them to screw up, they're going to live up to your expectation."

"I don't expect them to be smoking it up in the barracks on the weekend," Reza snapped.

Emily held up one hand. "Sergeant Garrison, thank you for getting straight to the heart of the matter. What you're talking about is not simply about drug abuse. You're talking about soldiers who are self-medicating. Instead of using the proper channels to seek care, they're choosing instead the easier path of smoking marijuana, or what is it you called it? Spice?"

"It's synthetic marijuana, ma'am," Garrison said.

She'd had no idea there was such a thing, let alone that soldiers were smoking it. "Thank you. Regardless of their drug of choice, the reason for using is often to deal with symptoms of anxiety that they're otherwise managing or not managing very well."

Reza lifted his hand and she swallowed the flit of nerves in her belly as she pointed at him. "Yeah, well, I've got real warriors who need help who won't go to the damn R&R Center because there's all these slick-sleeved little punks in there trying to get out of drug charges."

It was a cold statement, one that shook her, reminding her that this was not a sympathetic room. And that Iaconelli was not a sympathetic man.

"You raise an interesting point, Sergeant Iaconelli. The facts are that most of our suicides over the last two years have been among first-term soldiers who have never deployed," she said, speaking loudly to cover the nervous waver in her voice.

Garrison straightened where he'd been leaning against the wall. "Y'all know I got blown up a little over a year ago. I had a really tough road back. The thing I learned over that time is that our boys are struggling. Whether we see it or not, our boys need our help." He turned his gaze to Emily.

Reza scowled and shook his head. "Look, Garrison, you're not the only one who got blown up downrange. But the point I'm trying to make is that it's our boys who won't go get the help because of all the ash and trash taking up the appointments."

Emily held up her hands but Garrison interrupted her. "Ike, you need to shut your damn mouth. Just because you drink yourself to sleep every night as therapy doesn't mean someone else doesn't need a different way to cope."

"Fuck you, Garrison," Reza spat. "I'm the reason the rest of your platoon came home from the last deployment."

A red-haired sergeant stood. His right hand was bunched in what looked like a perpetual half grip and it took Emily a moment to realize that it was a prosthetic hand. Her skin went cold. She'd never seen physical evidence of the war this close before.

"Girls, girls. Can we please listen to the good captain explain to us the services she offers? I for one would like more information on how to not accidentally almost kill myself in the future."

The room groaned beneath the joke and Emily saw his name tag. Staff Sergeant Carponti. His eyes lit with an impish grin and she wished she knew the story behind how the young sergeant was able to defuse the anger between the two big sergeants with such ease.

"That's not funny, Carponti." Reza settled back against the wall.

"It was my accidental overdose. I'll make jokes if I want to," Carponti said. "You can't because that would just be wrong on multiple levels. But I can make all the inappropriate jokes I want." He turned and grinned in Emily's direction and she instantly liked him. "How do we fix this shit, ma'am?"

"There are no easy answers," Emily said once everyone's attention was off the two combatants. "But while Sergeant Iaconelli mocks the issue of bad homes, the simple fact is that the generation of soldiers we are dealing with have been raised differently than many of us were. A large portion of our force comes from broken homes, have been victims of trauma at a very young age." She deliberately avoided looking in Reza's direction. "What I'd like you all to think about is the fact that many of you are combat veterans. Many of you have lived through terrible experiences as adults. But how would your life be different if you'd been beaten as a child? Or sexually abused? You can mock the younger generation and say they're weak." She paused, scanning the faces of the warriors in front of her, looking for any sign that her words were breaking through their hardened shells. "Or you can look at the fact that some of them are even functioning as an act that takes the greatest strength."

Emily hung back as the crowd of officers and sergeants filtered from the stuffy classroom. There had been no further outbursts as she'd continued the discussion but she'd lost one very important player.

Reza had stared at his feet for the rest of her briefing, his jaw pulsing with more and more anger as she'd gone on. Something had struck a nerve with him and she had no idea what.

She also did not know him well enough to approach him about it. But that did not mean the worry would leave her alone.

She stuffed her notes into a plain manila folder as the sergeant major approached. He was a hard, weathered man, a man who'd spent too much time in the sun without sunblock. Who smoked and drank and lived life as hard and as fast as it would allow him.

"Thank you for coming, ma'am," Giles said, offering her a hand that swallowed hers whole. She felt engulfed. Surrounded.

"Thank you for letting me go off topic," she said quietly. "I think we do too much slidesmanship in the army and I haven't been around that long."

He grinned and it lightened the bleak darkness in his eyes. "Don't say that too loudly. You'll get kicked out of the officer corps."

She smiled and folded her arms over her chest. "Do you think anyone listened today, Sergeant Major?"

His gaze shifted to some distant battle and for a long moment, there were ghosts dancing in his eyes. He came back to himself with a grim set to his jaw. "I think so. Maybe one or two. But sometimes, that's all you can do. And sometimes, it's enough. Good job today."

He left abruptly and Emily wondered if this was what life was always like when dealing with men like this. Still, she had the feeling she'd been given high praise from a man who did not look like he handed it out easily.

She picked up her hat and her papers and started for the door, somewhat disappointed that no one had stopped her to ask questions. Usually at least one or two soldiers lingered after her briefing, wanting more information. Usually it was for a "friend." Today, though, there was no one.

The stigma against getting help was alive and well at Fort Hood.

She tucked the folder beneath her arm and started for the door. The hallway was old and beaten down, decorated with photos from the battles of this war and legends of previous wars. She didn't linger, uncomfortably reminded that she had no combat experience. That she was not welcome in this part of the post.

She slid her sunglasses on as she stepped into the bright Fort Hood afternoon, grateful that the day was nearly over. She wanted to go for a run. Needed to cleanse the toxic hostility from her skin.

She rounded the corner and stopped. Reza leaned against a black Harley Davidson, arms folded over his chest, his expression as grim and forbidding as it had been inside.

She could keep walking. Ignore the hostility screaming off him. She didn't know him. Didn't know why he'd chosen to wait for her outside the classroom, but her senses were not tingling alarm. At least not the kind of alarm that made her think potential psycho.

No, this alarm was something else entirely. Something she was too afraid to acknowledge.

She could walk around him and avoid him but that would be the coward's way out. It would be admitting that he unsettled her. She lifted her chin and headed in his direction, toward her waiting vehicle.

"You've never experienced pure hell on earth until you're in the middle of a firefight," he said quietly. "There is nothing like the feeling of piss running down your leg as you're throwing everything you've got at an enemy that would drag your carcass through the streets if you lowered your defenses."

She stopped in front of him, unsure if she met his gaze or not between her black-rimmed sunglasses and his. She glanced down at his chest and at the stack of black badges over his heart. "This one is the combat action badge, isn't it?"

He looked down at the knife encircled in a wreath. "Yeah. Why?"

She frowned. "Because you're right," she said quietly. "I

don't know what it feels like." She glanced down. "I'd like to think that my first time in combat, I won't cower in a bunker, too afraid to move," she whispered. Lifting her gaze again, she found the words she needed. "I'd like to know I won't be a liability on this next deployment if the base gets attacked."

Her words surprised him. She could see it in the slight part of his lips, the sudden absence of tension in his jaw. "What do you think you're asking for?" he asked, his voice rough.

"You have a field training exercise coming up, right?" She tried to find the words she needed but she was still learning the language of the military.

His lips curled in a faint smile. "Yeah."

"I'd like to tag along. See what your soldiers do." She tipped her chin. "I'd like to understand better. Would you be able to make something like that happen?"

Would he be able to make something like that happen?

Would he like to be held down and have a smiley face drawn on his nuts? Sure, why not. Every day brought a new experience; why not bring a psych doc out to an infantry company's training exercise?

Because what was the worst that could happen, right?

"Why?"

"Why what?" she asked.

"Why do you want to understand something you will never be part of?"

She offered him a funny sort of smile, a smile that hid a thousand secrets. A smile that reminded him that there was still goodness left in the world. A smile that shined a light on the dark part of his soul. "Let's just say it's intellectual curiosity and leave it at that."

He frowned down at the tightly buttoned-up captain and had the strongest urge to see what would happen if she unbuttoned enough around him to relax. She made him want things that he'd long ago given up on wanting for himself.

He was not meant for relationships. He managed to hurt everyone important to him. It didn't matter if it was intentional or not. She was out of his league and he knew it but the stubborn tilt of her chin stroked admiration to life inside him. His little captain had faced down a room of combat vets today and hadn't even blinked.

"You're one confusing lady," he said quietly.

"Keeps guys like you on their toes."

He met her gaze sharply. Her eyes danced in the mid-afternoon sunlight. If he didn't know better, he'd guess she was flirting with him.

"What are you doing, ma'am?" he asked, his voice rough.

Her throat moved, the muscles tight beneath her skin. "That's the first time you've used any military courtesy with me," she said. "That's the problem. I wear the uniform but guys like you, they don't see me as one of you. I want to feel like a soldier. Like we're on the same team." She paused, her fingers tightening around the notebook she cradled in one hand. "I want to understand what it is that you do."

"No you don't," he whispered.

Reza narrowed his eyes, searching her face for any hint of deception or ulterior motive. But behind the polished demeanor, he caught a glimpse of a hunger, one that he'd known well once upon a time.

Her need to belong was a palpable thing. He could practically feel it coming off her in waves. And yet, the way she stood in front of him, eager to go out to the field with a bunch of dirty nasty infantrymen...it loosened something inside him. Something he hadn't realized was bound.

Something that wanted to curl up with her and simply feel her heart beat against his. It shocked him with the strength and power of the urge. For once it overpowered the urge for a drink and it rocked him back on his heels with the force of it.

"Going to the field isn't going to help you understand us any better." *Only bleeding in combat would help you understand.* But he kept that thought to himself.

"It's not like I'm planning on going in Combat Barbie and coming out GI Jane or anything," she said dryly.

Reza laughed because her words were exactly where his thoughts had been heading. "That's good." He straightened, curling his fingers to resist the urge to touch her cheek again. "Look, I'll do what I can. No promises. But I need your help in return."

"Sure."

"I need you to find Sloban's packet. I've been getting the runaround from your office for a week and I need answers."

She frowned and jotted Sloban's name down in the little black moleskin notebook. "The name doesn't sound familiar but I've done so many files, I could have missed it. I'll check the log today."

"Thank you."

Her smile was blinding and he wondered if her eyes were lit up like her smile. "This means a lot to me," she said softly.

His throat tightened. "Remember you said that. Do you have your kit?"

A tiny frown burrowed between her eyes. "Kit?"

Reza took the notebook from her hand and jotted down a phone number. "Call these guys and get your gear issued. I'll let you know if I can get approval for you to come to the range with us."

Her smile was blinding. "Okay. I'll e-mail you as soon as I find Sloban's packet."

He leaned back on the bike and let her go, biting the side of his cheek to keep from calling her back. From asking her what she thought she was going to accomplish by going to the field with a bunch of knuckle draggers.

Here was his tight, buttoned-up captain, asking to go to the field to see what he did for a living. This same captain who put one of his soldiers in the hospital because he wasn't able to go to the field. Wisniak did everything he could to escape training. Emily had just asked for it.

Therein was the difference. He could train someone willing to train. He could build up a kid who was weak. But he couldn't make a man of character out of someone terrified of his own shadow. Who used the system to malinger and avoid his responsibilities.

So he'd take Emily to the field. Maybe he could understand her need to protect everyone.

Maybe he could understand what it was about her that called to him. That made him lose his mind and want something he could not have.

Because she didn't understand. Some people couldn't be saved. It was as simple as that.

He had warriors getting ready to go back downrange. Maybe if he helped Emily understand what they did, she could help someone before someone else got hooked on drugs like Sloban had.

Maybe he could make a difference one more time before he got her out of his system entirely.

He swung one leg over his bike and contemplated trying to make it off post without his proper safety gear. Deciding he'd had his ass chewed enough recently, he pulled his helmet on, idly wondering how he was going to survive being ragged relentlessly by the guys for bringing a female to training and knowing that was just a convenient lie.

He felt something when he was around her. Something he hadn't felt in forever. Alive. Like there was something filling the dead space inside him.

She touched a part of him he hadn't realized craved touch and now that it had been awakened, he wanted more.

Craved it more than the need for the alcohol that burned through him.

What the hell was he supposed to do about that?

Chapter Five

It was quiet. The kind of quiet that felt like a thousand tiny spiders crawling up his spine. The kind of quiet that could only be found in the middle of the night in the heart of the western desert outside of Fallujah. Every so often, a burst of automatic weapons fire would punctuate the dark and then silence would fall again—unnatural, heavy.

The silence of death and dying. Because death surrounded his platoon's position. They were not where they were supposed to be. There was nothing around them in any direction but darkness edged with the eerie green light from his night vision goggles.

And the radio silence carried with it the whispering seduction of the Reaper whose name they bore. His skin crawled in the darkness. Fear clawed at his belly like a live, crawling thing.

They'd taken a wrong turn. It had taken everything Reza had to keep the platoon sergeant from shooting the lieutenant on the spot.

They argued behind him in hushed tones, their whispers carrying on the midnight wind. Reza stared into the eyepiece of his night vision goggles, watching the desert for motion, keeping busy to deny the fear a foothold. He didn't want to die today. Not today.

He blinked as the sickly green shadows twisted in front of his eyes. Story's face melted into view. He blinked. Twice. He had to be seeing things. Story was dead. His lungs squeezed tight. He tried to suck in a breath but his lungs fought him.

Story's face melted into Wacowski's. And then another. And another. Until the faces of his friends blended into a writhing mass of green light.

Sloban laughed in his face. Reza jerked, his lungs locking up, his throat not cooperating. He struggled to break the fear's grip on his lungs but then the face melted and shifted once more.

And Emily was looking at him, her shadowed blue eyes filled with blame and sadness.

Reza bolted awake in the driver's seat of his car, his skin pulled tight against his bones as his heart attempted to break free from his chest. Fear skittered over his spine like the Reaper dancing over his grave and he shivered, turning the truck on to warm up the cab against the early morning chill. He threw his arm over his eyes and counted to one hundred by threes. The fear did not retreat but then again, Reza hadn't expected it to. It was always the same nightmare. Faces dancing in the desert, like specters beckoning to him from across the river Styx. Mocking him for their deaths. His failure to keep his boys alive.

Emily wasn't dead. Neither was Sloban.

His head was just screwing with him. The nightmares always screwed him up when he detoxed in Iraq.

Fuck, man, Emily had been dead. He scrubbed his hand over his face and covered his mouth. She wasn't his to protect. Wasn't his to mourn.

Reza sat there, gripping the steering wheel. The flask in

his glove box called to him. Whispered seductive things. Just one sip. One and it would push away the nightmare's lingering grief and fear.

One sip, right? He could do that. Hating that he was such a miserable failure, he reached into the glove box. The flask was cold beneath his palm. He sat there for a long moment, holding it. Staring at it.

Needing it.

The clock on the dashboard said five twenty-six. He made it a habit of getting onto post early, before the crush of traffic at the main gate that backed up Highway 190, sometimes for miles. He didn't always sleep in the cab of his truck but he hadn't been sleeping well lately. The nightmares had been getting worse and he was running on about four hours of bad sleep a night. He dragged his hand through his hair and wondered if he'd get back to sleep or if he should walk into the company ops and check his e-mail.

His brain danced over the nightmare again and again, the faces of the dead tormenting him. Mixed in together, enemy and friend alike. All dead.

Death, apparently, did not recognize divisions like religion or uniforms. Reza had told himself that he'd done what he needed to do to bring his boys home. But alone in the dark, it no longer seemed like a good enough reason to have led the charge full bore into battle like he had. The Queen of Battle had whipped him into a frenzy more than once.

And every time he'd told himself it was justified. It was the right thing to do. That if he didn't kill the enemy, then it could be one of his boys hanging from that bridge in Fallujah or being dragged through the streets of Mogadishu.

He'd grieved more than once over the friends he'd lost. But he hadn't expected the guilt over the enemy dead to weigh on him as well.

War was something he was good at. But there was a price.

Wasn't there always? The dead refused to let him go. And he punished himself when they didn't do enough. The flask warmed in his hand. A means to dull the pain, so that the guilt wouldn't eat at him.

Just a little to keep the monster inside him placated enough that it wouldn't consume what little was left of his soul.

Just one sip. Just one and he could forget. At least for a little while. He scrubbed his hands over his face once more, then put the flask back into the glove box.

He couldn't bring back the dead. And the grief would always be with him.

Maybe tonight, if he still hadn't slept, he'd take a drink. Just one. Just to take the edge off so he could sleep.

Until then, he had work to do. And he had to be sober to do it.

Cars and trucks were slowly filtering in. The parking lot would fill and some desperate private would soon be trying to squeeze an Escalade he couldn't afford into a motorcycle parking spot or next to a dumpster. And once a week, Sarn't Major Giles would catch someone and the bad parking would stop for a day and then pick right back up again.

Funny that a man who excelled at leading warriors in combat was reduced to bitching about parking on the grass back home.

Was that what they'd gone to war for? So that people could complain about parking?

Reza walked into the battalion headquarters and headed up the short flight of stairs to the operations office. He figured he might as well try and do things the right way for once when it came to training, especially since he knew the ops officer. Captain Evan Loehr had been his company commander once upon a war and while they'd always gotten along relatively well, it hadn't been until Loehr had started dating Captain Claire Montoya that Reza had really gotten to know the man behind the uniform. Claire was Reza's sister in every way but blood. He was pretty sure he would be dead if not for her coming to bail his happy ass out on the run to Baghdad back in the early part of the war. They'd gone through war together and she'd stood with him until the very end, when his drinking had gotten the best of him.

He hadn't been able to protect those he cared about from the worst of himself.

He was just like his father, after all.

His heart clenched when he remembered her crying over him in that hospital bed a few months ago. God, but he'd fucked up royally. He couldn't stand to think of the disappointment in her eyes if he started drinking again. He rapped on the doorjamb as Evan shot the middle finger at his computer monitor.

"Obviously, some of Claire's bad habits are rubbing off on you," Reza said by way of greeting.

"I hate this computer," Evan muttered.

"Isn't it a little early to be swearing at the electronics?"

"Very funny."

Reza leaned against the door to the cubicle. "How's Claire?"

"Hating life out at NTC," Evan said with a wicked grin. The captain's face lit up when he talked about Claire. God but Reza was glad she'd found someone who loved her for who she was.

She used to joke that she was going to be a crazy cat lady. But beneath the joke had been a very real fear that she was too broken to love.

Evan was a good man. And as long as he kept Claire happy, Reza wouldn't have to rip his spine out.

Win-win all the way around. So long as Reza wasn't the one who hurt her.

Because he had no doubt that Loehr would do the same to him.

"Why does that make you smile?"

"Because she's loving every minute of life in the 3rd Cavalry Regiment." There was an odd note in Evan's voice when he spoke of Claire. A note that made Reza relax a little more.

"Glad to hear she's not getting her ass handed to her out there," Reza said lightly. She'd been offered a rehab transfer after the epic screw-up in Colorado and she'd taken it. A hard penance in a hard unit but Claire was up for the challenge. "Speaking of getting their asses handed to them, I have a rather... unorthodox request."

Evan stopped where he'd started typing. He picked up his coffee cup and took a sip, studying Reza quietly. "This ought to be interesting."

Reza sighed and folded his arms over his chest. Better now than never. "One of the psych docs wants to come out and observe training." Reza was proud of himself. He actually managed to get the statement out without choking on it.

Evan frowned. "So why are you asking me?"

"Because you're the ops officer and that's normally how these requests would come if it was an official tasking."

Another sip of coffee. "And this is not an official tasking because..."

"Because she's treating a few of our troopers and she wants to know what it is they face on a daily basis to get a better idea of the stressors in their lives." The truth. A simple, honest request.

"Okay."

Reza blinked as Evan set his coffee cup down. "Okay?"

"Okay." Evan glanced up from where he'd started typing. "Why do you sound surprised?"

"Just expected a little more argument, that's all. It'll be worse than having civilians on the battlefield."

"Marginally. She's had some military training, right?"

It was Reza's turn to frown. He hadn't the slightest clue

what kind of military training she had, if any. Maybe she'd just been handed her uniforms and told to report to Fort Hood. Stranger things had happened. "I have no idea," he admitted.

"Well, find out. And make sure she doesn't accidentally set off any pyro."

Reza winced at the jab and flipped Evan off. "Very funny."

Evan cracked a grin as Reza left the office and headed down to his own.

Fifty-six e-mails waited in his inbox. He skimmed the contents, clicking immediately on the first note from Emily.

> Still haven't managed to locate Sloban's file. Have escalated to next level within department. Highest priority.—E

He'd asked her for help finding Sloban's packet and she was keeping her promise. Something so little meant so damn much to him right then.

Every day was another day that Sloban struggled to show up.

He wasn't using, though. He swore it.

And Reza wanted so badly to believe him.

But he knew firsthand how hard the monkey was to shake.

Emily tossed her body armor down on her office floor with a curse. She turned at the sound of soft laughter behind her. Olivia stood in the doorway, her favorite white and red coffee mug cradled in both hands in front of her.

"I never thought I'd hear the day where you'd cuss," Olivia said.

"Yeah well, you try putting together your Inceptor Body Armor," she growled, "without instructions. There is not a single person in this entire clinic that knows how to do this."

She glared down at the pile of gear. "There's pouches and pockets and straps and..."

"And lions and tigers and bears, oh my," Olivia said.

Emily glared at her friend. "Not funny."

"It's a little funny. Seeing you flustered like this? Totally funny." Olivia moved closer to the pile of gear sitting next to the empty plastic bags it had come in. She toed an empty pouch. "Did you just pick this up?"

"An hour ago. I thought it would come put together. I mean, who just hands a soldier a pile of gear and says 'here you go, figure it out'?"

"That would be the U.S. Army," a male voice said. A male voice that she was becoming all too familiar with.

Emily turned at the sound and tried to ignore the way her entire body stood up and took notice. Reza was a big man without any gear on. But now, wearing full body armor, he stood in the doorway of her office and consumed the space around him. The body armor made him look massive, like a warlord, dressed for battle. There was something different about the shirt he wore beneath his body armor. It hugged his skin like a t-shirt instead of being the normal loose-fitting uniform top she wore.

"Are you serious?" Emily said when she realized she was being incredibly rude by staring at him.

"It comes with instructions," he said mildly. She narrowed her eyes as the edge of his lips curled suspiciously.

"I'm quite certain that no live human being wrote those instructions." Beside her, Olivia laughed quietly. "You're not helping."

Olivia laughed harder and eased around Reza toward the door. She stopped and patted him on the shoulder. If Emily hadn't been watching him carefully, she might have missed the slight flex of his jaw as Olivia's hand slid away. He stiffened and eased back, out of her way.

"Have fun with this one, Sergeant," Olivia said. "I don't think she's ever been camping." Olivia stepped out of the office, leaving an awkward silence behind her. Emily shifted uncomfortably.

Reza's eyebrows lifted over the edge of his glasses but they drew down again the moment he saw the state of her body armor. He pushed his glasses to the top of his head, studying the pile. A slow heat crept up her neck at the disapproval she saw in his eyes.

He glanced up at her. His dark eyes were the color of whiskey, deep malted brown. "You've never been camping?" he asked.

Emily folded her hands in front of her. "Do I get kicked out of the cool kids club if I say no?" she asked quietly.

Saying nothing, he crouched down by her gear and started laying out pieces side by side.

"My dad used to take us camping," he said softly, sorting through her gear.

"Who is us?" She knelt down next to him, trying to figure out how he was sorting all the pieces.

"My mom and me." He started lining up things that looked like they were vaguely the same.

"Why do you sound so sad when you say that?" she asked.

"She died two years before I joined the army." The muscle in his jaw pulsed. His neck was tight. He paused for a long moment. "I'm sorry," he said shortly.

"Why are you sorry?" It took everything she had not to reach for him. There was such a rawness in the bleak sadness in his voice.

It was a long moment before he answered. "It's not important," he said quietly.

There was more there, something dark. Something that tugged at her and made her want to go into the dark shadows she saw in his eyes.

But there was something more, something that urged her to wait. Her gut said he wasn't ready, that he'd opened up without meaning to.

"Wouldn't you be more comfortable if you took that off?" She motioned to his body armor.

He said nothing for a long moment as he set two smaller pouches next to each other. "I've done more uncomfortable things than this in this gear," he said after a while.

"Like what?"

"Sleep. Eat. Bleed."

She froze. "You've been shot at."

He didn't stop sorting. "Shot. Blown up. Sure. It's an occupational hazard."

Emily watched the efficient movement of his fingers as he continued laying out the pouches on the chest of her body armor. He had rough-looking hands. Veins stood out against his dark skin. Coarse hair dusted the backs of his wrists, disappearing beneath the uniform t-shirt. A black watch encircled his left wrist. There was no wedding band mark on his left hand.

Faint white scars marked his knuckles. She wouldn't have seen them unless she'd been looking. She searched the moisture-wicking fabric of the t-shirt, looking for any sign of scars on his body. He spoke of getting shot at like it was akin to stubbing his toe. The muscles in his jaw bunched; the veins in his neck strained against his skin.

"You can keep staring at me or you can pay attention to what I'm doing so you can do this yourself." He stopped, holding a small, roundish pouch in his right hand. When she didn't move, he sighed roughly. "What are you staring at?"

"You've been shot?" Emily cleared her throat. "I mean, I know it's not unrealistic and all but . . ."

He shifted then to pin her with those intense dark eyes. "What do you think I do in the infantry? Hand out candy and flowers?" He turned back to her gear. "Winning the hearts and minds is some slogan for officers and talking points on cable news. I just want to bring my boys home from the fight." His throat moved and he yanked the glasses off his head and tossed them onto a nearby chair. "All right, pay attention. You want your ammo pouches where you can easily access them and where they don't hinder your movement."

She blinked at the abrupt transition. "I have no idea what you just said."

He turned to stare at her, his eyes glittering darkly. "Which part?"

"Any of it."

"Ammo. Ammunition? The little bullets you put in the magazine and shoot people with." He frowned. "You know what a magazine is?"

Emily pursed her lips as heat crept up her neck. "Can I just not answer any more questions?"

She wanted to shrink away from the harsh irritation she saw looking back at her. She braced for an ass chewing of epic proportions, prepared to take it. She wanted to understand his world but she didn't even know what questions to ask.

"All right, look," he said after a long moment. And when he continued, there was a wealth of patience in his voice. "When you deploy, you'll have something called a basic load of ammo. You'll have more in your vehicle. You'll need to get proficient with your weapon because rapid reloading is a learned skill that takes a lot of practice. Your magazines, where you carry your extra ammo, go here, like on my kit."

"Kit?"

"Short for rifleman's kit," he said pointing to all the equipment on the floor. "Slang for all of our gear."

Emily nodded and looked at the magazines he wore tucked into his body armor pouches, trying to keep up with the new language he was throwing at her. "Is that a basic load?" she asked, gesturing toward the magazines strapped to his chest.

"It's more than basic load." He met her gaze. "I like to go loaded for bear. Soothes my PTSD."

She tipped her head and studied him, trying to figure out what kind of man would admit to a disorder that held such a stigma. The edge of his lips curled into a faint smile. "It was a joke, ma'am," he said softly.

"Emily," she whispered. She swallowed, locking her eyes with his. "My name is Emily."

"Emily." Her name a caress on his lips. A deep, rumbling sound, deep in his chest.

She couldn't look away from the dark intensity of his eyes. The shadows she saw there were deep, etched into the creases around his eyes. There was something compelling about the man. It went beyond the physical power. Beyond the broad shoulders and wide chest and rough hands.

He'd been driven hard his entire career, she realized. Like an old war horse, ridden into battle again and again. A man who'd gone to war so many times, he was convinced he needed it. He loved it.

She looked at him and wondered if he'd ever simply stopped the carousel and tried to get off. The scars on the backs of his hands, the lines around his eyes, suggested otherwise.

"Sometimes, the jokes you guys tell throw me off," she admitted.

"Black humor. It's a valuable life skill." His lips twitched. "Now then, would you like to learn how to put your gear together?"

And just as abruptly, the man she saw behind those eyes was gone, replaced by the surly sergeant determined to teach her how to put her "kit" together.

Her naiveté should have pissed him off. Part of him *was* pissed that the prim and proper little captain would try to crawl inside his head. He reminded himself that she'd only asked a simple question, a question that any cherry who hadn't deployed asked.

"Your ammo pouches go here," he said. He slipped the thick strap through its slot on the body armor.

She watched what he did, her quick gaze taking in every movement. "What is it like?" she asked softly.

Questions like that haunted him because he didn't know how to answer. "Which part?" he asked.

"Deploying."

He swallowed. How to tell her about the long hours of boredom, the days with shitty rations and no place to sleep but on the back of his truck.

"It sucks," he said. "There's not a lot of ways to kill the time."

"How do you pass the time?" she asked.

He paused, figuring she didn't need to know that his first few weeks deployed were always spent puking his guts up and generally trying to hide the crazy. Maybe this time would be different. Maybe this time, he'd beat the seductive addiction that called to him every time he'd managed to make it home. "I don't have a lot of free time. Soldiers take up a lot of it." He slid a pouch meant for grenades in the space that would cover her heart. "And this is a good place for a flashlight or a head lamp."

"You've lost a lot of friends." It wasn't a question. He felt the tingling of anxiety tightening against his heart.

"Yes." *Please don't ask if I've killed someone.* Because he couldn't bear to see the flicker in her eyes. The silent judgment.

He closed his eyes as the sleeping demon inside him surged and thrashed, sparked to life by the memory of a question asked far too often with no regard to the weight of the words.

As though killing was something he did for fun. Like

some kind of real-life video game where the person on the business end of an M4 got to hit the reset button and come back to fight another day.

Like it didn't claim a piece of your soul each time you had to decide between the man on the end of that front sight post and your boys. It wasn't a hard decision.

Until it was.

"Where'd you go just then?" Her voice penetrated the melancholic introspection. He'd become such a buzz kill. He needed to go have a stiff drink to chase the memories back to the dark corner where he normally kept them.

Except he didn't drink anymore. He shook his head, avoiding her gaze. "Sorry. Got distracted."

She reached for him then, her fingers curling over his. His skin heated where she touched him. "Reza," she whispered.

He was tempted, so tempted to turn his palm beneath hers. To capture her fingers and see just how far she wanted to take this thing between them.

He met her gaze, offering her a wry grin. "You don't want to go crawling around inside my head, doc."

Her throat moved when she swallowed. "Maybe I just want to get to know you a little better."

It was his turn to swallow. His mouth went dry. So he hadn't been misreading things.

There was something there, something shimmering and new and filled with brilliant promise between them. It was so bright it fucking blinded him.

Once more, he tried to do the honorable thing and pull away. Because he hurt everyone he cared about.

It was how he was wired. Hadn't his dad beat that message into him?

"That's probably not a good idea," he said. His voice grated against his ears but even as he spoke, he knew it for a lie. Something as simple as her touch woke a dark and twisting need inside him.

Made him crave more.

She was close. Close enough that he could lean forward if he wanted. Brush his lips against hers and see if her mouth was as soft as it looked. He wanted to nibble on her bottom lip and feel her skin beneath his fingertips as he kissed her.

He needed to focus. They were going to the range today and he couldn't be thinking about her like this if he was trying to teach her how to shoot. "Where's your IFAK?"

Emily frowned. Reza almost laughed at the expression on her face. She was priceless. "My what?"

He kept forgetting she didn't speak the language. "Your first aid kit. Where is it?"

He pulled his thoughts back from the brink of inappropriate as she leaned forward on her knees. "Do you have any idea what you're looking for?" he asked, his voice rough.

She looked back over her shoulder and Reza's entire body tightened. She had no fucking idea how sexy she was at that moment, army uniform and all.

She knelt in front of him, pushing up on her knees with a frustrated sound. "I have no idea."

His gaze dropped to her lips, parted in frustration. She was there, just there.

And Reza surrendered to the temptation. He leaned in. Slowly, so that she could back away if she wanted to. Slowly, so as not to frighten her off.

Slowly, until his top lip brushed hers. A gentle nudge. A hesitant question.

And her soft, yielding answer as her bottom lip opened, just a little, just enough as she leaned in, opening to his touch.

He'd done stupid things in his life before and he would do stupid things again. Of that much he was certain.

But his brain didn't register the movement as stupid.

It was like waking up from a long sleep. Warmth spread inside him as he traced her lips with his tongue before sliding against hers. Pleasure spiked through him when she leaned in, bracing one hand against the body armor covering his chest.

He wanted to lock her door and lay her down on that pile of gear and strip her naked and learn everything that she liked.

But they were at work and at any moment, someone could walk by her office.

Officers and enlisted weren't supposed to get involved and Reza damn sure wasn't about to ruin her life with a single moment of indiscretion.

He eased back, swiping his thumb over her bottom lip before putting more space between them.

"Was that an IFAK?" she whispered, her eyes sparkling.

Grinning, he shook his head. "Not exactly," he said. She was going to mess up her hair in the field today. He wondered if she knew that.

He had the sudden idea that she might not care. She came across so proper but there was a wildness in his little captain.

A wildness he'd gotten a tiny taste of just then.

A wildness that he wanted to taste again.

He laughed then because he needed to do something to subdue the arousal wafting through his blood like a hit of the purest alcohol. "Get out of the way, knucklehead," he said, more gently than he felt.

He always ended up taking care of the strays in his platoon, the kids with no father, a bad home life. And he'd never admit it but he needed them as much as they needed him.

Maybe if he'd managed to protect them, he could make up for failing to protect his mom from the violence in their home. It was a stupid fantasy. Like he was searching for something he would never find. Something he should have known better and given up on a long time ago.

Emily wasn't like that. She knew what she wanted out of life, knew what she was doing.

She was stronger than he'd ever been or could ever hope to be.

He spotted the first aid kit under the chair and leaned forward to grab it. Emily reached for it at the same time. It was something out of an old movie. His hand closed over hers. He was instantly aware of her soft skin. The fragile feel of her bones beneath his, the echo of that kiss burning against his lips.

She froze the moment his skin connected with hers and there was a scattered fear that looked back at him for the moment he held her in his grip. And then as soon as it happened, it was over. He released her, the burn of her skin against his penetrating his flesh, a hunger twisting and rising inside him, craving more.

She said nothing and he let the silence stand. Whatever this was, it was complicated.

It always would be where Reza was concerned.

"Ready to try it on? Stand up and let's see how it fits." She opened her mouth, looking dubiously at the pile of gear. He tipped his chin, studying her. How could someone so stubborn be so unwilling to ask for help? "You don't know how."

She shook her head. "Got it in one."

"All right, watch me. You see these straps here?" He pulled on two Velcro tabs near his abdomen until they tore free. Dropping them, he let them fall, banging behind him like a heavy tail made of military equipment. "Lift this and there are two more straps underneath." He pulled those free as well and showed her how to lift the body armor over her head. "Got it?"

She looked between hers, still a shapeless lump on the floor and his, straps flailing like a Muppet on too much caffeine.

"One more time," he said. "Watch me."

He lifted the body armor over his head then secured first the straps closest to his belly and then the outer straps.

She knelt down and lifted her kit, stumbling a little under the weight. It would take some getting used to. She ripped the straps open on her body armor then struggled to lift the awkward mass over her head, and he made no move to help her. She needed to be able to do it herself. Even if he did it just this once, it would breed a dependency. She needed to know how to do this kind of thing. It was one of the basics that saved lives.

She struggled to get it over her head but finally she swung it into place. She searched for her straps and managed to secure both sets.

It was such a simple thing she'd done. An ingrained task that Reza could do without thinking. But for this civilian turned soldier, it was an accomplishment. She looked up at him with such pride in her eyes that he suddenly no longer saw Emily Lindberg, psych doc.

He saw Emily and a hundred other young soldiers before the war touched them. Saw her need to be inducted into the warrior caste without ever knowing what it cost.

But she wasn't just another soldier. She was Emily, and just being around her was doing something to his insides, something twisting and writhing and hungry.

Something possessive. She wasn't his. She couldn't be.

But he had the strongest wish that she was.

Chapter Six

We have to swing by my battalion headquarters before we head out to the training area."

Emily followed Reza out into the bright Fort Hood morning, trying to get used to the weight she now carried in the form of her IBA. The weight was evenly distributed around her torso but it was still bulky and uncomfortable. Reza wore his like it was a second skin. She wondered if he had some kind of superhero gene because the man positively radiated power.

Yeah, her lady parts were getting all quivery. She really was pathetic. She'd done so well keeping distance between herself and the temptation of so many well-built, honorable men. The kind of men who would cause her mother to faint.

She peered at Reza as she walked next to him. His skin was darker on his jaw, the shadow of his beard already making an appearance. She caught herself wondering how often he shaved.

She rubbed her hands together and he glanced down at her. "Where are your gloves?" he asked as they approached the Humvee in the parking lot.

"What gloves?"

There was nothing but the silent pulse of his jaw. "Here." He peeled his gloves off and thrust them at her. "I'll get another pair out of my truck."

"Why do I need gloves?" she asked, sliding her hands into the too big gloves. They were still warm from his skin and she smothered a ridiculous heat that spread through her body from the echo of his touch.

"Ammo shells, broken glass, shards of metal. All kinds of good reasons." He climbed into the passenger's seat of the Humvee and said something to the driver, a skinny, dark-skinned kid who looked like he was about twelve.

Emily climbed into the backseat behind the driver and simply sat for a moment. Her first trip in a military vehicle. There were divots running down the center of the truck and a tarp separated the front from the back. There was some kind of radio system between Reza and the driver.

And the noise. As soon as they started driving the engine rumbled to life, drowning out all thought, all sound. It was a constant roar, like standing in the entrance of a cave as the sea rushed in. The thin seat beneath her vibrated and she felt every bump, every brake check.

She glanced at Reza, who was constantly checking the mirror to his right and the road in front of him. When they stopped at an intersection, he shouted something to the driver but she couldn't hear him. The driver gunned it through the intersection and kept going.

The transition from the hospital complex to the area owned by First Cav was stark. Everything on Fort Hood was dated, but the buildings that housed the various battalions of the First Cavalry Division were ancient. Some of them looked like they should have been condemned and yet they stood proudly emblazoned with their unit logos and guidons waving in the easy spring breeze.

It was funny how the transition was subtle. The pride that

the officers walked with over here. She hadn't believed the hype about the division. Everyone ran around post saying "First Team" when they saluted her on those rare occasions that she ventured out of the clinic. They had to be faking that kind of enthusiasm, right? But as she rode deeper into Cav country, she started to think that maybe they really did believe that stuff about being America's First Team.

They rolled to a stop beside a headquarters building sheltered beneath old oak trees. The driver killed the engine and Reza shifted back to look at her.

"You coming or you want to wait here?"

"What are we doing?"

"I need to check on a training plan to make sure that nothing went wrong on the range."

Emily smiled but before she could speak, Reza's lips curled ever so faintly at the edges.

"Come on. I don't have time to translate right now."

The driver shot Reza a funny look but said nothing. Emily wondered at the relationship differences that seemed so much more stark over here. The soldier barely spoke to his sergeant but when he did, it was with a reverence akin to awe.

Granted, she grew a little more and more in awe of Reza the longer she spent time around him, but somehow she figured he'd be more comfortable with his men.

"What's on your mind, doc?" he asked as he flashed his ID at the staff duty sergeant.

"Just wondering why the driver didn't make conversation," she said after a moment, following him down the hallway and trying not to feel like she was rushing to keep up.

"We don't take warm showers together, if that's what you're asking."

Emily laughed quietly. "Was that a line from *Heartbreak Ridge*?"

"You didn't strike me as a war movie kind of girl." Reza stopped short, studying her. "Are you honestly telling me you've watched that movie?"

Heat crept up her neck. "Before I signed up for the army, I wanted to know what I was getting myself in for. I watched every war movie I could find."

Reza simply stared at her, his dark eyes glittering. She was sure he was laughing at her. "You know those were Marines in *Heartbreak Ridge*, right?"

"Of course."

He cracked the barest grin. She supposed it was better than yelling at her, so there was that. She followed Reza down the hall toward two double-wide doors that led to a wide open cubicle farm.

"Sloban's here," Foster said. His face was streaked with dirt and dust and sweat. "Needs to see you before you head out to the range. Who's this?"

Emily stiffened as the young sergeant in front of her snarled as she walked up behind Reza.

"Doc from the hospital," Reza said next to her. "Where's Slo?"

"In the ops."

Beside her, she felt Reza stiffen. She was embarrassed, both professionally and personally, that they couldn't find his packet. Foster's eyes swept over her in a way that made her feel judged and found unworthy. She knew the empty space on her right shoulder set her apart, just like the knowledge that she was medical and not combat arms. Had his gaze been any more suggestive, she might have added the fact that she was also female to the list of reasons why his resentment was a tangible thing.

"We got to find that damn paperwork, Sarn't Ike. The commander has been giving Sloban shit about his medical file."

Reza said nothing as she followed him out of battalion and toward his ops. It was a dirty place. Run-down with a fine coat of dust settled over just about anything that hadn't moved in the last week. It was a long way from the sparkling buffed floors of the hospital or her clinic. It felt like another world.

Emily frowned as they rounded the corner and into the ops. There were five soldiers in there but instantly she knew which one was Sloban. His hands were in a constant state of motion; his eyes were haunted and hunted.

He wasn't one of her patients but he was one of Reza's soldiers. She walked over to him. "We're working on finding your medical packet," she said softly.

Sloban turned those haunted eyes on her and she felt a coldness to the very pit of her soul. He opened his mouth but no sound came out. After a moment, he looked at Reza.

"She works at the mental health clinic. She's trying to help us find your file," he explained. His voice was gentle. Soothing. As though he was trying not to spook the kid.

"My log says I sent it back to the board people," she said. "We'll find it."

"Can't you just make copies?" Sloban asked.

She shook her head. "I wish it were that simple," she said. She didn't remember his file. She wished she did.

Foster sighed hard. "Well, at least we know where it isn't. Sloban is losing his fucking mind, you know that, right, Sarn't Ike? The commander is being a real douche to the guys with medical issues."

"Got it. I'll talk to him." There was an odd note in Reza's voice that hadn't been there a moment before. He glanced at Emily, his hand on Sloban's shoulder. "Give me a few minutes, okay?"

She nodded, wishing there was something she could do to ease the strain and the fatigue she heard in his voice.

It was the fatigue of a warrior who'd fought one too many fights with no end in sight. Sloban was just one more soldier. One more life he could touch.

But who was there to hold him up when he stumbled? Who did Reza lean on in the bad times?

She sat in the company ops as he disappeared behind closed doors, a sinking feeling in her gut that she knew the answer to that question.

He had no one.

And that simple realization broke her heart.

Reza closed the door behind Sloban, fighting the urge to take a wire brush to Foster's backside. He wasn't really sure what had Foster's panties in a bunch and he didn't really give a shit, either. His attitude had sucked the last few days and Reza was itching to get him to the gym to beat the living shit out of him on the combatives mat to make him talk about whatever was eating him. Foster got PMS about once every six months and it took a good bout in the ring to get him to open up. Usually he had women problems but as far as Reza knew, there was no one serious in Foster's life right now.

Unless he counted the stripper down at whatever name the club in Harker Heights was going by these days. Foster had been spending far too much time in that shit hole.

Foster wasn't his main worry. Sloban was, and right now Sloban looked like he was ready to climb the walls inside Reza's office.

Reza pulled up a chair diagonal to Slo. "What's going on?"

Sloban's hands shook as he tried to find something to do with them. He said nothing. Reza didn't expect him to. Since he'd gotten hooked on meth all those months ago, he didn't say as much as he used to.

The warrior he'd known was now gaunt and strung out

and pockmarked. His skin stretched too tight over his bones, his eyes were haunted.

"Are you using?" Reza asked.

Sloban looked down at his hands. "I'm trying. I'm trying so fucking hard not to screw up again, Sarn't Ike." He looked up, his eyes watery. "I need to go home. I can't fucking stay here and keep waiting. Why is it taking so long?"

Reza glanced at the door. Emily was trying to run down the packet. It was more than anyone else in the medical system had done for any of Reza's soldiers.

But it wasn't enough. And Sloban was running out of time. He knew it. He could see the hunger in the kid's eyes.

"If you use again, Marshall will stop the medical board with a court-martial," Reza said slowly. "Slo, you got to stay clean."

Sloban's throat moved, his eyes darting around the room. "I'm trying."

"How can I help?" Reza asked.

Sloban's answer was a flat smile. "Just get me out of here. That's all I need."

He reached over and squeezed Sloban's shoulder. "I'm working on it. Just stay with me a little longer, okay?"

Slo looked down at his hands and nodded. As promises went, it didn't measure up but it was the best he could expect. The warrior Sloban had been was long gone.

But Reza wasn't going to abandon the kid. He had no idea where the packet could be and short of raiding the hospital commander's office, there was little he could do other than keep calling over there three times a day.

Sloban stood and Reza followed him out of the office. Emily stood by the door, watching everything going on around her in stoic silence. The kid slipped by Emily without so much as a glance. The entire office seemed to breathe a collective sigh.

Reza looked down at her as she stood. The body armor

made her movements awkward. "You okay?" she asked as she followed him out of the company ops.

He said nothing for a long time. What could he tell her? That he knew the hunger that Sloban fought? That he knew how hard it was to stay sober and clean?

That he knew how this ended and it terrified him?

"I have to be," was all he said instead.

She said nothing. But after a moment, her hand rested on his shoulder at the edge of his body armor.

A simple gesture, nothing more. But the marks on his arms burned where she touched him.

What would she say if she saw what he'd done to his body over the years? How would she react to the scars and everything else?

But instead of brushing her hand off, he simply reached up and squeezed it gently.

And for a moment, it was enough.

He rapped on the door frame to Teague's cubbyhole. "Where's Captain Loehr? I need to make sure we've got clearance for the MOUT site today."

Teague grinned and stood. "Perfect timing. I need a ride out to training."

"There won't be any training unless we get the green light from Captain America."

Teague held up a folder. "You mean this? I swear, one range fire and you've turned into a timid little baby kitten afraid of his own shadow."

Reza swore under his breath, wishing Emily wasn't standing right there watching Teague show his ass—figuratively, of course. He wondered how long it would be before Teague tried to hit on her.

The thought made Reza's spine stiffen as he glanced over at her.

Emily raised both eyebrows, her lips twitching. "Range fire?"

Heat crawled up Reza's neck, along with a strong desire to throttle Ben Teague. "I may or may not have been involved in an incident involving a small fire here at Fort Hood."

"Ha," Teague snorted and grabbed his helmet. "He burned down three hundred acres of training area last year."

"It was an accident," Reza snarled. "Get your shit and let's go. We're burning daylight."

"It's always an accident," Teague said. "What's she doing here, anyway?"

"Wants to observe training," Reza said, stuffing the paperwork in his cargo pocket. "She's putting together an officer professional development program and asked for help."

He saw Emily open her mouth then snap it shut as the wisdom of the lie took hold. It wasn't actually a bad idea. He could practically see the shape of the good idea fairy forming in her thoughts. She pulled out a little moleskin notebook and jotted something down before climbing into the back of the Humvee.

He wondered if she always carried it even as she struggled to stuff it back into her cargo pocket. He watched as she moved, her body strong beneath the body armor. He'd thought she was prim and proper when he'd first met her but he was wrong.

The woman was so much more than she appeared. Dedicated. Smart. And so damned sexy.

The vehicle rolled out of the parking lot and headed to the MOUT site, leaving him to his thoughts for the moment.

That kiss still burned on his lips. A foolish gambit, one he wasn't going to regret but one that he couldn't repeat.

No matter how much he might want to.

He'd given up drinking and boozing. At least, that's what

he kept telling himself. But with Emily, there was something more there. A need. A desire for something more than a stolen kiss or an office flirtation.

He felt a pull of something real, something stronger than just sex.

Something that terrified him with the strength of it. He was trying to be the soldier the sergeant major wanted him to be. The warrior his men deserved. If he couldn't get clean and stay clean, how was he supposed to expect his men to do it? He wanted to save the remains of his career. He wasn't sure he could even go to bed with a woman without being shitfaced drunk.

He couldn't remember the last time something like that had even happened.

Sex and alcohol were all twisted up inside him and he damn sure wasn't about to admit his own personal psychosis to her.

He'd kissed her. She'd kissed him back.

It would have to be enough. Because the truth was, he didn't trust himself to try anything more.

He swallowed the bitter pill of frustration as they pulled into the MOUT site a few minutes later. Life was so much easier when he was drinking.

"Ready to get your ass whipped?" Reza asked.

"Oh yeah. I'm going to lay your ass out flat," Teague said, pulling on his gloves.

"You wish, pretty boy. You better wear a face mask 'cause I'm going to double tap you right between the eyes," Reza said. Reza tapped his own forehead.

Emily came up beside them, adjusting her hair beneath her helmet. He had no idea how to help her with that. Claire would have been able to give her some pointers on that one but Claire was in California right then. Emily was on her own as far as her hair was concerned. "Um, can I be the complete and total newbie here and ask what you're talking about?"

"You don't know what we're doing today?" Teague looked at her with an expression close to bafflement on his face. He looked back at Reza. "You didn't tell her?"

"Tell me what?" Emily sounded like he was dragging her toward a darkened pit filled with slithering things.

"We're going to a shoot house."

"A what?"

"Shoot house."

She went very still. The kind of still that made Reza think she was second-guessing her decision to come out here. "What's a shoot house?"

"A building where we go shoot each other with sim rounds."

"And sim rounds are..."

"Very painful," Teague said with the wicked smile of someone who knew exactly how painful they could be.

Teague was enjoying her discomfort far too much. "Go see why they've stopped." He was used to bossing the captain around. Teague was a good guy but he was ADHD boy. Needed someone to step on his neck to keep him focused and out of trouble. Teague unsupervised was a recipe for disaster. Reza wondered just how much of that was real and how much of it was a façade Teague put on to avoid any major responsibility. "What's wrong?"

"You're going to shoot each other?" Emily sounded shocked.

"With fake bullets."

"You just threatened to shoot him in the face."

Frustration at her naïveté snapped at its leash inside him, surprising him with its intensity. "Haven't we had this conversation before? The one where I explain to you that we're not giving out candy and roses when we're busy winning the hearts and minds?"

"Stop putting words in my mouth," she said more sharply than he'd anticipated. Something had gotten under her skin in between leaving the office and coming out here. He wanted to know very much what it was.

But he didn't know how to ask. "Then what is it?"

She opened her mouth to speak, then snapped it shut. "Never mind. I'm tired of you laughing at me because I don't know anything about the world you're from."

Reza stepped close, until his body armor almost brushed against hers. "I'm not laughing at you, Emily," he said, keeping his voice low. "You've never been to combat. You've never seen men die because of actions you've taken or worse, actions you did not take. You're untouched by all the death and dying and killing that smothers a man's soul." They were alone near the truck. He did not bother to rein in his urge to brush his knuckles against her soft cheek. "You have no idea how rare and precious being untouched by the war really is in my world."

She didn't flinch beneath his touch but she also did not acknowledge it in any way. Her skin was soft, satin beneath the rough ridge of his knuckles. Her breath was a scattered thing, coming in fits and huffs.

He wanted to tell her more, so much more. Wanted to satiate her curiosity to know about the war and send her back to her protected office, where she would never have to venture out into the real world.

A knight in shining armor would want to protect her. Cherish her.

Reza was no knight. He was a warrior. A man who fought for what he wanted. But with Emily, those things were no longer clear. And for the first time in his adult life, he turned away from a woman who'd trembled beneath his touch. There was more to Emily Lindberg than Reza had realized. So, so much more.

If this went any further, he would ruin it. He always did. There was nothing in his life he didn't screw up and he very much did not want to screw this up.

He wanted to keep her on her pedestal. Keep her unsullied by the war and the world he lived in. He pulled his gloves out of where she'd stuffed them into a small pocket. "Make sure you wear these today," he murmured.

Reza felt Emily hesitate before she climbed the hill toward the MOUT site behind him. His gaze fell to his gloves on her hands, and an unexplained warmth spread somewhere in the vicinity of his belly as he watched her.

He wasn't entirely sure what the hell had happened to him. Not so long ago, he'd gone up one side of her and down the other for keeping information about a soldier from him. Not so long ago, he'd told her she did not belong in the army.

Now she was out at the range with him, wanting to know about the world he lived in.

A world he didn't want her to know. The scars on his body were testament to the ragged ugliness of war.

She'd watched movies about combat. He'd led men in combat. Bled with them.

What on earth had possessed him to bring her out here?

He knew what it was and it pissed him off. If she was going to deploy, maybe something she learned today would save her life later. He hated to think of her in a bunker with rockets landing all around. His stomach twisted hard. He wouldn't be there to keep her safe.

People like her simply didn't recognize the world for what it was: a cruel, hard place that would crush the best of them. It was a world that required exactly what they were about to do: train.

If he couldn't protect her, he could train her. At least a little. A little was better than nothing.

If she backed away from the shoot house, he wouldn't let her go. She needed to do this, to see this in training where it was safe. No matter how much he wanted to protect her from the smoke and chaos of war—even a mock war like they were getting ready to wage today—the simple fact was she was going to deploy. Better to learn what she could here today rather than head to the desert with zero training. The threat of violence was a very real thing in his daily life and if she was going to deploy, she needed to understand that.

He watched her as she approached, careful to keep his expression neutral.

Part of him wanted her to run, to turn away from the violence of his life.

But another part of him, the dark part, wanted her to join him in the muck and the mire. That darkness held a powerful lure, a quiet shame mixed with the pride: he was good at what he did.

She flexed her hands in those gloves and his guts clenched. *Down, boy.*

"You ready for this?" he asked as she stopped next to him.

She peered up at him intently through her army-issued protective glasses. They were at least three sizes too big. "Is one ever really ready for something like this?" She didn't look nervous but he heard the stress in her voice.

"Would it help you to know that I'm looking forward to this? This is the fun stuff I signed up for." Not the killing parts. No, not those. But the force-on-force mock fights? That was the fun stuff.

"Fun? Are you serious?"

"Hey, Sarn't Ike, check this out!" One of his old lieutenants, Miller, ran up from the entrance to one of the blown-up windowless buildings of the mock city. He lifted his shirt, showing a brilliant purple and red welt on his side.

"That shit's going to hurt like hell tomorrow," Reza said with a low whistle. "Did the medics check you out?"

"I'm not fu— Nah, I'm good," Miller said, stopping himself once he realized there was an officer present. "Ma'am." He saluted and Emily returned the courtesy.

Reza almost shook his head at the sharp perfection of her salute. She obviously hadn't learned the half-assed officer salute that so many officers passed off as real customs and courtesies. He watched her expression change from horror to pure curiosity.

"Is that—"

"Some of the guys were screwing around, Ma'am. Doesn't hurt that bad." Miller had turned about as red as the bruise on his side.

"How did that happen?" she asked, peering closer.

Miller glanced at Reza for permission and Reza nodded. Unless he was mistaken, that bruise had come from an epic case of fucking around and he didn't mind Emily hearing that. She needed to see the fun side of the guys in addition to the fucked-up stuff inside their heads. Maybe if he could get her to see them as people, she'd stop thinking of them as victims.

"Couple of the guys cornered me. I let my guard down and well . . . there you have the results."

Reza grinned, feeling the warm comfort of familiarity slip around him as Miller ran back toward his boys. This, Reza knew. This was the only thing that kept him from crawling back into the bottle. A chance to lead his boys again.

He wasn't in charge today. No, that day was still a long way off. But he wanted—no, he *needed*—to be back with guys like Foster and Miller. With captains like Teague.

"Just follow me and stay close. It might get a little loud." Reza watched as she tried to get her bearings over the sounds and the movement and the noise.

People who had never been to combat didn't understand the chaos on the battlefield. It was oh so easy to second-guess the actions of the men and women on the ground when the videos captured everything, but in the thick of the fight? Yeah, it was never as easy as the video games and armchair quarterbacks made it seem. There was too much smoke, too much yelling, far too many people.

One wrong choice and the squeeze of the trigger ended a life. It might be fun, what they did in the shoot house, but that fun ended the minute they rolled with real rounds in the chamber.

"A little loud?" She was shouting. "I'm not sure it can get any louder."

"If you're still talking to me in a few months, I'll take you out on an op in the tunnels. You want to talk about loud."

"Tunnels?"

"We do tunnel training because we never know when we have to go below the cities, or literally in tunnels."

Her eyes widened slightly as though she was only just starting to grasp the variety of situations his boys faced. It was fascinating watching the scales fall from her eyes. She took everything in. Watched with a fascination that told him she wasn't missing anything.

Her brows drew down in a slight frown. "What?" he asked.

"Nothing. You're just... You're different out here." She tipped her chin at him. "More intense. You really do enjoy this stuff, don't you?"

The strange feeling in his belly unfurled completely, spreading warmth wide through his blood. "There is nothing better than leading men in combat," he said over the noise.

Nothing until he held that experience up next to the possibility of touching Emily again.

What would he give up for a few more minutes alone? To

touch her the way he wanted, to feel her soften beneath his mouth and his fingers.

An explosion ripped through the noise and he ducked, more on instinct than anything else. When he looked over at her, her jaw had tightened in determination.

And Reza fell a little harder.

Chapter Seven

Emily had never been so terrified in her life. For the last three hours, she'd watched grown men run around shooting each other with tiny rounds that looked like miniature lipsticks.

She felt alive. More alive than she'd ever felt before in her entire life. Even when one of those tiny rounds had slammed into the concrete next to her face, she didn't want it to end.

Her blood pounded through her veins, slammed with adrenaline and fear and laughter. She'd never heard so much trash-talking, ever. Her father's country club would never be the same to her again. There was an easy comfort in the way the men bonded, the way they'd mostly adjusted to having her on the mock battlefield with them. She covered her mouth with one hand, hiding her smile. Her mother would be so ashamed of her thoughts right now. Her behavior was most unladylike.

And she was loving it.

But there was something else, something she hadn't counted on. Reza. He shadowed her as they walked through the shoot house, his big body blocking her when the guys got a little too close. He wasn't obvious about it. He was just there. Solid. Steady.

Her shield. It was not something she might have appreciated otherwise, but the shouts of the men when they got hit by the rounds was enough to set her nerves on edge with a prickle of fear. How badly did it hurt?

She'd actually shrieked at one point when a burly specialist had crashed into the wall near her, only to practically bounce back to his feet and charge back into the fray.

It was terrifying. It was exhilarating. She'd never felt anything like the raw power of the sound of weapons reverberating off her breastbone or the exciting chaos of rounding a corner and wondering what skulked down the next hallway.

They were outside now, taking a break for lunch, if one could call the food product contained in a Meal Ready To Eat, or MRE, actual lunch. She bit back a growl of frustration as she tried to open the thick brown plastic that encased the foodstuffs. She glanced longingly at the knife Reza had produced from a hip pouch and then she blinked and her MRE was snatched from her hand. A flick of his wrist and he'd sliced the top off and handed it back to her.

"You need a knife," he said mildly, "when you deploy."

She started pulling each item out of the pouch, reading the heavy black letters carefully. There were half a dozen pouches inside the first pouch. Applesauce. Ham slice. A tiny pouch with a little folded napkin, a mini bottle of Tabasco sauce. Salt, pepper. A spoon. It was a complete three-course meal in a bag. "Is this really a ham slice?" she asked. "And do we eat so many MREs in Iraq that I'd need a knife?"

Reza gazed at her and she tried very hard not to notice how drop dead sexy he looked right then. He leaned back on his helmet and his body armor. His patrol cap was kicked back high on his head like a ball cap and he'd rolled his sleeves up in the warm afternoon sun. There was a hint of black ink beneath the edge of one sleeve. Funny, she hadn't thought about whether he had tattoos. Now, though, she wanted to know more.

His uniform was wet from sweat and his combat t-shirt clung to his body. And oh, what a body. The man was powerful and gorgeous, but it was not the power that attracted her at that moment.

It was the kindness he was showing her. A kindness she had not expected from him. The rough sergeant who'd laid into her on more than one occasion was relaxed. Not snapping at her. It was like he'd put on a different attitude toward her completely: he was more mentor than sergeant right then.

"Sometimes. We went without food back in OIF 06-08. They couldn't get the jackasses who were running logistics to come to our base. Some of the wives sent care packages but it got to the point where we'd have fought over a ketchup packet."

Emily stopped where she was, trying to figure out how to open the package of crackers, figuring crackers and cheese were about all she could stomach right then. "How long did you go without food?"

"Couple days where we had nothing left. Then the brigade commander found out about it and flew in some supplies."

"How did the commanders not know there were bases without food?" She was shocked.

Reza shot her a baleful look. "You have no idea how much a commander is responsible for. Logistics are one of those things that are supposed to take care of themselves."

"Food should be one of those things," Emily insisted. "There's no way anyone should not know that."

Reza smiled and it was carved in bitter sadness. "There are so many things commanders don't know. That they can't know."

There was something deeper in those words, something filled with hurt and darkness and pain. She reached across the space, squeezing his forearm gently. "And there's some things they're supposed to know," she said. "I deal with all kinds of commanders and I'm shocked at who they allow to lead soldiers."

Reza shook the tiny bottle of hot sauce into the gray pouch in his hand. "You're talking about Marshall, aren't you?"

Emily thought back to the captain who'd called her a very foul name for refusing to change one of his soldier's profiles. "Him. And others. They turn into petulant children with bad tempers when they don't get their way."

Reza laughed sharply then took a long pull off his Camel-Bak. "I'll have to remember that the next time Captain Marshall is crushing my nuts over something stupid." He stuck a plastic spoon in his pouch and stirred. "Marshall's a dickhead but sometimes, he's not a bad guy."

"You could have fooled me. He's going to drive one of his soldiers to kill himself. The man has no compassion."

"Maybe he has other things besides compassion driving him. Compassion almost got him killed back in OIF 2."

"OIF 2?"

"Iraq 2004. The first couple of rotations into Iraq were OIF 1, OIF 2. Then the years started getting split and we started calling them things like OIF 06-08."

"Ah. What happened to Marshall in OIF 2?" She was curious now. Despite his being an unrelenting ass, Emily was curious how Reza would justify the captain's actions.

"He was a lieutenant, brand new. First deployment. He'd found a group of women and children. Two of the kids had been shot and left in a bongo truck."

"By us?"

"No one knows, honestly." Reza concentrated on whatever he was mixing in front of him. "His platoon tried to get them to the local hospital. The truck was rigged to blow. He lost two of his boys trying to save a couple of Iraqis who died in the blast, too." Reza pinned her with a haunted look.

Emily swallowed a bite of stale cracker and thick, viscous cheese. It caught in her throat and she washed it down quickly with a sip from her bottled water. She wanted to ask more about the things that shaped Reza. Wondered what had turned him into the hardened warrior who sat calmly eating his lunch and talking of a war she'd only seen on TV.

Reza pushed away the memories and focused on the little captain next to him. She was a sneaky fox; that was for sure. She'd found a way into his head and that irritated him. It irritated him more that he'd gone down memory lane and remembered that Marshall hadn't always been such an asshole.

At the same time, it meant she was damn good at her job because he hadn't even realized it. If he wasn't careful, she'd have him confessing to a hell of a lot more than someone else's memories.

There were things he wanted to confess and it started with stripping off her clothes and doing inappropriate things. Would her entire body flush if he used his mouth on her?

God, he was so screwed. He couldn't concentrate if he was thinking about her standing naked and exposed in front of him.

But the more the thoughts lingered, the more he wondered if he could do it. If he could be with a woman—with this woman—without being shitfaced drunk.

"Okay, so after you finish your lunch, you want to give it a go?"

Emily stopped chewing. "Give what a go?" she asked carefully.

"The shoot house. I'll get one of the guys to let you borrow their weapon and you can try to clear a room."

"I'm not really sure what that means," she said quietly.

Reza couldn't help the grin that escaped. "Just like what you saw all morning. You shoot bad guys."

"Are you serious?" She sounded terrified and excited. Her eyes lit up and her lips parted just a little. Enough to draw his gaze and make him think about nibbling on the corner of her mouth. Every little thing drove him closer and closer to the edge of doing something stupid.

The hitch in her voice reminded him of the first time he took any scared private through a shoot house. There was a glint in her eyes and she tipped her chin.

"I'll go with you," he said quietly. "And the guys will take it easy on you. You've got gloves, you've got body armor and eye protection."

"But I could get shot."

"With a sim round." He didn't want her hurt but she needed to do this. She needed to experience this firsthand. It was as close to war as he ever wanted her to get.

"I've heard you guys complaining about how bad those things hurt all morning. I'm not exactly into S and M, you know."

Reza chuckled softly. "Scared?"

"So?" she said, lifting her chin.

He leaned toward her, his voice low. "Then think of how much you'll be able to relate the next time a kid comes into your office and talks about how scared he was the first time he got blown up?"

Emily narrowed her eyes at him. "That's a dirty trick."

"It's why you wanted to come out here, wasn't it?" She was going to do it. He'd struck her deeply with that comment and she might be prim and proper but she had too much pride to let him win.

He watched her nostrils flare as she took a deep breath. "Okay, fine." She stood up and started pulling on her body armor, slightly less awkwardly than she'd been earlier that day.

He stood and pulled on his own kit. He stopped as she tightened her helmet chin strap to keep it from falling into her eyes. She was chewing on her lip as she dressed for battle and tried to look like she knew what she was doing.

"Emily," he said softly. "I've got your back. I won't let you get hurt."

She stopped where she was fiddling with her gloves and looked up at him. For a brief moment, the chaos behind them at the shoot house fell away. They were engulfed in a world of silence. He almost reached up to stroke her hair off her cheek. The urge to kiss her then was overwhelming and it was sheer willpower that he didn't move any closer to her.

"I know," she whispered. Her throat moved as she swallowed and he suddenly badly wanted to drag his teeth against that scattered pulse. "I trust you."

Three little words nearly dropped him to his knees. They destroyed him, knowing she was placing her faith where it wasn't deserved. Where he couldn't keep it safe.

She trusted him.

"Ready?"

A deep, steadying breath. "Sure, why not. Let's go get shot at."

She sounded so sarcastic, he couldn't resist the laugh that escaped him. "It'll be fine. A couple of bruises if you actually get hit on your arms or legs. Think of them as battle scars."

Her gaze drifted back to his body like it had earlier. He'd found her curiosity about his scars off-putting earlier, but now? Now his blood warmed as her gaze trailed over his arms and chest. He cleared his throat roughly.

"LT!"

LT Josh Miller had grown up a hell of a lot since Reza had been his platoon sergeant. He strode up to Reza with a confidence that had been battle-born.

"What's up, Sarn't Ike?" Miller carried his weapon casually and there was no salute exchanged between them on the range. He wasn't sure when the rule of no saluting in a tactical environment had come into military history but it made sense.

No point in being sniper bait.

"We need to borrow a couple of weapons. Captain Lindberg wants to run through the shoot house."

Miller glanced at Emily, who stood stoically by his side, then back to Reza. "Sure thing, Sarn't Ike."

Miller would likely bust his balls later because Reza knew how it looked. And no matter that he *wanted* to sleep with Emily, the simple fact was that his reputation preceded him and everyone was simply assuming based on his past. He didn't want them thinking that Emily was just a cheap screw.

She was important to him. It was more than just wanting her to know this so she could do her job. He wanted her to know what it felt like—even if this was a bad facsimile of real life.

He glanced at Emily as Miller reappeared with two M4s. He handed her the first weapon and she immediately grasped the pistol grip and put her finger on the trigger.

"Okay, stop," Reza said, taking the weapon from her a little too abruptly. He handed his back to Miler, who was watching with interest. "Watch me. This is how you hold your weapon."

He demonstrated by angling the weapon across his body, the sling over one shoulder, the butt stock high against the pocket of his shoulder. "Look where my finger is," he said. His finger rested alongside the trigger. "You never put your finger on the trigger until you're ready to shoot something."

Reza let his own weapon hang in front of him as he took the second M4 from Miller. "Take the sling and put it over one shoulder. You want it tight but able to move." She held on to the weapon lightly as he adjusted the sling.

"It feels like the end of it is going to hit me in the face," she said.

"It won't. Keep it tight into your shoulder so you maintain control of it. The last thing you need is to hold it too loosely and have it bouncing around as you're trying to hit your target."

She swallowed nervously. "You mean a person, right?"

"Target," he corrected, uncomfortable with the direction of her thoughts. He stepped behind her and reached around her, encircling her body with his as he showed her how to lift the weapon and look down the scope.

She was small, so small, even wearing her body armor. He caught the scent of her shampoo, something clean and light that reminded him of sunshine.

"Remember how it feels when you have the weapon right. Tight in your shoulder. Pull back on it so you've got a good grip." His lips were near her ear, despite their helmets. She nodded, trying to get her head angled so she could see down the scope. A subtle shift but she leaned back into him. It was enough to send Reza's mind straight toward inappropriate thoughts. The kind of thoughts where she was naked and wrapped in his arms and he was...He moved away from her before he embarrassed them both. "Lower it." She did. "Now raise it." She did, trying to mimic his earlier motions.

"It feels strange," she whispered.

"Yeah, it will. Until you get used to it. This is just so you can get a feel for the chaos in a fight. Nothing more," he said roughly. "Ready?"

Another deep breath then she lifted her chin. "Ready."

Reza was in front of her, Teague behind her. She was the second man in the stack, so to speak, and while she had no idea what that entailed beyond literally being number two behind Reza, she was pretty sure she was going to pee her pants before this whole thing was over.

She slipped her finger over the trigger then caught herself and rested it alongside the trigger until she was ready to shoot. Teague pushed up against her back.

"Nothing personal," he said against her ear. "But we get stacked close so we can communicate through touch and don't have to talk."

So now not only was she pressed up against Reza's back but she had Teague pressed against hers. She was like an Emily sandwich, squished between two big warriors. She giggled.

Reza looked back over his shoulder. "There's no giggling in the shoot house," he said dryly.

"Sorry. Nerves." She tried to breathe but Reza was close enough that she couldn't really catch a deep breath.

"Okay, so we're going to go in and try to control the hallway. Captain Lindberg, when I kick in the door, you'll come in and crouch down, and shoot continuously until we're all in the hallway. I'll tap you on the shoulder when it's time for us to get up and start moving down the corridor. Don't stop shooting unless you run out of ammo. You remember how to change your magazine?"

She nodded, knowing she had absolutely no clue as to whether she was going to be able to do that on the run.

"We're not going full speed, okay? We're just going to walk through it."

"Then how will it be confusing?"

Behind her, Teague laughed. "You'll see."

"Okay, get set." Reza flipped the switch on his weapon and assumed an odd half-crouch.

Teague pushed her against Reza's back. After what seemed like a long moment, Emily felt Reza tap her arm. She reached back and tapped Teague and felt the movement in his body as he shifted into her ever so slightly.

And then all hell broke loose.

Reza literally kicked in the door and moved so fast Emily stumbled from where she'd been leaning on him. Somehow she made it into the hallway where rounds pinged off the wall and splattered near her head. She flinched and closed her eyes, curling up on her knees.

"Start shooting, sweetheart!"

She had no idea who shouted at her but she managed to open her eyes and lift her weapon. Soldiers at the end of the hall kept popping their heads into the hallway but they were gone before she managed to get a shot off. She squealed as a round exploded next to her head on the wall.

"Keep shooting!"

She squeezed the trigger, the gun recoiling against her shoulder so many times she was sure she'd have a bruise later. Someone grabbed her by her body armor and lifted her up. "We're moving."

Sounds exploded around her and the smell of sulfur and chalk burned her nose. She couldn't think in the chaos. She was barely aware of Teague shooting over her shoulder and Reza to her right as they walked down the hallway.

She squeezed the trigger again and nothing happened. She squeezed again and again. Only clicks.

"Change magazines!" Reza's voice, calm, barking orders.

She fumbled to drop the magazine from her gun and her fingers got stuck trying to get the magazine out of her ammo pouch.

The weapon was snatched from her hand and back

before she could count to three, reloaded and ready to go. "Let's go."

Everything from there happened too fast. They started walking down the corridor. Then a soldier jumped out, followed by two more. One lay on his belly in the middle of the hallway and started shooting. There was no place to go. Her fingers froze on the trigger as the rounds started thudding into her body armor.

Terror clutched her throat. And then a brilliant starburst of pain as her hip and thigh were pounded with what felt like a thousand rounds.

"Endex! Endex! Miller, what the fuck was that?"

Reza's voice came from far off. His face came into focus as the smoke cleared. He'd long ago passed pissed. He was livid.

"Fuck, are you okay? Emily," he said, his voice rough. "Look at me. You're okay."

Her eyes burned with tears she refused to shed. Her hip was on fire and she wasn't sure she could walk. "Holy shit that hurts," she whispered when she was sure she wouldn't embarrass herself by crying.

Reza smiled gently. "Come on, walk it off. I'll check it out when we get out of here."

She nodded shortly and limped out of the shoot house. She managed to hand Miller back the borrowed weapon.

"Sorry about that, ma'am," Miller said with a worried grin.

Reza smacked him upside the back of the head and Miller flipped him off. Reza shadowed her on the long, painful walk to the truck.

"You okay?"

She nodded. "It hurts," she whispered, her voice humiliating her as it cracked.

"Let me see how bad."

She looked at him like he'd grown two heads. "You want me to pull my pants down right here?"

"Other side of the truck. I need to see if you're bleeding or not. Nothing kinky, I promise."

She made a wry grin but the prospect of possibly bleeding caught her attention. "These can break skin?"

Reza shot her a look that said "obviously" then followed her around the truck. She reached beneath her body armor and unbuttoned her pants. Reza knelt in front of her and gently eased the flap open, pushing the fabric aside so he could see her hip.

She looked down, overpowered by the sight of the big man on his knees in front of her. With a single movement, she reached out, her hands resting on his shoulders.

He looked up, concern etched onto his features. His eyes were dark, his mouth hard. His tongue slid over his bottom lip, his throat tense as he swallowed. "You're okay," he whispered.

Emily was glad for two things at that moment: one, that she hadn't actually peed her pants and two, that she'd worn sensible cotton panties that morning. He didn't seem interested in her underwear, though, as he let out a low whistle.

She felt his fingers slide over the sensitive skin near her hip bone. She shivered beneath the hard echo of the pain. His fingers were rough on her skin. Gentle. "This is going to hurt like a son of a bitch tomorrow," he said quietly.

"How bad is it?"

"You've got a bruise the size of an apple on your hip bone. It probably bruised the bone. We need to get some ice on that before long or you're going to be walking funny tomorrow."

He brushed his thumb along the edge of the bruise and she felt the echo of pain next to the gentle stroke of his touch. He tugged her pants closed, his knuckles brushing over her hips as he buttoned them. "But you're not bleeding," he said quietly. His voice was thick.

Her hands shook as she tried to take over and button her own pants. His fingers brushed hers as he helped her, deftly flicking the buttons closed and fastening her belt.

"It's the adrenaline wearing off," he said, motioning toward her hands. "It's normal."

"It feels like I'm never going to stop shaking," she confessed.

"You will. Ready to head back?" He glanced at his watch. "If we stall long enough, you won't have to go back to the office."

She smiled, and felt shaky and weak and alive, her blood humming with latent energy that she didn't know how to process. "I don't think I can go back to the office like this, anyway." She looked up at him, afraid to put into words the question she wanted to ask.

"Why not?" His voice was dark. Deep. Sensual. She couldn't reconcile the sound of his voice now over the rough commands he'd barked in the shoot house.

"I've never felt this keyed up. I don't think I can type with my hands shaking like this. Do you have to go back?"

His nostrils flared as she looked up at him. She hoped he wouldn't make her say it out loud. She had too much energy, too much something running through her veins and all of this centered on the man standing in front of her.

"What are you asking me, Emily?" His voice rang heavy with echoes of war.

Her own felt heavy with a neediness she'd never felt before. She opened her mouth but there were no words for what she needed. At least not words she normally used. They were unfamiliar. Raw and hungry.

His gaze locked on hers. Powerful emotions radiated from his dark eyes. Turmoil and chaos and dark promises she didn't have the words for.

She wanted this man. This man who'd gone to war with her over one of his soldiers, this man who'd taken her to training because she'd wanted to understand his world.

This man, who stood, rough and ready in front of her, power radiating off him and feeding the need that vibrated inside her.

His throat moved. Out of the corner of her eye, she saw his fists clench. This was not an easy decision for him. She wanted to ask why but was afraid he'd come to his senses and say no.

Finally, he spoke. "Get in the truck," he said roughly.

Chapter Eight

The ride back to the clinic was quiet. At least, as quiet as a ride in a tactical vehicle could be. Reza's thoughts were filled with heady, slow images. Fantasies involving a prim and proper doc who'd frozen in the hallway today and gotten herself shot.

She didn't realize that the place she'd been shot had been near an artery. He hadn't been joking or flirting when he'd directed her to drop trou and show him her wounds. She'd been bruised, badly, but nothing had broken the skin.

And now she was riding the adrenaline high that Reza had long ago developed an addiction for. He could see it in her eyes, watch it in the shaking of her hands. He was used to it.

She was not.

She wanted to go home with him. He saw it in her eyes, the swollen oh of her lips as she'd looked at him. He wanted her. There was no denying he'd been unable to get her out of his head since the first time he'd met her. But he didn't want her when she wasn't thinking clearly.

He didn't want any regrets the next morning after the adrenaline had worn off and her blood had settled back into normal. They changed vehicles at the headquarters parking lot and she sat in silence as he drove her back to her clinic in his personal truck.

She twisted her hands in her lap as she sat quietly. He deliberately parked in an empty parking lot behind the clinic and killed the engine.

"How are you feeling?" he asked, twisting in his seat to look at her.

"I'm good." Her voice was throaty and thick. Husky.

Then she looked at him. Her eyes were pale, pale blue and heavy-lidded. Her lips were swollen, slightly parted. She looked ready for a nap and he had the strangest urge to pull her into his lap.

"Emily," he whispered.

He lifted his hand then, and slid his palm over her cheek. Her skin was soft and smooth. He rubbed his thumb over a smudge of dirt on her cheek. Her lips parted a little more and he was dying to taste the sweetness of her mouth.

Their breath mingled as he hesitated, unsure of himself with a woman for the first time in a long, long time.

In the end, it was Emily who spanned that final distance between them. She brushed her lips against his, a faint, hesitant kiss like a butterfly against his mouth. He groaned low in his throat, fisting her hair in a tight grip and pulling her toward him.

His blood boiled from that hesitant touch. An urgency burned through him as he angled his mouth over hers. He wanted to consume her, to draw into his lap and feel her thighs spread across his hips.

Instead, he savored that first brush of his lips against hers. He nudged her top lip open with his, felt her breath on his mouth. Her tongue retreated against the gentle touch of his and he followed her, wanting to feel the glide of her tongue against his. Hesitant, her tongue touched his and he was lost.

He groaned deep in his throat as her tongue slipped into

his mouth. He resisted the urge to consume her and let her explore, until he could capture her tongue and suck gently.

Her surprised gasp burst against his mouth and he felt the slow burn of satisfaction unfurl in his chest. He tightened his grip on her bun and angled her mouth until he could taste all of her. He deepened the kiss, unable to resist the urge to take. He surrendered to the need, releasing all the unspent adrenaline and passion from the firefight into that single moment.

Emily was lost, drowning in a sea of sensation and touch and taste. He was power and rage—caged energy. He vibrated beneath her touch where her fingers curled into his upper arms. Raw strength held her close, encircling her. Protecting her even as he plundered her mouth.

Arousal like she'd never felt throbbed between her legs. Nothing she'd ever experienced could describe the pure sensation of the mixture of lingering fear from the range with the raw passion of his kiss. He kissed like he lived. Unhinged. On the edge. He consumed her like he owned her and the power and confidence in his every move poured into her with that kiss.

He couldn't say who came up for air first. At some point, he'd captured her face with both hands and cradled her now, his touch gentle and restrained. He licked her bottom lip, sucking gently as she caught her breath, pouring every ounce of restraint into gentling the ferocity he felt.

"Reza." His name was a prayer. He smiled against her lips.

"Hmmm."

"You really know how to kiss," she whispered.

He laughed deep in his chest, brushing his lips against hers again.

"Thanks. I think."

"Oh no, thank you," she said, opening her eyes. "I've never felt anything like that."

Her words were a purr, a caress against his cheek.

"It's adrenaline," he said, pulling her against his chest.

"Still?"

"You'll crash soon," he said. "When it wears off, you'll need to sleep."

"How do you do that in combat?"

"We manage," was all he said, not wanting to talk about war with her kiss still warm on his lips. "You should get home before you fall asleep," he murmured, brushing his lips against the top of her head.

She lifted her gaze until she met his and her eyes were filled with dark promise and a need that flattered him. "Will you follow me home?" she whispered.

Reza's throat went dry. "Is this really what you want?" He wanted her to be sure. Because he wasn't. He didn't know if he could do this, was terrified of screwing it up.

She nodded, remaining silent. The only other movement was a slight flex of her fingers on his arms.

He kissed her like the world was ending, then urged her gently from his truck, watching her to make sure she was steady on her feet. And his blood tightened in his veins as he followed her off post.

This was a mistake but it was one he couldn't stop himself from making.

She could feel him behind her. He radiated energy and heat as she fumbled getting her key in the lock. Sweat slicked her body and she felt his gaze on her back.

She wanted this. She wanted him. This had nothing to do with her past, nothing to do with a revolt against her family.

This was something just for her. Just him. A man who was big and powerful and strong and used everything he was, everything he had to protect those he deemed worthy of protection.

She turned as he closed the door behind him. Her space looked tiny with him in it. She *felt* tiny next to him and tipped her chin up to glance at him. She licked her lips, trying to banish the sudden dryness and find something to say that wouldn't embarrass her entirely.

"So we're here," she whispered. A tremor in her voice.

"Hmm." There was a warm, rich laugh in his. He lifted one hand, brushing his fingers gently over her cheek.

"Okay. I've never done this."

He leaned back, his dark eyes pinned to her face. "Sex or…"

She laughed at the question, at the shock in his voice. "I'm not a virgin, if that's what you're getting at." Her throat tightened as he stuffed his hands into his back pockets. The movement stretched the tight t-shirt against his chest and she could see the carved outline of muscle against thin fabric.

"Well, that's reassuring. It would be a hell of a lot of pressure to be your first."

Emily coughed and choked on a laugh. "Wow, I wasn't expecting that." Her gaze drifted down his body, her blood warming from his nearness. "Do you want to shower or something?"

A vein pulsed in his neck. "Do you want to wash my back?"

"I could." Light, teasing words in a space heavy with sensual heat.

He stepped toward her then, cupping her cheeks in his palms. "Careful, Emily. That's a hell of a lot of temptation."

She wrapped her arms around his waist. "I'm tempting you?"

"You have no idea." A strange note in his voice. One she would have to ask him about.

Some other time.

"I like that I'm tempting you," she whispered, her skin absorbing the heat from his body. She shivered and his fingers flexed against her cheeks.

"How long has it been for you?" he whispered as he pressed his lips to the edge of her mouth. His tongue flicked out to touch her skin and she shuddered as he traced the line of her jaw.

"Well, it's been almost two years since I found my best friend giving my fiancé oral sex, so you can probably figure it's been at least that long."

"Cheating sucks," he whispered, his breath hot on her ear. He nipped at her earlobe. "But did you just say 'giving him oral sex'?" There it was again, the laughter in his question.

"So?"

"Can you say 'blow job'?" His tongue traced over her ear. She gasped and arched her neck.

"I'm sweaty," she said, dodging his request.

"I think that's okay." He tugged her earlobe gently with his teeth. "If we do this right, we'll be sweaty again." He bit down. "Say 'blow job.'"

"Why is that important to you?" Her words were a gasp.

"Because I want to hear you say something dirty."

"I'm sweaty and I want to take a shower. Is that dirty enough?"

He hugged her close then, his laughter shaking through his body and into hers. "Shower it is, then," he whispered. He released her and stepped back. "After you."

He followed her into the bedroom, wanting badly to strip her naked and feast on her body. Her hands shook as she reached for the light. Nerves. Adrenaline wearing off. And sexual need burning over it all.

There was strength in this woman. A strength that appealed to him even as her teasing laughter eased him out of that dark space where he'd spent so long.

But there in the dark, for once, he didn't feel alone. And it terrified him, having another person there. A kindred spirit with the soul of a warrior. Her body wasn't marked with scars like his but there were scars there nonetheless.

She turned to face him, her expression tense, her eyes dark and aroused.

He wanted to watch her peel off her clothing. Wanted the lights out so that he could keep the scars on his body hidden a bit more. He wasn't ashamed of them nor of the art he'd covered them with but he didn't want to bring the war into the bedroom with them.

She took a step closer to him. Tugged at the hem of his combat t-shirt. His breath caught in his throat and it took everything he had to simply stand there and allow her to lift the shirt over his chest.

She'd said she trusted him earlier that day at the range.

It was his turn to trust her.

There was nothing in her life that prepared her to see a man of Reza's size and strength unclothed. Beneath the black t-shirt, his body was a prize. But when he took a step back and pulled the cotton over his head, her breath caught in her throat.

His body was not perfection. It was scarred and damaged, and laced across those scars he'd carved his own flesh with pitch black ink. Death's sickle cut across one pec and twisted in the robes draped down his left shoulder were names. She counted quickly. Twelve names and ranks on one bicep, each with a date carefully in line with it. On the other, places she recognized from the news. Fallujah. Najaf. Tal Afar. Mosul.

"What's BIAP?" she whispered, curling her fingers into her palms to keep from tracing the mournful letters.

He didn't want to answer. He closed his eyes as her fingers skimmed the names. Women had seen him naked before. But they'd never asked about the names or the places. Never asked about the reaper over his heart.

He wouldn't have answered them if they had.

But Emily. Emily asked.

And he had to answer her. Had to trust that she would take him as he was.

It was the greatest leap of faith he'd ever taken.

"Baghdad International Airport," he said, his voice thick. "It's the place I lost the first piece of my soul."

She'd seen war memorials carved into skin before. Many of the combat veterans she saw in her office had permanently inked their memories into their flesh. But none had ever struck her so viscerally. There was violence in those names carved into his flesh, an echo of the war carried close to his heart.

And over his heart, beneath the blade of the sickle, a single name. "Maliheh," she whispered.

"My mother." His throat moved. "I lost her when I was fifteen."

"Reza." His name on her lips was a prayer. For his soul. For hers. She no longer knew. But there was pain etched into his skin. More than the war had made him what he was.

"Don't feel sorry for me." He moved then, cradling her face in his palms, his big hands inexplicably gentle. "I wear their names to honor them. To remember."

"So much pain," she whispered.

"Don't pity me." Harsh judgment of his own actions. A warrior resigned to his fate.

She met his gaze then, closing her fingers over his. "I don't pity you, Reza." She brushed her lips against his. "I admire you."

His smile was cold, his eyes an abyss stretching into eternity. "Don't think you can crawl inside my head just because we're getting naked."

She stepped close to him then, because to do anything less would be an admission of defeat. Instantly, she was surrounded by the heat from his body. The black ink of the tattoo seemed to writhe against his skin, urging her to touch. She lifted her index finger, sliding it along the edge of Death's Sickle. She was almost surprised when her finger did not bleed.

"It's not your head I'm interested in," she whispered, threading her arms around his neck.

A smile, this time genuine, on those full lips as he kissed her deeply, his fingers tugging at her bun until her hair fell free down her back.

"I'm going to get you to say it," he said as he tugged at the zipper on her uniform jacket.

"Is that a dare?"

He made a noise as he captured her lips and pushed her jacket off her shoulders, then tugged her t-shirt free from her pants. "Beautiful," he murmured, tracing one finger near the edge of her bra.

She kissed him as he tugged her toward him, lifting her until she could wrap her arms around his neck and her legs around his hips. The bruise on her hip screamed at the pressure but the pleasure of his lips drowned out the echo of any pain.

"Where's the shower?"

She nibbled on his lower lip and pointed toward the door on the other side of the bed. He strode through the bedroom and each movement brought his erection in close, intimate contact with her aching sex. Never in her life had she been so aware of her own wetness, her own arousal.

He set her on the counter and reached into the shower, turning it on. Steam filled the small bathroom.

Then, his dark gaze penetrating hers, he finished what he'd started and began peeling off the rest of his clothes.

Emily Lindberg was a mystery. He'd never have guessed she'd have had a fiancé in a previous life or that he'd been dumb enough to cheat on her. This was a woman who was finding her own place in the world, experimenting with her own power.

Her gaze on him made him slow down. Untie his boots slowly. He felt her inspecting his tattoos and his scars and knew there was more she wanted to know.

She said she admired him. Only because she didn't know how hard he worked to stay sober. How much it was costing him to be there at that moment and not reach for a drink.

But for once, he wanted to untangle the mess of alcohol and sex. He wanted to feel, really feel, Emily's skin against his instead of using fast, fleeting contact to chase away more memories.

Maybe someday he would tell her just enough to appease her curiosity. Just a little. Because he wasn't ready to start unpacking all the shit in his rucksack. There was a lot of baggage there and the war was far from over. He needed to keep it stuffed down until the day came when he hung up his boots. Maybe then he'd start to examine the life he'd led.

Until then, he'd bury the memories like he'd been doing. He'd just keep it under control this time. He could do it.

He straightened and nudged his boots to one side. Steam made her hair curl around her face, dark ringlets clinging to her cheeks. Her breath came in short, quick huffs and he watched the gentle swell of her breasts as she breathed.

Her chest froze as he flicked open his belt. "It's not really fair that I'm getting naked and you're not," he murmured, opening another button on his pants. His erection was painful and tight. Her eyes darkened as she watched him drop his pants and toed them to one side. When he straightened, her gaze took in all of him.

A bolt of pure desire shot through him as her gaze landed on his erection. He was a big man and while he'd never had any complaints before, the way her eyes widened suggested she'd never seen someone his, ah, size before.

Her lips parted and he could see the uncertainty in her eyes. He crossed the small space and nudged her thighs apart, capturing her face in his hands and kissing her until she forgot her own name, forgot her fears and her insecurities. Until her fingers tightened against his back and she rocked gently against him.

The friction of her touch drove him wild and he pulled her closer. "You really need to lose the boots," he murmured, then knelt in front of her to tug on her laces. He pulled them off then peeled the olive green socks down her calves.

He framed her hips with his palms, careful about the bruise on her hip, then reached for her belt. "You're still wearing your clothes," he murmured against her lips.

"Well, we can certainly fix that." She scooted off the counter and opened her pants, pushing them down. She sucked in a breath as she bumped the bruise.

"You're still not naked enough," he said. He turned her gently and pulled her against him, tracing his hands down her sides, stroking her skin gently. He hooked his thumbs in her panties as he nibbled on her shoulder and pushed them down her thighs. Watching her in the fogging mirror, she rested her head against his chest as he stripped her bare.

Focusing on her pleasure allowed him to ignore his own uncertainty. He watched her lips part, felt the tension in her body, and forgot all about his need for a drink. Forgot anything but his need for this woman.

Reza was a solid wall behind her. His big body surrounded hers; his hands were dark against her skin. He spread his hands against her belly, then slid one down her body. She couldn't take her eyes off his hand as he traced one finger down the seam of her sex, a gentle, soft touch. A gasp escaped her as he stroked her, her moisture glistening on his finger.

"You're so fucking wet." His voice was a growl near her ear as he continued to stroke her. Nothing more than gentle strokes, not parting her, just coaxing her body to swell with her own slick pleasure. His erection was persistent against her lower back.

She had managed to keep her thoughts to herself. She hadn't wanted to admit she'd never seen a man of his stature. She closed her eyes and absorbed the pleasure of his touch. Trusted him.

"I really hope you'll keep your promise," he murmured near her ear as he pressed gently on her most swollen place. She cried out as a burst of pleasure popped inside her but the orgasm she craved was still distant and far off, begging to be released.

"What promise?"

"About washing my back." He released her then and stepped backward into the shower stall. Water sluiced over his big body, running rivulets over his dark skin. Dark hair covered his chest, curling down his stomach to the thick hair around his erection.

He held out his hand to her. It took her a moment to realize this was her last chance to back away from the power of the man. His body called to her but there was something more. The letters on those tattoos flexed as he moved to turn the water temperature up. More steam filled the bathroom, coating the glass of the shower door.

Emily held her breath.

And took that step.

Reza had never showered with a lover. There was something deeply arousing about having Emily's slick naked female body wriggling against his in the confined space. He poured some sweet-smelling stuff that echoed faintly of apples into his palm and rubbed his hands together.

He moved her hair out of the way and rubbed his hands over her shoulders before he massaged the tight muscles there. "You're going to be sore tomorrow," he said when she gasped after he found a particularly tight knot.

"You won't be?"

"Probably not. I'm used to it. You're not." He swept his soapy hands down her body, foam swelling beneath his fingers and trailing over her skin.

He turned her until he could cradle her against his body again, cleaning away the sweat and grime of the day as he aroused them both with his wandering hands. His cock ached every time she wriggled against it.

She was content to let him touch her, let his hands explore. He cupped her breasts and she moaned low in her throat as his fingers circled her nipples. And when he pinched one gently, her cry of pleasure made his blood tighten against his veins.

Hunger burned in him. He turned to rinse them both and she winced as his hand bumped her bruised hip. He kissed her, stroking his hands over her body to soothe the pain away. She relaxed against him, her body molding against his. His cock pressed against her belly and he rocked his hips gently against her.

Reaching behind her, he turned the water off, wanting—no needing—her on her back when they did this. He wanted to watch her face as he filled her, wanted to watch her eyes as he moved inside her.

She was in a daze, he realized, in part from the adrenaline rapidly leaving her body and in part from the dark arousal in her eyes. He tugged the towel from her body and lifted her into his arms, drowning in the taste and pleasure that was Emily.

She was overwhelmed. She'd never felt the intensity of the passion she felt as Reza's hands roamed her body, like he knew her better than she knew herself. She'd never known how good a man's touch between her legs could feel but she'd never admit that to him.

He wrapped her legs around his hips as he walked and she could feel the insistence of his arousal at the juncture of her thighs. He crawled up her bed and her body until he lay between her thighs.

She braced her hands on his chest. "Condoms?"

"I've got some," he said.

She tipped her head and studied him. "Were you planning on this?" she asked.

"No." A deep flush crawled up his neck and she wondered at the source. He crawled off her body and searched his pants. There was a tear of foil and she watched in fascination as he rolled it over the head of his erection and down the thick length of it. He looked up to find her watching him. He settled against her again. "You can still change your mind, Emily."

She frowned. "Why on earth would I do that?"

"You look like you're not sure about this." He nibbled on the side of her neck, scraping his teeth over that pulse point he'd seen earlier.

"I'm not sure about certain aspects of this but I'm sure about it overall."

Reza laughed and she felt it in his entire body where he rested against hers. "Which aspects are you not sure of?"

Heat flamed across her cheeks and she closed her eyes. He licked her neck, flicking his tongue over her ear again until she gasped. "Tell me," he urged.

He slipped his cock against her heat, stroking her where she was swollen. Her hips twisted against the sensual assault and she jerked and cried out.

He shifted and cradled her face in his hands. "Emily." His voice was a whisper. She met his gaze, her eyes glittering with uncertainty. "Emily, I've got you," he whispered.

He needed her mindless. He needed her not thinking

about the size of him and instead drowning in pleasure. He kissed her gently, sucked on her lips. Traced his tongue down her body, distracting her with his hands until he'd reached the center of her. He pressed his lips to that fist-sized bruise on her hip, then kissed her right where she was swollen.

Emily cried out as he suckled her, her hips bucking off the bed at the pleasure. He held her in place, draping one thigh over his shoulder as he continued the assault on her most sensitive flesh. She fisted her hands in his hair, needing something to anchor her before she shattered into a thousand pieces. And then he slid one finger inside her and she exploded.

She was shattered and limp from the most powerful pleasure she'd ever experienced when Reza crawled up her body and kissed her. She could taste herself on his lips, something warm and sweet against his tongue. There was a gentle pressure as he started to fill her.

Her body, still throbbing from his touch, stretched around him. She gasped against his mouth and shifted until he could slide deeper. He was a big man and he filled her, consumed her as his body inched deeper and deeper into hers.

She was so fucking tight, so good. So his. He reached between their bodies to stroke her sex again and she relaxed with a gasp, her body taking him deep, so deep.

He kept stroking her intimate flesh as he moved, sliding deep and slow inside her, giving her time to adjust. And then there was no more need as her body shuddered around him, gripping him tightly as she came again.

He kissed her deeply as his pleasure took over his control and he pushed into her body a final time. He came apart in her arms and it was only later as she lay curled against him that he marveled at the contentment that had followed his own release.

Chapter Nine

He'd been right when he'd told her she was going to be sore. Sore didn't even begin to explain all the pain in places she hadn't even known existed. Her hip ached every time she moved. Her shoulders felt like they were still carrying the heavy body armor, and between her thighs felt richly abused and sensitive.

She wanted him again. She'd awakened that morning, alone, his scent heavy on her skin, in her bed, and she'd wanted.

He hadn't asked to spend the night. She hadn't pushed. She refused to let the tiny fear that snuck into bed and cuddled up next to her chip away at her trust in this man. Instead she'd kissed him gently and closed the door behind him. Exhausted.

Satisfied.

And as she had fallen into a dreamless sleep, she'd been amazed at the tenderness this rough man had shown her.

Now, at the office, she was struggling to concentrate. Her brain was in a haze and the only thing she could see clearly was the memories from last night.

Her inbox chimed, yanking her out of her daydream. Captain Marshall, Reza's commander. "Hmm."

She opened the message.

Captain Lindberg, please send a status on the following soldiers' mental health evaluations.

   SGT Chuck Wisniak

   SPC Neal Sloban

   PFC Erol Spintz

   All troopers are pending adverse actions and the delays in their mental health evaluations are delaying proper adjudication of their separation actions. Your incompetence is impeding my ability to accomplish my mission.

   v/r

   JPM III

Emily smothered her irritation that Marshall was being so demanding. Apparently, he and Reza hadn't talked, because Reza had the latest information about those packets—except for Sloban's.

She tried to remember the compassion she'd felt when Reza had spoken about Marshall's past, but instead all she felt now was irritation that Marshall was so hard and unforgiving. She flexed her fingers and started typing a response.

"Whoever pissed you off, it's not really the keyboard's fault." Olivia stood in the doorway of her office. Her friend's hands were bereft of her favorite mug.

She sucked in a deep breath. "Can I just complain for one hot second about how rude some of these guys are? And I quote: 'your incompetence is impeding my ability to accomplish my mission.'"

"Someone needs some therapy chocolate," Olivia said, *tsk*ing. "Who's got you so pissed?"

Emily pointed at the computer. "Irritating captain of the day."

"Obviously," Olivia said dryly.

"What are you working on today?"

"About twenty-five legal reviews from the 3rd Cavalry Regiment. I've got a stack on my desk six inches high that's only getting higher."

"Can you see if you've got a packet on a kid named Sloban?"

Olivia nodded. "Sure, but shouldn't that be with final review board?"

"It should be, but no one can seem to find this packet and it's running up against the timelines from higher up." Emily fired off a terse response to Captain Marshall.

She glanced at her watch, wanting very much to call Reza. A slow smile spread across her lips.

"You look like you have a juicy secret," Olivia said, narrowing her eyes.

Emily burst out laughing, thinking about last night with Reza. "Maybe."

"Wait a sec... You went to the range yesterday and never came back. You didn't..." Olivia glanced over her shoulder then slipped into the office. "Spill in thirty seconds or less."

She said nothing as a flush crept over her skin.

"With Sarn't Iaconelli?"

Emily bit her lips together and nodded. There weren't enough words to express how knotted up everything was inside her. It was a good knot.

"And?"

"And what?" Emily asked.

"Okay, seriously? You have got to tell me more than that silly smile."

"There's not a lot to tell. He followed me home after the range and... yeah."

"Wow," Olivia said. "He made you speechless."

Emily grinned. "Pretty much."

"Oh, we're going to have to talk later." Olivia glanced at her watch once more. "Ah well, back to work. Want to get lunch later?"

"Maybe. I've got to tackle the triage now that it's blowing up."

"All right. Well, let me know."

Olivia disappeared into the hallway, leaving Emily alone with her thoughts and her aching body. It hurt if she shifted wrong. A good hurt, a reminder that last night had actually happened instead of just being a really great dream.

Her phone vibrated on her desk and she answered it automatically. "Captain Lindberg, may I help you."

"Captain Lindberg. It's Sarn't Iaconelli."

Her blood warmed at the sound of his voice. "Hello, Sarn't Iaconelli. What can I do for you today?"

"I wish I was calling for something other than business but sadly, duty calls. I wanted to give you a heads-up that Wisniak is on his way to your office. He's been put on the duty roster and he's freaking out about it."

She heard a thousand unsaid things as she jotted down notes. "Why would he be upset about being put on duty?"

"You don't really want my opinion on that," he cleared his throat. "Just listen to what he says and keep in mind that he was assigned duty."

She frowned, surprised and grateful that he wasn't trying to argue with her again about Wisniak being weak or spineless.

"Okay. Thanks for the heads-up."

"Sure."

He hung up and left her feeling vaguely disappointed that he hadn't called for pleasure. Her phone vibrated on her desk again and she looked down.

When can I see you again?
She smiled.

Reza finished reviewing the latest evaluation report, wishing that some of the sergeants in his platoon spent more time learning to read than shooting things on the range. Some of them could barely put together a coherent sentence and while Reza was a long way from being a Rhodes Scholar, he could at least figure out the difference between a noun and a verb. Most of the time, anyway.

He glanced at his watch, needing an update from Foster on Wisniak for the last ten minutes. Rage churned in Reza's belly at the malingering sergeant. While Captain Marshall was doing everything he could to throw Wisniak out of the army, it grated on Reza's last nerve that he had to send someone—again—to hunt Wisniak down.

He tried to consider Emily's opinion on the kid, he really did. But now Wisniak had turned up missing again and the irritation was back in full force. Foster walked in and plopped into the chair on the other side of Reza's desk.

"I am so sick of chasing this motherfucker down." Foster took out a pack of dip and stuffed a wad in his mouth. "You using this?" he said as he grabbed the water bottle off Reza's desk and promptly spit into it.

"Not anymore," Reza said dryly. He kicked his feet up on his desk, knowing Captain Marshall would immediately go into labor with kittens if he saw him with his boots on the desk. Reza was beyond giving a shit. They sat in silence for a long moment.

"Do you ever think Wisniak wakes up in the morning and goes 'man, I am a fucking sissy'?" Foster asked, fidgeting.

"What the hell is wrong with you?" Reza asked when Foster couldn't sit still.

"I was up all night drinking Red Bulls and playing *Call of Duty*."

"Oh. Lay off the energy drinks, man. You look like a meth addict." He sighed heavily, scrubbing his hands over his face, wishing he wasn't familiar with what meth could do to someone's life. "Anyway, I'm sure something like that goes through Wisniak's head every time he falls out of a squad level run." Reza wondered, though. What if he was wrong? An uncomfortable feeling settled around his shoulders, pressing down like a soaked wool blanket. "Man, why can't we get him out sooner?"

"Beats the shit out of me," Foster said. "Personally, I wish he would just go AWOL."

"Bite your tongue. Do you know how much paperwork that is?" He didn't want the damn kid to go AWOL. He just wanted him out of the army.

"Yeah, but then he's gone and we don't have to chase him down every time he doesn't get his own way." Foster leaned forward. "Do you realize this is the fifth time he's been to the R&R Center this month? And he's never pulled staff duty as long as I've been here."

"He pulled it once when we first got back. Then he started having all these appointments." Reza thought about all the times he'd had to change the duty roster to accommodate the Wisniaks while guys like Foster were left holding the bag. All the guys who couldn't keep their shit together and pull twenty-four-hour duty.

It burned that so many couldn't pull their own weight. That they depended on others to do the basic things that kept the army running.

"You ever think about some of the shit we did downrange, Sarn't Ike?" Foster's question came out of a long lull of silence that had hung between them.

"Sure. Who doesn't."

Foster rubbed the bottle against his temple. "Sometimes I think being downrange is better than being home."

"Don't say that. At least at home, you're not getting shot at."

Foster coughed and the sound that came out of him sounded suspiciously like "bullshit." "Whatever. I know you think about it."

"'Course I think about it. I think about all of them." Far too often. Sometimes he could still hear their voices in his head.

Foster spit into the bottle, his gaze distant and unfocused. "Yeah, well, the war sucks. I want to go back and blow something up." He looked up at Reza. "I know that like half of them are your cousins and all but I really fucking hate Iraq."

Reza flipped him off. "My mom was Iranian, shithead. Not every brown guy from the Middle East is an Arab."

Foster grinned and things settled back to the normal they both knew. "Yeah, well, Iraq still sucks. Anyway. What's on the honey-do list for today?"

"Head down to the clinic and see if you can't find out who the review board person is in charge of Sloban and Wisniak." He handed Foster the last known location of the missing packets and hoped that Foster could smooth talk one of the civilians down there into helping him out. "And they need to finish their processing over at the Copeland Center before their board files are complete." Reza closed down his computer and stood up.

His cell phone vibrated in his pocket. Emily.

"Sarn't Ike."

"Reza?" Emily sighed and he heard the distress in her voice.

"What's wrong?"

"I need someone from the chain of command down here immediately."

He turned away from Foster, lowering his voice. "What's wrong?"

"Can you come to my office?"

"Emily, am I the right person for this? If there's something that needs to be reported, you need to go through the right channels."

"I don't know what the right channels are, Reza." She sighed hard. "I need your help." A whispered plea.

One he couldn't turn down.

Emily stood the moment Reza walked into her office and closed the door behind him.

She didn't expect him to cross that small space. Or to put his hands on her shoulders.

Or to see the worry in the dark lines beneath his eyes. "What's wrong?" His voice was flat, calm, but laced with unspoken worry.

"I'm fine." A single palm on his chest, her fingers pressing over his heart. "I have a situation that I don't know how to handle."

He took a step back and her skin protested the lack of warmth from his closeness.

"Why didn't you ask your supervisor?"

"Because this involves an officer." She lifted her gaze to his. "Your commander."

She thrust a sheet of plain white paper at him. "Read it. Then tell me what to do."

He scanned the handwritten notes quickly, then read it again. His jaw tightened as he read more slowly the second time and heat crawled up his neck. By the time he looked up at her, he radiated pure fury. "Are you kidding me?"

"I wish I was. It explains why Wisniak won't pull duty and why he's having such a hard time any time he's around Captain Marshall and some of his minions."

"Emily, he's alleging he was hazed at the duty desk by Song and Peters, and Marshall knows?"

"It happens," she said quietly. "The army isn't immune to hazing."

"I know that," he snapped. "Marshall might be an asshole but he wouldn't ignore something like this."

"So you think Wisniak made all this up?"

Reza read the paper again. "Damn it," he whispered. "You need to call the cops."

"I don't have to alert the chain of command?"

He shook his head and handed her back the paper. "Not in this case. They'll find out soon enough. Call the cops. Make the investigation official." He swallowed hard. "It'll keep it from getting buried that way."

Emily's hands shook as she picked up the phone and dialed the MPs. Her voice wavered as she reported the information she had to the special investigator. The entire time, Reza stood big and steady in her office. He was furious. That much was obvious but she couldn't figure out why.

She wanted to know. Wanted badly to ask. But she didn't. Instead, she finished the report and hung up the phone. "The special agent will be by as soon as he can. Sadly, this is the fourth hazing incident reported on post this week."

Reza released a sharp breath and some of the tension eased out of his shoulders. He crossed the small space, resting his hands on her shoulders. She needed the comfort of his touch.

"What happens now?" she whispered.

"Now I go brief the sergeant major and get Wisniak moved someplace where he'll be safe."

She frowned and he caught her. "What?"

"I didn't think he mattered to you," she whispered.

He lowered his hands and looked away for a long moment. "Maybe I've been going about this all wrong." He met her gaze. "Maybe you're right."

"Reza." He stopped near the door, his head bowed, his hand on the knob. "Do you believe him?"

"What I believe isn't important."

He closed the door behind him, leaving Emily alone with the feeling that she'd done something horribly, horribly wrong.

"Are you fucking kidding me?"

"Sarn't Major, I would normally love to screw with you but not about something like this."

Reza stood at parade rest in Sergeant Major Giles's office, afraid to move and set the old man's PTSD off. Normally, Reza would have taken something like this to the battalion command sergeant major but in this case, whereas it involved the battalion commander's top company commander, Reza had skipped a level of command.

Plus, he trusted Giles. He might be a cranky old bastard but Giles had honor where there were few honorable men left. Generally, the higher one went in command, the more honor was merely preached instead of lived. It simply wasn't possible to maintain one's values. Not if one wanted to be successful, anyway.

"All right, Ike, if you say this is legit, I'll let the boss know. It's coming through the cops?"

"Yeah, Sarn't Major. I was there when the doc called the police."

Giles chomped on his cigar, and Reza felt like a hamster cornered by a hungry cat. "You were there?"

"Wisniak is in my company. The doc asked what she should do. I told her to call the cops and let the police sort it out."

The cigar twitched and Reza braced for the explosion. "I'll let the boss know."

Reza snapped to the position of attention and went to

leave. "Sarn't Major, Wisniak needs to be transferred out. He's made an allegation against members of this unit. There may be reprisals against him."

"No one is moving until we figure out if this is a legitimate complaint or not." Giles swore and threw his cigar down. He picked up the phone and damn near stabbed it with the amount of force he used to dial. "It's Giles. I need you to give me a room in your barracks. And it needs to be kept quiet." Pause. "Roger that."

Giles jotted down a phone number. "Call Sikes and get Wisniak moved across post. Don't tell anyone where he is."

Reza stuffed the paperwork in his pocket and turned to leave. "Roger, Sarn't Major."

"Ike?"

He stopped at the door.

"Next time, give me a heads-up before you tell someone to call the damn cops." His voice was laced with disappointment. Shame crawled up Reza's spine.

Shame that he hadn't trusted his sergeant major in the first place. Shame that the leaders Reza was supposed to advise and support were weak. Were bullies.

That he was one of them.

That he'd failed to protect the weakest among them.

He had no response to the sergeant major's silent admonition.

But the urge to drink ramped back up, twisting in his guts. Demanding that he do something to squelch the hunger in his soul for just one drink.

Chapter Ten

Reza had headed back to the R&R Center to pick up Wisniak, only to find out the kid had left without being seen. He headed back to the barracks, dialing Wisniak's cell phone repeatedly. It went straight to voice mail every time.

A sense of urgency rose up and threatened to choke him. Damn it, he had to keep the kid safe until the investigators could talk to him and verify his story.

And if Marshall was letting some of the guys haze members of the company...

It was going to take everything he had not to deal with that in his own special way.

Unable to shake the feeling that Wisniak was dangerously on edge, Reza swung into the barracks, praying that the kid was in his room.

The door was unlocked. Wisniak was there by himself, staring aimlessly at his computer. He looked up at Reza and blinked several times before he realized he was supposed to stand up.

He pushed shakily to his feet and attempted to go to parade rest.

Reza approached carefully. Rested a hand on Wisniak's shoulder and was shamed when the kid flinched away.

"What are you on?" Reza asked softly, keeping his voice level.

Wisniak's face blanched, followed by a deep red flush that started at his neck and moved up toward his hair. "Um. Welbutrin. And Xanax. I took an Ambien at midnight." He looked up at the ceiling. "I think."

"You shouldn't be here right now," Reza said. "We're going to pack up some of your stuff and take you to another barracks." His gut was screaming that the kid had taken the wrong meds.

Wisniak blinked again, his throat working just as slowly. "Sarn't Song said if I left my room, he'd have me court-martialed." His words were slow. Dull.

"Song doesn't get a vote," Reza said. He gripped Wisniak's shoulder tightly. "You did the right thing today," he said quietly. "But I'm worried you're not doing okay. Are you sure you've only taken what you're prescribed?"

Reza had seen too many troopers nearly OD on the toxic mix of meds the docs frequently prescribed. Warnings went off in his head.

The young sergeant's eyes filled as his face flushed deeper red. He lifted his chin and tried valiantly to keep it from wavering. "I'm fine, Sarn't Ike."

Reza clenched his jaw to keep the frustration pounding through him from overwhelming the scared soldier in front of him.

Something bad had happened to Wisniak. Something that had scarred him beyond repair. He'd heavily medicated himself just to survive whatever it was.

Reza knew the tendency all too well.

"I need to see what medications you took, okay?" He held up his hand when Wisniak's eyes widened. "You're not in any trouble. But you're not acting right. I've got a doctor friend of mine who I just want to check with and make sure you haven't taken too much of anything." He kept his voice gentle, his words calm.

The stillness stretched for an eternity and then Wisniak shook his head. "You're just going to tell Captain Marshall I took too much."

"I won't. I swear I won't. I need to check, though, or I'm going to take you to the emergency room." Wisniak needed to know that Reza was serious.

Another long moment and finally Wisniak nodded.

Wisniak lined up half a dozen pill bottles and Reza picked up the phone.

"Captain Lindberg."

"Emily, it's Reza." He paused, his next words nearly impossible to get out. "I need your help."

He read off the list of medications, not telling her that Wisniak was the soldier in question. She'd alert the cavalry and at this point, Reza wasn't sure he could protect Wisniak from whatever vengeance Captain Marshall had in mind.

"He needs to be checked out at the hospital." She paused. "Don't risk it."

Reza glanced at Wisniak, whose eyes were dull and looked like they were going in and out of focus. He took a deep breath. "Thank you."

"What's going on?" Concern echoed across the distance between them.

"I can't tell you right now." Silence greeted his honest answer. "I'll call you later?"

"Okay." An act of trust.

One he did not deserve.

He didn't make it back to his office. He'd meant to. Instead, he detoured out to Engineer Lake, needing time to put everything to rights in his own head.

He dialed Foster. "I need you to pull Wisniak's duty."

"Oh, come on, Sarn't Ike. That's bullshit."

"Foster, I wouldn't ask you to do this if it wasn't important." Wisniak was sleeping in his undisclosed barracks room. The ER doc had checked him out and said he just needed to sleep.

For once, it felt like Reza had dodged a bullet.

"Fuck me, Sarn't Ike. I haven't had a day off in a month." Foster had been running around with Ike after the delinquent members of his company. Bailing guys out of jail, picking them up before they went to jail.

Reza knew the pressure was building but he didn't trust anyone else right now. "Look, I know. I'll give you Friday off. Monday, too, if you don't bitch about this too much."

"Fine." Foster spit the word into the phone. "But you owe me."

Reza hung up, irritated by Foster's attitude. Foster didn't know about Wisniak's allegations and Reza couldn't tell him. He wanted badly to bring Foster up to speed but he couldn't. Maybe he could ask Teague if Marshall had any skeletons in the closet.

Reza turned the truck and backed into the trail. He pulled the flask from his glove box then dropped the tailgate. He sat for a long moment, watching the breeze stir small whitecaps in the man-made lake as he wrestled with the temptation to drink.

He twisted the cap off slowly, then twisted it back on. On. Off. Like his fingers belonged to someone else. Wisniak had accused Marshall of ignoring his complaints about being harassed. He knew that Song and Pete were assholes but he didn't think that they were running around hazing people into the unit.

He didn't want to believe that Marshall would have allowed this. He was a dickhead but to ignore threats of harm? Maybe it was just a prank that had gotten out of hand.

154 *Jessica Scott*

Marshall was fond of breaking in the new soldiers. Ensuring they had loyalty to the team first.

The MPs were going to talk to Wisniak tomorrow. And then all hell was going to break loose in the company. Marshall was going to be questioned and he was likely to completely lose his shit. But that wasn't the worst of it.

The ugly truth settled around Reza's heart. He twisted the lid again. On. Off. It would be so easy to chase away the cold stone in his heart with a shot from the flask. *No one was going to believe Wisniak.*

That was the only thing that made sense. The stone was back, pressing on his chest.

"Fuck!" He slammed his fist into the truck bed. The brilliant starburst of pain exploded up Reza's arm.

"There are generally better-accepted ways of managing your anger."

He whipped around, surprised to see Emily standing there, chest heaving. She'd been running for a long time, judging by the sweat soaking her t-shirt. Her hair clung to her face.

"Are you managing yours?" he asked. He set the flask down on the tailgate. She didn't know he wasn't supposed to be drinking. And he hadn't yet.

Still, guilt crawled up his spine because if she hadn't have shown up, he likely would have been halfway through the flask.

God, but he missed the comfortable numbness sometimes.

"Better than you are, apparently." She motioned her head toward the truck. "Can I sit?"

He swallowed and nodded. He slid over and made room for her on the tailgate of his F-150. "You're a long way from post."

"I told you I liked to run out here."

"How far is it from your office?"

"Six miles round trip." Her breathing was slowing rapidly. "You okay?" She sat close enough that their upper arms touched. The heat from her body radiated through his uniform jacket.

"Sure."

"So being okay means drinking?" There was no accusation in her voice.

"Considering I did not start drinking at breakfast, this is an improvement," he said dryly. He almost told her about his problems with alcohol. About the accident in Colorado. About trying to stay sober and failing. Other than through deployments, this was the longest he'd ever gone without drinking and he was rapidly reaching his breaking point.

"Bad day?"

"'Bout normal." He picked up the pint. Twisted the cap. On. Off. "What are you running this far out for?"

"I got my hand slapped for taking too long on the medical board files." She sniffed. "Apparently they found Sloban's file today."

"That's bad?"

"It is when we're backlogged six months and every day I take trying to make sure the cases are evaluated properly is a day my boss has to hear about it from the commanders here on post."

"Considering your boss called my boss and I got my ass chewed because of it, I'm not exactly sympathetic. You could take longer. You know, be a pal?"

"I'll do my best." Emily grinned and pushed her hair out of her face. She sighed quietly, then shifted to lean against the side of the truck, her gaze dropping to the flask in Reza's hand. "You know what my parents said when I told them I'd joined the army, Reza?"

"You're an adult. Why did they even get a vote?"

She pulled her knees up to her chest and wrapped her

arms around them. "You don't understand the life I come from. My parents aren't used to being defied. By anyone, let alone their daughter."

"So what—you were supposed to marry some idiot banker's son and instead ran off and joined the circus?"

"Bentley was a senator's son, actually."

"Really? Wow, you're slumming pretty hard with me, huh?"

She frowned slightly. "I'm not slumming with you. You have more honor in your little finger than Bentley has in his entire body."

Reza looked down at the pint, uncomfortable with that look in her eye. She looked at him like he was some kind of hero—and he was nothing of the sort.

"So you caught your best friend with your fiancé's dick in her mouth and decided to join the army?" he asked, changing the subject away from his alleged honor. His honor was nothing but a bad joke. A convenient lie that people used to overlook the worst of his sins.

"It was more than that but yes; that was part of it." She rested her forehead in her palm. "I visited the VA hospital in Boston once with my friend. It was such a somber place. And I remember this woman there. She was sitting in the lobby. Off to one side, by herself. She looked so lonely. So sad. My friend just wanted to leave but I couldn't...I couldn't not talk to her." She swallowed hard a couple of times. "She was trying to get her husband an appointment but was told there was a five-month wait." She paused. "I'll never forget the desperate sadness in her voice. Like she'd just given up."

"What did you do?"

"I tried to send him to my father's clinic." She lifted her gaze to his. "His name was Mike Richards."

"Was."

"He killed himself while his wife was at the VA, fighting for him." Her voice broke and she blinked, looking away.

"So then why aren't you there?" He shook his head. "Never mind. Boyfriend, right?"

"Ex." She met his gaze. "I wanted to make a difference and all I feel like I'm doing is putting out fires."

Reza shifted. "Welcome to the army. That's all we ever do." He twisted the cap back on. Set the pint down by his hip. "I don't think I've ever met anyone who managed to get ahead of everything."

"That's so cynical," she whispered.

He shrugged and let his gaze drift down her exposed legs. "I suppose cynical is just a way we get through this stuff," he said.

"There are other ways to cope with stressors in life."

"You sound like a shrink," he murmured. But then he glanced up. Surprised to find her watching him, her eyes dark, her cheeks flushed. What would she do if he touched her? He reached out, cupping her calf, still slick with sweat.

She stilled, her eyes going wide as he slid his hand down her smooth skin. She was slick and soft and hot beneath his touch. Her lips parted.

But she didn't pull away.

"You can't be serious?" she whispered. "We're outside. In broad daylight." And chasing those words was arousal, hot and pulsing through her veins, settling between her thighs.

"You've never gotten naked outside before?" His voice was thick.

"Not next to an army airfield," she whispered. She felt foolish. There wasn't anyone around for miles.

"Trees overhead." He inched his hand higher up the back of her leg. "I hear it's great stress relief."

"Getting naked or getting caught?" She gasped as his thumb stroked the inside of her knee. Such a simple touch. Electric and erotic. "I have to go back to work."

He shifted then to crawl between her thighs. He captured her between his body and the truck. "You don't need anyone's permission for this," he whispered against her mouth. "Be wild for once."

She expected he'd kiss her but instead, he simply shifted and pulled her onto his lap. Her shins banged against the bed of the truck but none of that mattered when he pulled her flush against him. "This is your idea of wild?"

"It's a start," he said, his hands sliding up the back of her jersey. She shivered at his light caress against her skin.

"You can't be serious?"

"I'm always serious when it comes to sex," he whispered against her mouth. "And it's a great alternative to what I had planned for stress relief."

"Would that involve crawling into that pint?" she asked, threading her fingers behind his neck. "I thought you didn't drink anymore."

"I don't." He kissed her. "But that's a long story and I much prefer this technique if you're up for it."

His fingers wandered over her back, slipping beneath the wet shirt. Was she seriously considering this? The thought of getting naked in the back of his truck was...it was forbidden. Something she'd never dreamt of trying when she'd been younger. The fear of getting caught added a delicious spice to the arousal coursing through her veins.

It stunned her how much she wanted this. Wanted to feel the kiss of the air against her bare skin. How much she wanted to feel the wild abandonment he brought to life inside her.

"I've never done it in the backseat before," she whispered against his mouth.

He grinned and it was feral and hungry. He urged her into his lap to straddle him. His big hands found her hips then he slid off the back of the truck and climbed into the backseat.

"I'm sure we can figure it out." He lifted his lips toward hers, his gaze on her mouth.

There was something powerful about her position. She slid her arms around his neck, threading her fingers into his soft, short hair. She brushed her top lip against his, a tentative gesture. His mouth opened but still, he let her retain control.

She flicked her tongue out, tracing the line of his lips. A shudder ran through him and his fingers tightened on her hips. His tongue met hers, a gentle caress between their lips, and excitement purred through her. She swallowed and eased back, enjoying the way he watched her. His wide full lips were parted.

Patient.

Waiting.

Letting her take control.

She licked her lips then leaned in to press them against his. Felt him shudder beneath her touch. Cradling his cheeks, she angled her mouth over his. His lips parted beneath hers, opening beneath her touch. A click of teeth and his tongue slid along hers, a sensual dance.

He was dying. A thousand slow deaths as she kissed him. He fought the primitive urge to drag her out of those sexy running shorts and slide into her. She was driving him insane with her sexy kisses and sensual sounds. He gripped her hips and she winced, a gasp that was not pleasure against his mouth. "Sorry. Hip still sore?" he whispered.

"It's better than it was," she murmured.

"I'll be more careful." He leaned up, capturing her mouth before she could get too far away. "But we've got to get you out of those shorts."

"I'd much rather get you out of those pants." She reached between them, fumbling with his uniform belt until it slid free. She flicked open the buttons on his pants and paused, her eyes widening. "No underwear?"

He shrugged, his lips parted, his eyes heavy with the anticipation of her touch. "Laundry day." His voice was hoarse. "Touch me," he whispered when she hesitated.

He guided her hand to his aching cock and almost died of pleasure from her gentle grip. He squeezed her hand tight around him and showed her the rhythm. He started to release her hand and let her stroke him.

"Don't let go," she said. He looked up to find her watching their hands intently. She lifted her gaze and their eyes collided. He'd never seen anything so fucking sexy as he guided her hand over his erection. The way she watched him, like this was the first time she'd ever done anything illicit. Anything without permission.

"Honey, if I don't let go, we're going to have a hell of a mess on our hands," he murmured against her mouth. "Pun intended."

"Oh." A gasp, filled with arousal and heat and longing.

He kissed her then, pulling her close so that he could feel her heat against him.

He thanked the new truck fairies that he'd had the foresight to get a full-sized pickup, one with a backseat that had room in spades. He pushed the front seat forward as Emily shucked out of her shorts, then pushed his pants down as she crawled back into his lap.

"Condom?" she whispered. Her body was taut against his. He reached between their bodies to find her soaked. Swollen, so swollen.

He shifted and urged her to rub against him. Her heat surrounded him, caressing his cock until he thought this was going to have a disappointing ending for them both. Instead, she shifted unexpectedly and slid down his length with an audible gasp.

"Fuck, did I hurt you?"

Her breath came in short quick bursts. "No. I need...

I..." She pressed against him, her body shuddering around him. "This. I need this."

He shifted then and arched his hips into hers. She cried out then started to move. Slow and deep, she took him, clenching around his cock until he thought he'd die from the simple pleasure of watching her move.

He leaned his head back and half-closed his eyes, letting her move, letting her find what felt good. And when he reached between them to stroke her softly, she whimpered but kept moving, riding him deeper. And then a little harder.

He stroked her until that first shudder broke over them both. She lost the rhythm and he found it, gripping her hips and holding her as he slid deeper, deeper into her. The cascade of emotion started with the tiniest wave of her shuddering pleasure. It continued, stronger and stronger until he clutched her to him and surrendered a piece of his soul.

Chapter Eleven

H̲ow much trouble are you in at work?" he asked as he parked behind the clinic.

"Nothing drastic," she said. "I just have slight perfectionist tendencies and I don't like screwing up."

He leaned toward her then, threading his fingers into her hair. He urged her to look at him. "You're not screwing up. You're trying to do a good job," he whispered against her lips.

"I'm not being very successful at it," she said, blinking rapidly.

"Yes, you are." It was weighing on her, more than she'd admitted at the lake. He brushed his lips against hers. "What are you doing later?"

"Working."

He narrowed his eyes at her, then nodded. She was dodging him. And normally it wouldn't bother him except that now he wanted to know what she was hiding. Why had she gone for a six-mile run in the middle of the workday if she was just blowing off steam?

Reza looked longingly at the glove box as he drove back toward his company operations area. After-lunch traffic on

Fort Hood sucked balls on a good day and today was not a good day. He'd already inched past three fender benders and at least two civilian cops handing out tickets.

Why couldn't people just put the phone down and drive? Hell, he couldn't fathom not paying attention to the roads as he drove. He clenched the steering wheel with his left hand as he flipped through the radio stations. A tight band squeezed around his chest until he realized he was holding his breath.

A single hard breath and the band released. "Stairway to Heaven" came on the radio at the same time as his phone started vibrating in his pocket. He pulled it out and put it on speakerphone. "Sarn't Ike."

"Sarn't Ike, it's Foster. We've got a small problem."

"What's that?" Lovely. He was stuck in traffic and they had a small problem. The day was shaping up to be a real winner at the rate it was going.

"Sloban is missing. And his roommate says he may or may not be riding around with a pint of Patrón and a nine mil."

"Tell me this is some kind of joke." The tension around his heart was back and it brought friends, stabbing his heart with a thousand tiny nails. Adrenaline pounded through his veins, gearing up for action.

Because if Sloban had a gun, there was going to be high adventure somewhere on post.

"Apparently, he got the notification that his medical evaluation board results denied he has PTSD. He's getting thrown out of the army with nothing." Foster's voice held a hard edge, the kind of edge Reza was used to hearing when the shit and the fan were making babies. "Are you near the R&R Center? You might want to head back there. His roommate said he was going off about the psych docs."

Reza glanced around him at the traffic. He was pinned in

on three sides but if he went over the median and busted a U-turn, he could get back there easily.

To hell with it. He'd deal with the cops later.

"All right. Have you called the MPs?" Reza swore under his breath. "Never mind. Just get some guards posted on the building so he can't get in if he shows up. I'm heading back to R&R."

"Don't get shot. I'm going to be pissed if I have to deal with Marshall and friends by myself."

Reza grinned. "I'll do my best, honey." Reza dropped the phone into the center console of his truck and waited for the car in front of him to inch forward a little bit more. Scanning his surroundings, he offered up a prayer to the traffic gods that there were no cops around. Flipping on his four-way flashers, he eased the truck over the median and then gunned it once he was in the opposite lane, cutting off a Humvee.

The Humvee's horn blared but he ignored it. His blood pounded in his veins as he mentally started running through the various scenarios. Sloban could already be inside. He could have a gun.

Reza really didn't want to get shot. Not today, anyway, and for damn sure not by one of his guys.

At the R&R Center he pulled into one of the handicap spots. Screw it; the cops could ticket him if he didn't get blown halfway to hell. He scanned the parking lot quickly, looking for Sloban's shitty white Bronco, and didn't see it.

Wishing for his body armor, he walked through the front door of the clinic. Nothing looked out of the ordinary. The receptionist had the same blank stare that she'd had earlier when Reza had tried to get information from her about Wisniak. At least, that was until she looked up. Her eyes widened once she recognized Reza. "Sergeant—"

"Ms. Walters, I'm not here to argue with you. I need you to clear the lobby of folks."

She stood, canting one eyebrow, hands on her hips. "I'm sorry, Sergeant Iaconelli, but you don't get to give orders here."

He slammed his palm against the counter. "Listen, lady. Someone in this clinic just told one of my joes he's not getting a medical discharge from the army. We suspect he's got a weapon. So you can stand here and argue with me or you can clear the fucking area. Your choice."

Her dark skin paled. She grabbed her purse, her movements jerky. "Don't forget your ID card," he reminded her.

She scuttled out the back door silently. She hadn't breathed a word to any of the troops in the waiting room. Coward.

"All right, listen up. I need all of you to grab your gear and head out of here." He reached out, stopping a young female private who looked like she was about twelve from walking out the front door. "Head out the back." He had no idea if Sloban was going to come in the front door or the back but Reza figured it was a better idea to ship people away from the front door. Sloban wasn't smart enough to conduct an actual assault on the building if he was coming here.

Reza waited until the last soldier had departed the waiting area, then started back toward the front door.

"Just what do you think you're doing?"

Reza glanced over his shoulder to see one highly pissed-off Emily. If they didn't get shot, dear Lord was he in trouble.

Reza's features were stretched tight, his breathing quick. She was close enough to see that his nostrils flared with each breath. He looked tense and alert.

Just like he had at the shoot house.

"You need to clear the area."

She raised both eyebrows. "What's going on?"

His fists clenched at his sides. The movement drew her

gaze and she noticed how big his hands were. Hands that had been on her body less than an hour ago. Veins crisscrossed the dark skin. Her mouth went dry and she told herself it was from the fierce anger looking back at her.

"Someone in your clinic decided that Sloban's PTSD was caused by the drugs he was smoking instead of his time in the combat zone, and now he's pissed. He could be heading anywhere but I'd bet my life he's coming here." There was censure in his voice and Emily flinched. "Someone should have probably broken the news to him a little more gently. Now we've just got to keep him from blowing the place up and we'll be good to go."

"Tell me you're joking?"

His smile was grim against the dark of his skin and he glanced at her slick right sleeve that sported no combat patch. "You should worry when I'm not making jokes," he said, leaning back to check the door.

He pulled a vibrating phone from his left shoulder pocket and peered out the front door. "Yeah?"

Emily stood back, unsure of what to do. She'd never been in combat and she hadn't really paid attention in officer school when they'd done the combat training. Reza pushed the door open a little.

"Yeah, I see the truck. MPs are en route. Got it." He scowled and slipped the phone back into his pocket and pushed through the door. Over Reza's shoulder, she could see an ancient white Bronco yank into the parking lot. A minute later, the door opened and Sloban tumbled out, at least halfway to wasted, gun in hand.

He was tweaking on something. His movements were jerky and quick.

"Wait." Reza stopped and turned back at her movement. "What are you doing?"

"I'm going to go talk to him. What's it look like?"

"You realize that is massively stupid, don't you?" She took a step forward. "Last time I checked, I was the doctor here." Her skin tightened over her bones and she fought the fear that crawled up her spine to wrap around her throat. She was afraid. She should be better than that by now. She expected him to look at her with disdain but instead, something softened in his eyes.

"It's okay, Emily," he said softly. "He's one of mine. I've got this."

He stepped into the bright Fort Hood afternoon.

What kind of a man walked toward the threat of violence instead of away? Everyone else she knew would have smartly left and let someone with a heck of a lot more skill handle the situation. But the big sergeant she'd made love to less than an hour ago headed out to face down a soldier on the edge.

She blamed the little flip in her belly on nerves as she crept toward the door. She couldn't very well hide in the corner while Iaconelli did this on his own. She was a doctor. This was what she did. It took her thirty seconds to find her courage. Then she followed him into the light.

Sloban walked slowly toward the front of the clinic. He was using. Reza could tell instantly by the way his hands were in constant motion, especially the one holding the nine mil. Sloban's eyes were sunken and hollow and rimmed with red.

He felt her presence behind him as he stepped from beneath the shade tree overhanging the front door. Emily had been white as a sheet only seconds ago when he'd told her he was going out to talk to Sloban. He'd figured her natural fear would keep her inside and out of his way.

Apparently, self-preservation was not on her list of strong points. Second only to domestic violence situations, dealing with a strung-out druggie was the worst type of situation to go into. Well, except for house-borne IEDs. Those were always fun, too.

"Dude, this isn't the way you want to go out," Reza said quietly to Sloban. He wanted to turn around and shout at the dumbass captain behind him. Why the hell hadn't she stayed inside and let him handle this? Did she think this was some kind of friggin' game? The kid in front of him, who had once been a decorated combat veteran, was twitchy and strung-out. His face was pockmarked with sores—some scabbed over, others still fresh and raw. Reza's soul ached at the emptiness that looked back at him. Sloban had been part of Reza's platoon once upon a time. He'd been a fucking warrior on the streets of Baghdad and had gone house to house with him in Sadr City.

But one too many nightmare scenarios had twisted something inside the shadow of the man looking back at him now. One too many explosions that had left him covered in his buddies' blood. One too many sleepless nights in the bunker as the world blew up around them.

Reza knew full well what it felt like to want to numb the pain. But he'd never resorted to meth. That was just stupid. Here Sloban was, destroying himself, all because he was trying to get away from the assault from his own brain.

"Sarn't Ike, the army fucked me. Totally fucked me." Sloban gripped the nine mil in his hand like an old-school mobster, waving it for emphasis as he spoke. "*She* fucked me. Her and all these goddamned doctors who think they know what we do." He jabbed the gun over Reza's shoulder in Emily's direction.

Reza stepped to the side, blocking Sloban's view of Captain Lindberg and moving directly into the path of his weapon. "You don't want to do this, Neal. This isn't the way to get them to listen to your case."

"They're not going to listen to me!" Sloban raked his

hand through his stringy hair. "They said I'm an addict. I won't get shit from the VA now. I can't get the fucking memories out of my head. They broke me, Sarn't Ike. I begged not to go on this last deployment. You know what Captain Marshall said? Suck it up, pussy." He scrubbed his hands over his face. "I am not a fucking pussy." His eyes filled. "I did everything the army asked me to do," he whispered. "Everything."

"I know, buddy." Reza took a single step forward. "I know. And we'll get it figured out. I'll help you write to your congressman. I'll take you to see the Corps commander. We can figure this out, okay? But this isn't the way to do it."

Sloban shook his head, his dirty hair falling across his empty eyes. "There's nothing else to do, man. They don't want to pay for what they did to me. They don't want to talk about how fucked up this war is. They just want people like me to go away."

"That's not true."

"We can fix this." Emily's voice was soft though filled with terror. She was directly behind Reza. Fear pitched in his guts. "I'll go back and re-look at your file."

"I am not a file!" Sloban screamed, raising the gun at the woman now standing at Reza's side. "I am a person. A fucking person! I'm not a number. I'm not a file. I'm not something the army can just throw away!"

The world slowed down and ground to a halt.

Sloban flicked the safety off.

Reza dove.

The echo of the nine mil shattered the afternoon.

Chapter Twelve

The lights from the ambulance bounced off the buildings around them. Some jackass really needed to turn off the sirens. It wasn't like they were in a hurry to get anywhere.

Sloban had been dead before he hit the ground.

Reza stood near his truck, holding a coffee cup and sipping it slowly.

He'd finally opened the flask. He didn't think anyone would give him shit about having a drink right about now.

Hell, he needed something a whole lot stronger than a few shots of vodka to get the smell of charred skin and smoking blood out of his nose. The laced coffee was helping, but not nearly enough.

He watched the chaos play out before him, feeling detached from the world around him. His heart rate had long ago slowed back to normal. He was lucky that he wouldn't have a strong crash response after the adrenaline stopped pumping through his system, otherwise he'd probably be ready to take a nap. Other than needing a clean uniform, he still had to go back to work. He was sure that Captain Marshall was going to need a full report, PowerPoint slideshow, and executive summary with note cards before Reza could go home for the day. Douche bag.

The paramedics covered the body and lifted Sloban's remains into the back of the ambulance. It was only after they moved that he saw Emily standing beneath an old oak tree with Colonel Zavisca. She didn't really appear to be listening to whatever the colonel was saying. She had her arms wrapped tightly around herself. One hand was repetitively rubbing her shoulder and her face was still pale and drawn. Colonel Zavisca patted her back awkwardly and walked back toward the waiting MPs.

Sighing and knowing full well he should be going in the other direction, he started across the small yard. She didn't acknowledge him until he was practically on top of her.

"Here." He thrust the coffee cup toward her. It was like a curtain lifted from her vision as she looked first at the coffee cup and then up at him.

"I don't drink coffee," she whispered. "But thank you."

Reza offered a grin he wasn't really feeling. "Make an exception. It'll help get you through the rest of this."

She glanced skeptically down at the Styrofoam cup. "What's in it?"

"Bug juice. Just drink before you friggin' collapse."

Her hands trembled as she took the cup, then with a deep sigh she tossed back a solid gulp.

And promptly choked. Her eyes watered as she coughed. Reza took back the cup before she spilled. "What was in that?" she asked when she could speak.

He smiled and felt some of the detachment he'd felt snap inside him, letting him feel the warmth of the sun beating on his neck. "Special brew."

She swiped at her eyes. "I thought you gave up drinking."

He wasn't going to answer that one honestly. "Today's an exception," he said quietly.

"That was a dirty trick."

Reza lifted one shoulder, watching a hint of color come back into her cheeks. "You look better now."

"How can you be so calm?" she asked, tipping her head to peer up at him. A single ray of sunlight glinted across her cheek.

Calm? That wasn't how he would describe the lack inside him. It wasn't how he'd explain the total emptiness he felt as the adrenaline wore off. "Guess I'm used to stuff like this."

"That is a really sad commentary on your life," she whispered. Already she looked steadier on her feet, more solid, instead of as if a stiff breeze would knock her over.

"It is." He shifted and turned toward the departing ambulance. "I knew Sloban before..." His voice cracked and he cleared his throat roughly. "Before he got hooked on the bad stuff. He was a good kid. Lots of potential. Something broke him." Reza looked down at her, noting how close she stood. Color had come back into her lips. "Eventually, war breaks everyone."

She studied him quietly and for the first time in Reza's life he wanted to simply sit. Not move. Not drink himself into oblivion or fuck until he passed out. Just sit in a stillness that didn't echo with the taunts of the dead. It was a strange sensation and not completely unwelcome, but a little unnerving.

"Why do you still stay in, then? Why not get out of the army before it breaks you, too?"

He smiled wryly. "Who says it hasn't broken me already?" He rubbed his hand over his face and took another drink, then offered her the cup, surprised when she took another, if smaller, sip. "This is the first time you've been around something like this, isn't it?"

"Yes. Not a whole lot of death at home."

"Where's home?"

"Outside of Boston. You?"

"New York."

She handed him back the cup. "You don't sound like you're from New York. You don't sound like you're from anywhere in particular."

"I've been in the army long enough to bleed any accent out of me." He kept the rest of his comments to himself. He wanted to make sure she was good to go before he headed back to face Marshall.

His phone vibrated in his pocket. "Speak of the devil," he mumbled. "Yes, sir?"

"Haven't you seen my phone calls?"

"Been a little busy here," Reza said, taking a long pull off the coffee cup. It was pretty sad that he needed strong alcohol more to deal with his company commander than he needed to deal with a kid killing himself right in front of him. Shit, he was a disaster.

"I needed a situation report for the battalion commander an hour ago. I'm pulling into the parking lot now, damn it, since you haven't answered the phone."

Reza glanced up in time to see Marshall's big black Toyota Tundra whip into the tiny R&R Center parking lot like it was a sports car on a closed track. Reza slid the phone into his pocket then handed the cup to Lindberg. "I'll be back in a few minutes. Here, you look like you need a little more."

She smiled and the way her eyes warmed did something to his insides. "From the sound of that conversation, you may need it more than me."

He grinned. "Yeah, but I'm used to dealing with douche bag officers. Part of the duty description of an NCO."

He stalked toward Marshall, praying for the gods of patience to smile down on him. It would not do well for him to punch his commander. Sergeant majors tended to frown on things like NCOs assaulting their officers.

*   *   *

Emily wrapped her hands around the warm cup and sat down on the ring of paving stones circling the tree behind her. Reza was right: Whatever was in that cup was helping keep her upright. All she'd wanted to do was go home, take a shower and curl up in the dark safety of her room. She wanted someone to wake her up and to be able to start the entire day over again.

The nightmare of Sloban putting the gun beneath his chin and pulling the trigger was enough to make her soul bleed. Every time she shut her eyes, she saw him do it again, over and over in slow motion.

She opened her eyes, refusing to descend into the morass of the memories, and watched Reza walk toward one very angry captain. The other captain was almost as tall as Sergeant Iaconelli but much thinner. Where Iaconelli was big and wide and looked built for strength, the captain was wiry.

Other than their uniforms, they looked like they came from two different worlds. The captain was tense and angry, the ends of his dusty brown hair fading into the angry purple of his face. Reza shook his head and jerked his hand in her direction.

Why would they be arguing about her?

Sucking in a deep breath, she stood and crossed the small yard, the dead leaves and dried grass that she'd learned marked the Fort Hood summer crunching beneath her combat boots. The other captain's voice held barely restrained fury. Reza was calm and unruffled, as stoic as he'd been throughout the morning's ordeal.

"I don't really give a shit if the Corps commander was here, Iaconelli. I needed to update the brigade commander and I missed a critical window on the reporting requirements."

Reza stuffed his hands in his pockets. "One of your

soldiers is dead and you're worried about a report." He didn't raise his voice but Captain Marshall's face went white. Emily couldn't tell if it was from fury or shame.

Marshall jabbed his finger in Reza's chest. "You're out of line, Sarn't Ike. Completely and totally out of line."

"What are you going to do, tell the sergeant major I was too busy dealing with a dead body to answer the phone? Go ahead, sir. Knock yourself out. And while you're at it, add in the part where you revoked Sloban's pass privileges and ordered him not to do any more drugs. It'll make you look like a real fucking hero."

Reza had almost gone to jail that day. Marshall had done everything he could to punish Sloban for his addiction. Reza had gone over his head to get the kid sent to rehab.

Was it just too hard to comprehend that you couldn't give a soldier a direct order not to use? Not when they were addicted to the hard stuff.

"I told that soldier not to do drugs!"

Reza's temper finally snapped and he took a step toward his commander. He stopped short of actually striking the man. "He was a fucking addict, you asshole. You can order him not to do a lot of things but you can't order an addict not to use. I'm done with this shit. Do you have your precious fucking report?"

Marshall took a deep breath, his hands clenched by his sides. "I'm going to let your flagrant disrespect slide because of what happened here today. But watch yourself, Sergeant. One day, all the awards on your chest aren't going to fucking save you."

Marshall stalked off, slamming into his big truck and tearing out of the parking lot. Reza turned and almost plowed into Emily. She held up the cup. "You can definitely use this more than me," she said.

He seemed to visibly relax as he took the cup. He didn't seem to feel the alcohol at all. "You doing better?" he asked.

"I'm fine. But do you have to deal with that guy on a daily basis?"

"He's my esteemed company commander. We suspect he was potty trained at gun point."

He took the cup from her and lifted the lid off, peering into the now empty cup. It had numbed something sharp and stabbing inside her. Missing though, was the comfortable fuzz in her head, like there normally was when she'd had a glass of wine. "You haven't answered the question, Ma'am."

She smiled up at him, seeing a crack in the deep mocha steel of his skin. "I thought I was Emily," she said softly, wishing she could take back the words that had stung him earlier.

"Only if you still want to be," he said, his mouth curling in a faint smile. There was something about his smile, the way it eased the hard lines around his mouth. Like he didn't spend nearly enough time smiling.

She tipped her chin. "It just dawned on me that your name is Reza Iaconelli. What kind of a name is that?" She needed the distraction.

"Italian and Iranian."

"It seems like there's a joke in there somewhere," she said quietly.

"It probably has something to do with too much body hair."

Emily laughed out loud, then covered her mouth as several bystanders shot her looks. "I'm sorry," she whispered. Sobering, she folded her arms over her chest. "I feel so guilty for laughing right now."

Reza stood a little too close, close enough that she could see a shaving nick at the corner of his mouth. Close enough that people would start talking if she didn't step back.

But right then, she didn't care if the whole world started

talking about their relationship. She needed him. More than anything.

At that moment, she couldn't walk away. Couldn't tear herself away from him and the solid support he provided by simply offering a cup of liquor to help get her through the terrible afternoon.

"You shouldn't feel guilty for laughing," he said, his voice rough. "We all have different coping mechanisms."

"What are yours? Other than drinking, I mean."

Something shuttered down on his expression and it hardened. The warmth that had been there a moment ago was now gone, severing the connection that had been growing between them.

"You don't really want to know." He twisted the cup in his hand. "I've got to head back across post before Captain Marshall crushes my nuts."

She offered him a sympathetic smile. "Yeah. We wouldn't want him to hurt those."

She slapped her hand over her mouth again, her face flaming hot. Reza laughed quietly, the lines around his lips softening. "You going to be all right?"

She nodded, sobering at the reminder of the day's horror. "Yes. I'd just as soon you leave before I have any more of my boot for lunch."

He lifted his hand and for a moment, she thought he was going to slide those rough fingers over her face. Instead he rested his palm on her shoulder. The solid warmth steadied her. "Make sure you take some time for you today. This may hit you . . . later."

She smiled thinly. "I thought I was the counselor here," she said weakly. "Shouldn't I be saying that to you?"

He grunted and lowered his hand, saying nothing, silence in the middle of chaos.

Chapter Thirteen

An hour later, Reza parked his truck in the first sergeant's parking spot, and tried to figure out how to give his statement to the commander without wanting to punch him in the head.

Sloban was dead because of Captain Marshall, and that Reza could not forgive. Maybe Marshall hadn't pulled the trigger himself but he was responsible nonetheless. Sloban had been through some bad shit downrange. Very bad shit. The kind of bad shit that people wrote books about. The kind of shit that ended up in the Army's Lessons-Learned database that no one paid attention to. But it was also the kind of bad shit that the Army liked to pretend didn't really fuck people up in the head as much as it really did.

Because hell, every soldier should be able to see their buddy get their legs blown off and come home just fine, right? Add in that Sloban's wife had run off with his brother—how was that for family loyalty—and Marshall's relentless push to throw Sloban out of the army for misconduct—and the kid had finally just snapped.

It wasn't going to be easy facing his commander. Reza reached into the glove box for the flask. He wasn't so stupid as to risk getting an open container violation riding around on post with a vodka bottle in his truck. Then again, the rent-a-cops that checked their vehicles at the gate weren't the most astute individuals. They saw what they wanted to see. Unless they happened to have a military working dog at the gate who was trained to sniff out alcohol. But that hadn't happened to date so Reza wasn't overly concerned about it.

He sat in his truck and tossed back a shot of vodka straight up, trying to figure out how he was going to keep his temper in check, and felt like a fucking failure for tossing back another one. Marshall was probably having kittens because Reza had deliberately taken his time getting back to the company ops office.

Goddamn it. He'd finally broken. He'd been sober for months. All that hard work was fucking gone.

Just like Sloban.

He rubbed at his eyes with his thumb and his forefinger, then rested his elbow on the door, hoping he didn't have to see the sergeant major before today was over. Giles would know in a heartbeat that Reza had been drinking and somehow, Reza figured it was safe to assume the old man wouldn't stick his neck out to save Reza's ass one more time. He wasn't getting hammered. He just needed a little bit to take the edge off. He was fine.

Today was an exception if he'd ever seen one.

He'd get through the rest of the night then he'd sober up for tomorrow. He'd get back on track then.

Tonight? Tonight he needed the help.

His cell phone vibrated in his shoulder pocket. "So much for a moment of peace," he mumbled. Frowning, he saw a text from Captain Claire Montoya. *Are you okay?*

He smiled faintly. Trust the mother hen to check up on him. *I'm fine. Shit day at work.*

His phone vibrated again. *Don't lie to me. I heard about the shooting.*

I'm fine. Gotta go brief Captain Asshole about it.

He supposed he should be glad that someone gave a shit about him enough to check up on him and in reality, he was. But there were things about him that Claire would never understand and that he'd never tell her. Personal angst and childhood trauma and blah blah bad memories blah.

He took another pull from the vodka to steel his nerves then slipped the flask beneath the driver's seat.

The company operations was a madhouse. He pushed through the back door and came into absolute chaos. The company supply clerk was red-faced and pink-nosed. She'd been crying. Damn it, he wasn't ready to deal with other people's grief. Her eyes widened when he walked in and he glanced down.

Fuck. He still had blood on his uniform. That was not going to go over very well. Nothing said "triggering flash-backs" like walking around in a bloodstained uniform. Jesus, he was going to be the reason fifteen dudes lined up at the R&R Center for counseling after this.

He wondered if Captain Marshall had called the chaplain. You know, for people with legitimate grief issues. Or as Marshall liked to call them, candy pants, crybaby sissies.

The full weight of his own hypocrisy nailed him dead center. He'd said the same thing about Wisniak the other day.

He was cut from the same cloth as Marshall, apparently.

Guilt rose up to choke him.

"I don't suppose that Captain Marshall would under-stand if I headed home to change first?" he asked the supply sergeant.

Pressing her lips together, she shook her head. "He's pretty pissed right now, Sarn't Ike."

Reza sighed. "Figured as much." Bracing for the reaction

of his troopers and hating himself for not changing first, he walked through the company ops.

Silence fell over the ops personnel as soon as he pushed through the door that separated company supply from the main office. Foster was there, looking grim and harried, undoubtedly from Marshall's demands.

"What the hell is taking Sarn't Iaconelli so long to get here from R&R?" Marshall's voice carried over the silence then faded as he realized he was the only one talking. It was another moment before he came out of the tiny closet that doubled as his office.

Marshall was six feet tall and believed himself to be bullet-proof. His dirty blond hair was cut into a military high and tight and Reza was convinced that Teague was not far off the mark about his potty training happening at the end of a gun. Patience was not in the man's vocabulary, as witnessed by his excessive use of the word "now." And while Reza had him by about three inches and twenty pounds, Marshall was convinced he could go toe to toe with Reza.

"Sorry I took so long. Was busy trying to get the blood out of my uniform."

Marshall's gaze drifted down Reza's body and back up. He fought the urge to cross his arms over his torso. Somehow, Reza didn't think Marshall would appreciate his attempt at sarcasm, such as it was. "I need the rest of the information for an update to the initial Serious Incident Report."

"I'm fine. Thanks for asking."

Reza was reasonably certain he saw smoke coming out of Marshall's ears but he said nothing else. Instead he walked into the first sergeant's office and slipped his ID card into the computer to log on. He clenched his fists as he waited for the computer to load, refusing to acknowledge the slight trembling in his hands.

He was fine. He'd been through worse shit than this. He

just wanted to give Marshall the information he needed so he could go burn the blood-covered uniform and then get back to work.

A quiet rap on the door drew his attention from the blue computer screen. "What's up, Foster?"

"Just wanted to give you an update. I called the chaplain already and he's on his way down here as soon as he gets done with the battalion commander. And we've already pulled Sloban's emergency data sheets for the brigade casualty affairs officer."

Reza studied Foster closely, looking for any cracks in the man's cool demeanor. His behavior was typical. Stay busy after something bad happened. Busy was easy. Busy meant not having to think about whatever bad thing had happened that day.

Busy kept your mind from drifting into dark, uncharted territory. But Foster showed no signs that he was doing anything other than his job. Then again, he'd never really gotten along with Sloban.

"Thanks Foster. That's two things off my list of shit to do."

"Yeah, well, I only did it to keep Marshall from stepping on your neck. He's freaking out about Sloban. The man does not handle pressure well."

Reza entered his password on the computer then glanced back up at Foster. "None of us should be taking this well," he said quietly. "Thanks for keeping your cool. I'll take it from here."

Foster looked like he was about to say something but then snapped his mouth closed. After a moment more, he said, "You probably need to change your clothes, Sarn't Ike. Especially if you're going to stick around today."

He glanced down at his ruined uniform. "Yeah."

There was really nothing else to say.

*   *   *

The sun was still shining brightly through the office windows when Emily's hands started shaking. The duty day had long ago ended and now the silence hung on, echoing down the empty hallways.

She sank into her cheap leather chair, following techniques she'd long ago started preaching to her clients. Breathing deeply through her nose, she didn't fight the feeling. Rather, she let it take her. Let it fill her up and expand beyond her body. Her breath penetrated the panic, pushing away the lingering fear.

She folded her hands together in her lap and simply was.

Her fingers shook as the grief and the fear and the relentless memory replayed over and over and over.

She breathed deeply. Inhaled slowly, letting air fill her lungs. Praying for a calm that escaped her.

Reza. She wanted Reza. She wanted to check on him. To see how he was holding up.

To feel his arms around her. To lean on him. Just a little bit.

She had the sneaking suspicion that he'd been leaned on too much for too long. There was a reason he no longer drank. That much she was sure of.

And she wanted him. Wanted to be with him when the grief tore through her. Wanted to be there so he wouldn't be alone. She closed her eyes and felt his big rough hands push her down once more, digging into her flesh, but when she tipped her chin to look into his ebony depths, the soft black emptiness looking back at her offered calm. Her breathing slowed as she gave herself over to the comfort of her fantasy.

Here was a man who didn't ask for permission before he took. Who dominated simply by being in the room. She wanted to rest there in the shadow of his body. Wanted to feel the heat from his flesh penetrating hers.

She felt his hands on her hips again. Felt the gentle kiss of air as he stepped directly into the line of fire from Sloban's weapon.

Her heart tightened at the mere thought of the weapon. Her lungs refused to cooperate. She tried to release the sensation, tried to let go of the stifling pain but nothing worked.

She closed her eyes, trying to think of what Reza would do. She rubbed her hands over her face. He probably didn't have panic attacks. He'd handled the entire thing with little more than a shot of whatever had been in that coffee cup.

And that's what worried her. The alcohol in that cup had been strong, stronger than anything she was used to. And as long as she'd known him, he'd been avoiding alcohol.

His hands hadn't trembled. His voice hadn't wavered. He'd been stoic and steady and calm. And he'd made her laugh during a time when, well, laughing didn't really seem the thing to do. Psychologically, she realized that dark humor was a way to cope with a tragic situation. In reality, it felt both good and wrong all at once. It was a feeling she knew well, one she'd struggled to avoid in her life since joining the Army, getting as far away from the bad decisions as she could. But some habits were harder than others to break.

She glanced at her cell phone then flipped open a file on her desk. There in bold red ink was Reza's phone number.

She could call him. She could pick up the phone and see how he was doing. It wouldn't make her look desperate, right? Or like she was trolling for a hot and sweaty release in the Texas heat?

She'd just been through a crappy situation with him. It would be a completely innocuous phone call.

So if it was so innocent, why did she hesitate?

Sighing quietly, she threaded her fingers together, forcing herself to be still and *think* before she picked up the phone.

Somehow she'd come to depend on him in the short time she'd known him. He'd become somewhat of her Guide to Life in the Military, at least life outside the protected walls of her clinic. She'd wanted to escape the Ivory Tower she'd grown up in but instead, she'd merely traded one for another.

The clinic was just as sheltered as her home had been. She clenched the pen in her hands, flicking the cap on and off. She was not going to let others rule her life. If she wanted to call Reza, damn it, she was going to call Reza.

Except she didn't pick up the phone. She wondered if it would be better to simply go to his place. She could find his address easily enough. It would be a violation of her ethics but still. A few strokes on her keyboard and she could know everything about him.

But right then? She just wanted to know where he lived.

Because she was a coward who couldn't pick up the phone.

There was no guarantee this would end up the way she wanted it to. There were no promises that he would even answer the phone, let alone open his door to her. Wouldn't it be better to simply let him go? Let him fade into a really great memory? Except she was tired of letting others make her decisions for her. Tired of hearing her mother's voice in her head every time she colored outside the lines, threatening to disown her if she didn't return home.

She could spend the rest of her life wondering what if. Because she was really good at what if-ing a situation to death. She glanced at her cell phone. At the computer where she could easily look up his address.

Or she could make her own decision for once and ask for what she needed from a big sergeant with strong hands and a good heart.

She dropped the pen onto her desk.

Unclenched her fingers.

And made her choice.

Reza walked into his house long after the sun had already set. His mouth was dry, his nerves shot to hell. His hand shook as he reached into the fridge and pulled out a can of Steel Reserve. He'd gotten through the day with the rest of the pint that morning. A second pint of vodka in his Red Bull at lunch.

He was comfortably numb but not nearly drunk enough.

He wanted to pass out. To fall into sleep and wake up some time tomorrow and find out that the miserable shit day had all been just a bad dream.

But the day had been slowly closing in on him as he'd finished up the endless reports and phone calls. Slowly the pressure had started crushing the air from his lungs and chasing any daylight from his soul. He sank into the ten-year-old couch that he'd been carting around since he was a private at Fort Stewart and kicked his feet up on the beat-up coffee table.

He'd stopped by the shoppette on his way home. Bought another six-pack of Steel Reserve that was now sitting in his fridge and planned to crawl into the bag. There was a bottle of vodka cooling in the freezer.

Sobriety was overrated for days like this.

He breathed in deeply as he took a long pull from the can, trying to chase the smell of burning blood from his nose. The scent of malt liquor burned the insides of his sinuses but did nothing to chase away the other smell.

Killing half the can, he closed his eyes, feeling the slow numbness he'd craved all day slowly seeping through his veins. He should have gone to the bar tonight. A bunch of the guys were getting together to commiserate but tonight, Reza couldn't summon the energy.

The wretched miasma of the day wrapped around him, pulling him down into the comforting embrace of the malt liquor.

He rubbed his eyes roughly with his thumb and his forefinger. They burned. Sloban was a fucked-up kid but he'd promised Reza he'd been holding it together.

Jesus, would it ever end?

Reza tried to swallow the lump that rose in his throat. It took a lot to wash it down. He sat up, resting his elbows on his knees, rubbing his face just to have something to do with his free hand.

The alcohol burned a path down his esophagus but it did nothing to dull the pain burning around his heart, threatening to crush him. He slugged back the rest of the malt liquor. It tasted faintly of rubbing alcohol. It wasn't that far removed.

He tossed the can in the trash and went for another in the fridge. The sergeant major could kiss his ass. He was crawling into a bottle tonight and he wasn't coming out until he was certain he wasn't going to shatter every time he thought Sloban's name.

He was halfway through the third can when his skin finally began to tingle. He glanced down. There was still blood on his uniform. Memories started circling.

Sarn't Ike! Oh fuck Sarn't Ike, it hurts.

Bush had died in Reza's arms because they'd been unable to secure a MEDEVAC site. And Reza, being a fucking failure of a human being, had never written to Bush's wife and told her that he'd loved her like he'd promised.

Well shit, this isn't how I planned it. Cooper was bleeding bad. The road outside Baghdad Airport was red with rust-colored blood and spent ammo.

Don't say that, Coop. Reza kept pressure on the wound. Someone shouted for a medic.

It'll be all right, Sarn't Ike. Get everyone else home, okay?

Coop. Jesus, Coop, look at me. Don't...

Coop had been a smart-ass to the very end. Reza tossed back the rest of the can and finally felt the buzz of alcohol starting to cloud his brain. But the pain in his chest didn't stop. Didn't ease back. He needed it to fucking stop.

Just one night. Just long enough for him to put everything back in the box and lock it down. He staggered to the kitchen and pulled the bottle of vodka from the freezer. His phone vibrated on the counter next to the sink. He ignored it.

It was probably Marshall, wanting to bust his balls over Sloban. Christ, it never ended. How the fuck was he supposed to know the kid was going to kill himself? Or threaten to kill Emily?

Rage surged inside him as he remembered the weapon pointed at Emily. He'd wanted to tear Sloban's fucking heart out when he'd seen the gun. He'd been too late.

The kid was dead because Reza hadn't been fast enough. The phone buzzed in the kitchen again. He walked past it, ignoring it. He twisted off the frozen cap and blew on the top of the bottle before taking a heavy pull. It burned like ice down his throat and the familiar numbness settled around his heart.

Oh fuck oh fuck oh fuck.

He set the bottle down on the coffee table and cradled his head in his hands, rocking gently, trying to get the memories to stop. He didn't want to see their faces again. He didn't want to feel their losses all over again. Fuck, he just wanted it to stop. He was tired of bleeding his soul out at the bottom of a bottle.

Another pull off the vodka and his heart was frozen in his chest. He pressed his palm against his breastbone and felt for a pulse. There had to be one, right?

Boom boom.

There it was. Still beating. Just minus the pain. The boom returned and he realized it wasn't his heart beating in his ears. Someone was at the door.

Who the fuck was at his door at this hour? It better not be Teague. He wasn't in the mood. He managed to get up off the couch but tripped on one of his boots. He staggered into the chair, stubbing his toe on the sofa. He swore loud and long and his toe was still throbbing as he yanked the front door open.

He was still sober enough to be shocked that Emily stood on his porch.

Chapter Fourteen

C an I come in?"

He was drunk. She could see that by the way he leaned against the door frame, barely upright. She'd come seeking solace from the day's events but looking at him then, she didn't think he'd be the person to give her anything but a hangover.

A hangover would be preferable to the horrible sadness she felt right then.

She was terrified that he was going to close the door in her face and she didn't know what she'd do if he did.

She'd called him before she'd looked up his address. And then she'd worried when he hadn't answered the phone. Fear had writhed with grief on the ride to his house.

Now, she wasn't so sure that had been a good idea.

"Why?"

"Why not?" she shot back. *Please don't ask me to leave. I'm terrified of being alone.*

"Because I'm not really fit for company tonight." He wasn't slurring but he was close.

"Neither am I." She swallowed, hard. The smart thing to do right now would be to walk away and leave him to drink quietly by himself. But something about leaving him alone seemed incredibly sad.

She'd never seen him drunk before. Didn't know how he handled his alcohol or how he would if he was—as she suspected—dealing with an addiction.

She took a single step toward him. He towered over her.

She reached out, placed her hand over his heart. It beat slow and steady beneath her palm.

He was real. He was alive.

It was a connection she needed. Badly.

"Can I come in?" she whispered again.

He was going to say no. She saw it written on his face. It was a long, long time before he answered.

"Sure," he said dryly, stepping aside to let her in then closing the door behind him.

The house felt like him. It was Spartan and functional. The couch was old and well worn and she could see his favorite place to sit. A bottle of vodka sat on the coffee table and drew her focus. She didn't know the history behind his drinking but from the looks of things, he wasn't doing too well tonight. She turned when the silence grew too heavy. He hadn't moved from where he'd stood near the door.

"What do you want, Emily?"

"I don't want to be alone tonight."

"You've got other places you can go. You don't want to be here right now."

"This is exactly where I want to be," she said. And she meant it. She didn't know how to ask how he was doing. Didn't know how to get him to open up to her. Didn't know how to ask about the drinking.

Didn't know how to tell him how much she needed him. "I think I'd like a drink," she whispered.

He opened his mouth to speak but no sound came out. She slipped away and padded to his kitchen. There was milk and orange juice in his fridge, along with something that might have been a cucumber at one point but now resembled a fuzzy, wet caterpillar.

Closing the fridge, she searched his cabinets and found nothing beyond a couple of cans of tuna and a couple of shot glasses.

She took the shot glasses. She didn't know the story behind Reza's drinking but tonight she didn't care.

She just wanted to forget.

She circled the old leather couch and curled into one corner after kicking off her shoes. She leaned forward and twisted the cap off the bottle. His lack of response was unsettling her resolve. Whispering in her ear that this was a terrible mistake.

That he hadn't really cared a damn thing about her before now and that tonight was just another ending.

Reza finally moved, approaching the couch and sitting in the opposite corner. His expression was blank, his movements rough.

She wanted to ask how much he'd had to drink but resisted. She wasn't here as a shrink, she was here as a lover. As a friend.

And as worried as she was about him, she suspected he didn't need to be poked about drinking. Not tonight.

It could wait. Not too long. But it could wait.

"So that's why you're here? To crawl into the bottle with me?" His voice was heavy, thick. As though he'd been about to fall asleep.

"I'm not here to crawl inside your head, if that's what you're thinking." She picked up the first shot glass and looked at it like it contained a foul poison. Frowning, she held her nose and tossed it back.

It burned. She managed to choke it down but then gasped. "Oh my God that burns."

Reza raised both eyebrows.

"Oh my God." Emily was still coughing, incapable of making conversation yet. Her eyes filled with tears and she breathed deeply when she could. "That's terrible. How do you do that?"

"I've been drinking since I was fifteen."

"That's when your mom died," she whispered. The burn spread through her veins. Her mouth felt numb. "Why?"

"Because what else was I supposed to do after my dad put my mom in the hospital?" He reached for the bottle.

"Oh, Reza."

"He beat her so bad she never woke up." He took a long pull from the bottle. "I'd tried to kill him that night. Tried to stop him from hitting her." He set it down hard on the coffee table. "Let me tell you, a skinny kid doesn't have a chance against a grown man." He reached for the bottle. He leaned forward, resting his elbows on his knees. "Let me ask you something."

"Let me get this next drink down."

"You might want to slow down before you end up puking on my bathroom floor. It's not nearly as fun as it sounds." Sarcasm. She glanced at him. Good. It wasn't anger. Or at least, if it was, it was well hidden.

"I've been drunk before."

"On wine coolers?"

"Ha ha ha. On wine. And a wine hangover is terrible."

"You haven't felt anything yet. Wait 'til you wake up tomorrow." He pointed at the shot glass in her hand. "I have a question."

Emily's eyes filled as she chased the next shot and this time it wasn't from the liquor. Ignoring the ache in her chest, she set the bottle down. "What's your question?"

Reza paused for a long moment. "Did you know Sloban was as fucked up as he was?"

"Is that the clinical term? Fucked up?" she asked, anger snapping in her chest. "No, Reza, I had no idea. I evaluated his medical records and endorsed the recommendation long before I met you or knew who Neal Sloban was. I'm sorry I didn't remember. I'm so goddamned sorry."

The silence stretched between them, cold and uncomfortable and filled with blame and guilt and a thousand other unnamed things.

"Soldiers die every day. Get used to it, sweetheart." There was no sarcasm in his voice. No blame. A cold, harsh comfort, from a man who knew far too well the weight of personal failings.

Tossing back the next drink, she set the bottle down roughly. She shifted so she could look at him. "Does it get any easier?"

Reza looked away and reached for the bottle. He took another pull. Shorter this time. "Not really."

Emily gripped her hands tight in her lap. "Oh."

Silence hung between them. The memory of the crack of Sloban's gunshot echoed in the quiet, a requiem for the dead.

He wasn't too drunk to see how badly she was hurting.

But nothing he felt compared to what he saw written into her features. Blame. Guilt. She wore them like a funeral shroud. Her eyes were red from crying, her nose pink. And now, she was sitting on his couch a little lopsided because she hadn't yet realized how hard the liquor had hit her.

Idly, he hoped she'd throw up because she might not be sober for quite a while. He had the distinct impression she wasn't a big drinker.

She stared into the distance. He knew what she was seeing. Sloban raising that gun. Over and over again.

Violence tended to do that. The images repeated until they drove you crazy trying to get away from them.

He hadn't wanted her here.

Hadn't wanted her to see him like this.

Part of him had thought he could handle it. That he could take a few drinks and start again tomorrow.

But it wasn't that simple. Now he wanted another drink. And another one.

He couldn't do that now, not now that Emily was here. And he found himself needing her more than he wanted another drink.

He shifted, leaning closer to her.

"Blaming yourself doesn't solve anything," he said, breaking the fragile silence between them.

She looked up and offered a watery smile. "Who else am I supposed to blame? I approved the eval that ruined his life." Her voice broke. "I didn't even know him."

Reza swallowed another pull from the bottle, decided she needed the truth. "Did you do it on purpose?"

"Excuse me?" Her outrage was slow to appear, her reaction time already dulled. Her speech slurred.

"Did you sit in your office and gleefully downgrade anything he'd reported? Did you do it to fuck him over?"

"Of course not." Her 's' was drawn out. Her eyes were glassy. It was a long moment before she moved. She crawled down the couch toward him, her movements wobbly and unsteady. And then she was there, pressed against his side, her head resting in the pocket of his shoulder. The smell of her hair brought tears to his eyes and he dug his fingers into them. He'd never wanted this for her. For anyone. The innocent fervor of her passion for her work had been refreshing. Unique. She hadn't been jaded. She'd wanted to make a difference.

And instead, she'd failed. In her eyes, she'd failed. It didn't matter that she was fighting a deeply flawed system. It didn't matter that one person couldn't hope to make a difference against the machine processing soldiers out of the army.

The generals wanted soldiers fit to fight. Guys like Sloban who'd done their duty should have been in a different category than guys like Wisniak, who'd never served in combat. Even then, knowing what he now knew about Wisniak, Reza wasn't so sure that was the right answer, either. People could talk all day long about systems and processes but at the end of Sloban's life, it had been Reza who'd failed, not Emily.

Another innocence lost. Another person he should have protected forever lost to the war just the same as if the enemy had struck him down.

Emily shifted against him as he reached for the bottle. Her hand curled over his heart and he realized she'd passed out. Good. She'd been falling apart when she crawled into his arms and though he hadn't planned on doing anything but drinking himself into a stupor tonight, a dark, wicked part of him was strangely touched that she'd come to him.

Part of him was grateful that she'd cared enough to check on him. She curled up against him now, her body warm against his. She'd descended into the blood and mud and her uniform now bore the dirty stains of war. But now, watching her lying on his couch as her tears dried on his t-shirt and her breathing slowed until it was steady and even, bitter regret crawled up his throat.

The war had taken its due from her today. There was no therapy to end the relentless replay of the violence she'd seen. She'd close her eyes ten years from now and the flashback would come, as vibrant and brilliant as if it had just happened.

He knew that. He'd lived it long enough to know the harsh road she'd been thrown on today.

Reza's soul was already blackened. The fresh horror of Sloban's death only added to the nightmares Reza had already lived through.

He raised the bottle they hadn't finished to his lips, swallowing down a lump of overwhelming sadness.

* * *

"You're awake."

Reza's voice rumbled beneath her cheek. She stopped trying to shift her arm to a more comfortable position.

Her head was no longer clouded with grief and vodka. "I wouldn't go so far as to say I'm awake. Semi-conscious might not be too much of a stretch."

His soft laugh vibrated through his chest and his arms tightened around her.

"How long was I asleep for?"

"I wouldn't say you were asleep, exactly. Passed out is a slightly more apt description."

Emily turned her face into his chest, grateful for the darkness that hid her embarrassment. "Sorry about that."

"Don't be. Shit days deserve shit endings."

She blinked until the shadows formed into things and she could see his face in the dim light. "What time is it?"

"No clue. You're lying on my watch." His fingers tightened on her back to hold her in place. "Don't worry about it."

"Are you sober?" she asked suddenly.

He shifted until he could look down at her. In the shadows his body surrounded her. "Sober enough. Why?"

"Because of this," she whispered, reaching up and threading her fingers in his hair. She tugged him down until his lips found hers in the darkness, until he moved his body between her thighs and simply kissed her. Kissed away the memories threatening to crush her. Kissed away the pain and the fear and the emptiness inside her.

She arched beneath his touch as they stripped off their clothing in the darkness. She didn't wait for him to reach between their bodies. She wanted to feel something other than numb. She guided him inside her, urging him deep before she was fully ready.

The moment her gasp broke the silence, he stopped. He

froze, refusing to budge. Slowly he pulled free of her body and sat up.

"What are you doing, Emily?" He didn't look at her, simply cast the question into the darkness.

"Obviously not having sex anymore," she muttered.

His laugh surprised her, his gentleness as he reached for her and pulled her into his lap even more so. "I won't let you use me to hurt yourself," he said against her mouth. "You can't bring him back, Emily."

She lowered her face to his neck, a quiet sob escaping her.

He didn't let her cry. He lifted her face to his, kissed her hard. Lost himself in her taste and touch. "You can't bring him back."

She wanted to be mindless. Wanted to forget.

But Reza whispered in the dark—warm, soft, senseless things. She closed her eyes and listened to the sound of his voice, felt the whisper of his breath on her skin. His touch slipped over her skin, stroked away the pain that ached in her heart. He teased her nipples with his teeth and she forgot her own name.

He laid her back on the couch. The leather was cool against her back, his skin hot against her front. He traced his fingers down her belly. She trembled beneath his touch. Lower he kissed, until he parted her sex with the tip of his tongue. She arched off the couch with a cry and let the horror of the day fade away. Her pleasure pushed away the darkness, filling the emptiness and pushing aside the grief.

She'd gone to him tonight. She could have dealt with her grief alone but she'd gone to him.

He licked his tongue down her belly, showing her with his touch the things she knew he couldn't say.

There were no words for the things inside her. No words to tell him how she felt when she was around him. He continued his sensual assault, taking her just to the edge and backing off. She eased her hips away from his mouth, tugging him up.

She wanted him inside her when she came. He teased her sensitive flesh as he crawled up her body, pausing only to roll a condom in place.

"Emily." He whispered her name as he slid inside her. He wrapped his arms tight around her and then he started to move.

Emily was beyond thought. Everything was pure sensation. The full tightness of Reza inside her, the fire that burned in her veins as he slid into her body again and again. She arched against him, wrapping her legs around his hips, her arms around his shoulders.

She kissed him as she came apart, not in a shuddering earthquake but in something so much more powerful. A deeper wave of passion crashed over them both and they fell together. Damaged. Wounded.

But together.

Chapter Fifteen

Emily was alive. At least, she thought she was. A series of explosions were cooking off inside her skull, in perfect rhythm with her heartbeat, and she was reasonably certain that there were a thousand ice picks stabbing her in her eyes.

She'd joined the army because she'd wanted to feel alive. She'd never felt more alive—and more wretched—than she did at that exact moment.

Something was wrapped around her like a snake, stealing the air from her lungs. She tried to move but whatever had her trapped was immovable. She shifted and tried to brace her hand and instead of feeling a mattress or a rug—or Lord only knew what else she thought she should have been lying on—instead her palm connected with warm skin.

A heart beat slow and steady against her hand. She swallowed the passing wave of nausea and tried to open her eyes. Daylight pierced her retinas and made her long for the deep darkness at the bottom of a well. Or at least beneath a warm blanket.

Squinting against the harsh daylight, she peeked at her surroundings. The first thing she realized was that she was definitely lying with a man. But not any man. Reza.

The next thing she realized was that they were on a couch. A couch she faintly recalled was deep, mahogany-tinted leather. She tried to shift and her skin stuck fast. Yep. Leather.

She wiggled and discovered that last night's mind-blowing sex had not been a drunken dream. She squinted as the remnants of last night came into view: a tipped-over bottle of vodka on the coffee table.

Oh Lord. Everything started tumbling back all at once. She vaguely remembered crawling down the couch toward him and hell, she'd cried like a baby. Then sometime later, he'd taken everything that hurt and made it not hurt as much.

And now Emily was lying on the couch, very much naked and very much hung over.

She nestled closer to the man who held her pinned between his big body and the back of the couch. Really, was it possible to feel more secure? More warm and comfortable?

Lying there, listening to him breathing, with his arms like steel bands around her, the slow beating of his heart beneath her flesh, sparked something inside her. Something she had never dared to believe she could have. Someone real. Someone who cared about her because of who she was, not because of her last name.

What she had with Reza was the first real thing she'd ever had in her life.

Blood pounded in her skull, threatening to leak out of her ears. As nice as lying in his arms was, she really didn't want to do the awkward morning after thing with him. Considering her very snug position between him and the couch, she was going to be hard-pressed to get out of there without waking him up. She could hope that he was as deeply asleep as he sounded but even that was no guarantee.

Slowly she nudged his arm off her shoulder. When it

sank into the couch without him so much as missing a breath between gentle snores, she released the breath she hadn't realized she'd been holding. Wiggling slowly, she inched down his body until she could get leverage between the couch and the space behind his hips. Hips that were for all intents and purposes covered only by a thick fuzzy blue blanket.

She was tempted to peek at the man in all his glory but somehow that felt a little too close to stalker behavior. Besides, she'd gotten her fill last night anyway.

It seemed somehow wrong and possibly illegal to look at a man—no matter how well put together said man was—while he was sleeping. Of course, she didn't think he was actually sleeping.

They were going to have to talk about last night. Not the sex. No, not that. But the drinking. She needed to know what she was dealing with—and she wanted him to trust her enough to tell her.

He'd been drinking a long time. That much she knew. Her heart broke for him all over again, thinking of the boy he'd been when his mother had died.

She finally extracted herself from the tangle of arms and legs and half-covered body parts on the couch and stood up. Emily groaned quietly as the movement set her skull to pounding all over again and went about finding her clothes. Good thing she didn't have to...

Go to work.

She glanced at her watch. Holy crap, it was seven thirty. She was supposed to be meeting her boss for a run this morning. Panic swirled in her guts. At least, that's what she hoped the sinking feeling was; otherwise she was about to ruin Reza's floor.

She dressed quickly, finding her cell phone beneath the couch. With one last stolen glance at Reza, who had not budged the entire time she'd been rummaging around looking for shoes, car keys, and cell phones, she slipped out the front door.

She fired off a quick text, then simply sat, alone in the quiet of the driver's seat, staring at his small house.

She should have left him a note.

Should have maybe said something cliché like "thanks for a good time."

"Or not," she mumbled, turning the key in the ignition.

She was going to be lucky if she got through this day without chopping up a couple of Excedrin pills and mainlining them in her office.

But she'd survived worse. At the moment, though, she couldn't remember when.

Reza watched her leave through half-closed eyes, still feigning sleep. He'd felt her move the moment she'd awakened but he'd stayed still, wondering what she was going to do.

The fact that he'd slept wrapped around her said something in and of itself, about the way their budding relationship had started changing the moment they'd first slept together. Nothing built on a foundation of yesterday's tragedy could survive an awkward morning after.

Truth be told, he never spent the night with the women he went home with. If he wasn't truly convinced that God had abandoned him a long time ago, he'd swear there was someone watching over him. But Emily had started drinking and after the day they'd had, he hadn't tried to stop her.

He didn't know why he'd told her about his mother last night. Wasn't sure why he'd let that fact slip out. He'd never told anyone else.

He'd just buried that pain, too.

And then the war had started and brought him back to hell.

He watched her tiptoe out of the house, unable to resist the temptation of watching her leave.

Fear rose up that she was leaving. That she wouldn't come back.

He shoved it down. She'd come here last night. She'd stayed with him despite how he'd tried to push her away.

A piece of the cold, empty wasteland inside him was less empty today.

He wanted her to stay. But he was too much of a coward to say the words.

So he watched her tiptoe from his house. And missed her the moment the door closed behind her.

He rolled onto his back and threw one arm over his chest, idly scratching his stomach. He supposed he needed to get up and get going. First order of business was to check on Wisniak. Then he needed to finish up all the admin chaos that had come out of Sloban's death.

He sighed and shifted on the couch. He wanted to pick up his phone and call Emily. Ask her to turn around and pull back into his driveway. To walk back through the front door and slide her arms around his waist so he could bury his face in her neck and just hold on to her and try to forget about the morning he still had to summon the energy to face.

He pushed himself upright and kicked his feet up onto the table, staring longingly at the empty cans on the coffee table. He had more in the kitchen. It was only a few feet away. Then he could get started on filling out the casualty paperwork. And making sure his guys were okay.

And somehow start to bury the memory deep so that he'd forget about the whole thing. For a while at least. Until Sloban's ghost joined the legion of others that refused to leave him alone and drove him back into the bottle he was trying so desperately to forget.

Something nagged at the back of his neck. Foster had

taken yesterday entirely too easily. Granted, he and Sloban hadn't exactly been BFFs but that didn't explain Foster's cool response to the entire morning's epic charlie foxtrot.

He closed his eyes and sighed. He was already late. What difference did it make if he slept off the hangover for another hour or rushed into the eight a.m. traffic? Breathing deeply, he caught the scent of Emily's shampoo on the couch pillow. Soft, sensual; it still reminded him of the beach.

His phone vibrated somewhere in the vicinity of the floor. He contemplated ignoring it but even that was probably too much. Marshall was going to be at it again, calling him, demanding to know why he wasn't at formation, why he didn't have accountability of his troops. Damn, sometimes he wished the sergeant major had simply thrown him out instead of tying him to this relentless parade of nagging and babysitting.

The phone stopped but before Reza could breathe a sigh of relief, it started buzzing again. Groaning, he rolled over, feeling around until he found the offending electronic. He didn't bother to look at the number before he pressed the little green button that answered the call.

That was his first mistake.

Claire Montoya's voice pierced his thoughts. "Where have you been?"

Panic wasn't one of Claire's strong suits but given yesterday's events, the fear in her voice was somewhat warranted. Granted, at some point in their relationship, Claire had appointed herself his guardian and well, Reza loved her. Sometimes, however, the mother hen routine went a little overboard. Reza grinned. Maybe he should tell her he wished she'd get pregnant so she'd have someone else to worry about instead of him. Somehow he doubted she'd appreciate the humor.

"Hi, honey," he said dryly.

"Not funny. I've been calling you since last night." Her tone softened. "Are you okay?"

"Yes, Mom, I'm fine."

"So you're being a dick about this," she said.

"No." He scrubbed his hand over his jaw, the bristles scraping his palm. "Sorry. I feel like shit and I'm just cranky." They'd argued fiercely about his drinking when he'd first come back from rehab several months back.

"How much did you have to drink?"

So much for that plan. "A couple drinks, then we went to sleep."

"We? What, are you the royal 'we' now? You and your dick make a team?"

Reza couldn't help but grin, despite the feeling that his skull was trying to split itself open. Vodka never seemed that good of an idea the morning after. Then again, few drinks ever did. But a stiff drink would more than heal his aching head.

"My dick and I are always a team, not that that is any of your business."

Silence greeted his comment.

"Damn it, Reza, you promised."

A lump rose in his throat. "It was just last night," he said. "Shit, Claire, don't cry."

"I'm not."

"Liar."

She made a choked sound. "Just tell me you're okay?"

"I'm fine, Claire. No range fires. Nothing got blown up." *Except Sloban.* "I'm getting in the shower and heading to work."

"Okay."

He paused. "Thanks for checking on me," he said after a long moment. Reza hung up the phone and summoned the willpower to get off the couch. He kicked his clothes into a pile near the bathroom and stumbled toward the shower.

A half hour later, he was mostly functioning. But he was not prepared for the text from the sergeant major's driver that he was wanted in the command group. Fifteen minutes ago.

The morning was off to a great start.

"Were you drinking?"

Reza stood at parade rest in Sergeant Major Giles's office behind closed doors and contemplated the end of his military career. He was a few years short of retirement. Unless he got them to throw him out for a medical reason, he'd leave with nothing.

One night. One goddamned night he'd fallen down and he was getting a wire brush run over his ass.

He could lie but he had the sneaking suspicion that Giles already knew the answer to his question.

Reza sniffed and scrubbed his hand across his jaw and decided on the truth. "Figured getting brains blown out all over me was a pretty solid exception to the no drinking rule, Sarn't Major."

Giles chewed thoughtfully on the end of his cigar. "Well, you get points for honesty," he said after a while. "What the fuck happened yesterday?"

A ghost slid up the back of Reza's spine. "I wish I knew, Sarn't Major." He sighed heavily. "I wish I knew."

"No warning signs? Nothing?"

"Nothing. He hid his meth problem pretty well until we caught him." Kind of like Reza had hidden his drinking problem until he hadn't. "Sloban never talked to anyone about having any issues." *And I didn't ask*, Reza thought bitterly. He'd left him at the mercy of dickheads like Captain Marshall. And by the time Reza had sobered up, it had been too late.

"Sit down, Ike." Reza sat. "What I'm going to tell you does not leave this office."

Reza nodded sharply but said nothing.

"The brigade commander has opened a formal investigation into Wisniak's allegations. Until then, he wants to keep everything quiet." Giles tapped his finger on the edge of his keyboard. "Is the kid safe?"

"Yeah, Sarn't Major. He's good."

Reza thought of the droned-out expression on Wisniak's face the last time he'd seen him. He was heading to Wisniak's room as soon as he was done here.

He'd fucked up with Sloban. He wasn't going to do the same thing with Wisniak.

The kid deserved better.

Reza was going to do better.

"How fast will the investigation move?" Reza asked, wondering how long he could keep Wisniak functioning and away from Marshall.

"Fairly quickly, I hope. The boss has called in some outside lawyers to get a fresh set of eyes on this thing." Giles leaned forward. "Here's the thing, Ike. Colonel Horace needs a damn good reason to remove Marshall from command and right now, he's got nothing but allegations from a kid who wanted the pay but never wanted to be the leader the rank on his chest demanded."

Reza nearly cringed as his own thoughts came back to haunt him. Everyone judged guys like Wisniak harshly. Including Reza. He had no idea how to fix something like this. Wisniak had made allegations against the company commander but the brigade commander wasn't going to act on them until he had all the facts. It was a prudent decision even if Reza disagreed with it. The important thing was to keep Wisniak safe.

"I believe him, Sarn't Major," Reza said quietly. He wondered if Wisniak ever had anyone believe in him.

Reza certainly hadn't.

Giles sniffed. "I do, too. Marshall's arrogant enough to think he can get away with this kind of thing."

He swallowed hard. Giles had never let him down. Not once. Not even when Reza had nearly ended his career over his drinking.

"Last night needs to be the last time you drink. You can't keep falling off the wagon."

Reza nodded.

If Wisniak was walking the knife's edge because of something that happened between him and Marshall, then taking him out of the company—essentially sending the message that something had happened—might tip him off the ledge.

Reza ground his teeth. He had to stay sober. Too many people were counting on him.

And he could not screw up again.

Chapter Sixteen

Emily walked into her office exactly one hour and thirty-six minutes late for work. Which meant the official start of her duty day was going to kick off with an ass chewing by her boss.

The secretary, Ms. Walters, looked down her nose at her as Emily walked by. She was late. She knew she was late. So why did Ms. Walters act like she was the avenging angel of the time clock? If Colonel Zavisca didn't care that Emily was a few minutes late, why the hell should Ms. Walters?

She needed to rewind the entire week and start over. Preferably without Sloban's death.

She walked into her office, dropping her tote into the chair near the door, and logged in to her computer. The absolute normality of the morning was contrasted by the utter chaos inside her. Hoping she still had a few minutes before Ms. Walters started the line of patients parading through her office, Emily headed to the break room to microwave some water for tea.

She needed just a few minutes to prepare for the day. She was not yet put back together enough to deal with what had happened yesterday. Her stomach flipped as the memory flashed through her brain for the thousandth time.

"Emily?"

She stopped on the other side of Colonel Zavisca's doorway. His office door was open, which was unusual. The man did most of his work behind closed doors. Emily suspected he had some control issues about people walking in on him, but left it alone.

It was not good form to psychoanalyze one's boss.

She took a single step backward, pressing the tea bag to the inside of the mug. "Yes, sir?"

"Emily, do you have the notes on yesterday's shooting victim?"

Emily said nothing for a long moment. All the euphemisms in the world. Anything to avoid calling Sloban by his name. As though somehow, in passing from this life to the next, he'd become less than a person. More of a memory. A statistic.

Anything but a person. A son. A brother. No, he was just the victim now.

Her lungs refused to expand to hold the deep breath she'd inhaled. Releasing it, she smiled faintly. "Yes, sir. I'm sure I do."

Colonel Zavisca leaned back in his chair, resting his fingers on the top of his head. "Are you okay?"

"I'm fine, sir."

"Coping okay? No nightmares or self-destructive thoughts?"

She fought the urge to frown. "No sir."

He didn't really want to know what she'd done for therapy last night. He wouldn't approve of her seeking out a man like Reza Iaconelli, and not just because Reza was enlisted. No, he'd warn her against a man like him.

It was a warning she didn't want to hear.

Because she didn't care that Reza was enlisted or

broken or damaged. She cared about him. Felt alive around him.

Zavisca frowned and leaned forward. "You're a terrible liar. What happened?"

She lifted the mug to her lips, sipping the tea gently. Mostly just to buy herself some time before she answered. "Nothing, sir. I just slept...poorly."

"Okay, then. I need you to update his information in the medical system. Big Army medicine conducts a formal review of all active duty suicides."

Emily frowned. It made sense. Still, the rational answer didn't chase away the lingering discomfort about the privacy of the dead. It felt somehow wrong, to open up his medical records to an investigation. "If it helps us identify any trends..."

She left her words hanging and Colonel Zavisca nodded. "Exactly. We've got a massive problem on our hands across the army and we've got to figure out how to identify those high-risk soldiers earlier and get them the help they need."

Ms. Walters took that moment to stick her head around the corner at the end of the hall. "Captain Lindberg, your first patient is here." Her voice had the thick rasp of a thirty-year smoker but her face was smooth and flawless, as though she'd never spent a day in the sun.

"Okay then." She turned her attention back to Colonel Zavisca. "I've got to get going, sir. I'm already fifteen minutes behind."

"Thanks, Emily." Colonel Zavisca looked down at his desk, then back up at her, opening his mouth, then snapping it shut. "Oh, Emily?"

"Sir?" Her stomach dropped.

"I hope there's nothing going on between you and that first sergeant that's been down here several times. One of the nurses said she thought you looked a little too comfortable with him after the shooting. He was in the victim's chain of command."

She turned slowly, sure there was a huge scarlet letter on her chest and baffled that her boss would make something out of her seeking comfort after a tragedy. "Sir?"

Colonel Zavisca cleared his throat. "Personally, I don't care where you spend your nights. But keep it out of the office," he said mildly.

Emily swallowed. "Roger, sir." A hoarse whisper. Her skin, cold. And beneath that, an odd sense of relief. Her boss didn't care if she was involved with an enlisted man.

She padded down the hallway to her own office, where her first patient of the day was waiting.

Wisniak sat in the plain white plastic chair outside her office. He looked tired but his eyes were alert. He stood and she rested her hand on his shoulder. "You look well," she said, barely masking her surprise.

He licked his lips and nodded nervously. "Sarn't Ike moved me out of the unit."

He took his normal seat on the small couch in her office and she slid around to sit in front of her desk. "This is a good thing?"

He nodded eagerly. "They don't know where I am. I can take a piss—I mean, I can go to the bathroom—without worrying if they're going to break into my room. I slept, ma'am. For the first time in months, I really slept."

"That explains why you look so much better." Relief was hot and prickled across her skin.

Wisniak looked down at his clenched hands. "I can't stay in the army," he said softly. "I don't fit here." He looked up at her, his eyes filled with disappointment. "I'll never get to deploy."

Emily glanced at her own right shoulder, bereft of the honored combat patch. She shouldn't judge but she also knew she was going to get her time in the desert. For her it wasn't a question of if; it was a question of when. "That's not necessarily a bad thing," she said softly. "Deployments break the strongest of us. Maybe you need to go figure out what's going to make *you* happy."

"I thought being a soldier would do that," he admitted. "Guess I got that wrong, huh?"

She smiled at him. "There's nothing wrong with figuring out that you want to do something different with your life."

She wondered how Reza had felt on his first deployment. Had he been scared? Emily was terrified of stepping foot into Iraq. She remembered how it felt to step into that hallway of the shoot house. The pure terror and adrenaline all mixed together. Absently, she stroked the mostly healed bruise on her hip. That day had been terrifying even though she'd known she wasn't going to die.

The squeeze of a trigger. A splattering of blood.

Memories rose unbidden and unbound. She was determined to shove them aside, to focus on the young private in front of her. She didn't have time to fall apart.

She'd failed yesterday. Today, she had to find the energy to fight the good fight and damn it, that meant focusing on Wisniak.

She'd find time to deal with her own *stuff* later. In the meantime, she had patients to see.

"Sergeant Iaconelli, my office. Now."

"Good morning to you, too, sir," Reza said, following Captain Annoying into his office.

"Is there a reason why you're just showing up at nine thirty? And before you say anything, it needs to be a really good reason." Marshall's head looked like it was about to explode. Reza supposed he should be glad that Marshall wasn't screaming yet but it wouldn't be the first time that

Reza had had to deal with an officer that cracked under the pressure. Combat, a dickhead battalion commander—the source of the pressure didn't matter and the reactions were legion.

Marshall, for example, was a screamer. Reza had worked for a lieutenant once who'd turned vicious when he was stressed out, calling subordinates names. Abuse was so much more than just fists and belts, he thought, standing at the position of attention.

Reza chafed under Marshall and men like him. Men who thought that the rank on their chest automatically made them right. "Stomach flu, sir. Couldn't get out of the bathroom to get to the phone." Couldn't have him asking about Wisniak. If he was pissed at Reza he'd forget about the soldier out of ranks.

It had happened too many times before for it not to work today. Marshall had no idea how to lead men.

"Do you have a sick call slip? A note from the doctor?"

Reza raised both eyebrows. "Guess you missed the part about me not making it out of the bathroom?" Marshall's jaw pulsed. Reza *almost* smirked. "No, sir, I don't have a sick call slip."

"Sergeant Iaconelli, if I make Sergeant Wisniak turn in a sick call slip for his appointments, what makes you any different?" Marshall's eyelid twitched. He was *that* close to really screaming. A little more and Reza would see one of the full-blown, epic tantrums that Marshall was known for.

Reza counted to ten and restrained his inner smart-ass. Channeling Teague right now didn't seem like the best idea. "I'm not going to wait in line for half a day to get a little piece of paper to tell you I was sick." The lie didn't bother him in the least. Marshall didn't deserve the truth. He didn't deserve Reza's loyalty or his trust and that had been the case even before Wisniak's allegations had come to light.

"You have stomach bugs a lot," Marshall said.

Reza couldn't resist any longer. "What can I say, sir? I have a sensitive tummy."

Marshall snapped, slamming his palm on his desk. "God damn it, Iaconelli, I am tired of your smart mouth! You're one step away from being relieved for cause. One more formation. One more missed work call and I will have your ass."

Reza lifted his chin. "Do it now. Don't wait and don't fucking threaten me. Sir."

"You think I won't? The sergeant major won't always be around to protect you."

Reza laughed bitterly. "Is that what you think? You're stupider than you look. *Sir.*"

"I am tired of your disrespect, Sergeant!"

"And I'm tired of you threatening people." Reza leaned across the desk, getting back in Marshall's face. "I don't know what happened between you and Wisniak, but I'm going to find out." He straightened. "You can count on that. Sir."

"I don't know what you're talking about." Marshall's expression didn't change. Not a flicker. Interesting. Marshall continued, ignoring Reza's veiled threat. "You're too busy drinking yourself sick every night to be able to lead soldiers. The only thing protecting you is the sergeant major. And I'm tired of it."

"Nice try, dickhead, but I quit drinking, remember?" Reza sniffed and lifted his chin, grinding his teeth. Last night didn't count. "And I'm reasonably certain that what I do at night is none of your business."

"It becomes my business when you can't make it to work on time."

"Do you want me to go get a goddamn sick call slip?" Reza snarled.

"I want you to get to work on time. I want you to keep your soldiers from killing themselves." The vein in Marshall's forehead pulsed wickedly.

Reza scoffed. "That would be a hell of a lot easier if you weren't putting them in a pressure cooker and letting them go off. How often did you harass the clinic to get the mental health evaluations sped up?"

"That's my fucking job," Marshall said. "We need to get rid of the ash and trash so we can focus on the real warriors."

Echoes of Reza's own words slapped him in the face. Cold prickled over his skin.

"Sloban was a real warrior," Reza said quietly.

Marshall stopped whatever he'd been about to say. For a brief moment, Reza considered that Marshall might actually have a heart attack and die on the desk.

The officer corps would be better for it. He wondered what that said about him, that the thought of Marshall dead didn't bother him in the least.

Reza swallowed. "Well, since it looks like we're done here, I guess I'll get to work."

"Everything isn't a joke, Iaconelli."

"Sir, if you think I'm joking after having Sloban's blood splattered all over my uniform yesterday, you've got a pretty fucked-up idea of a joke."

Marshall's nostrils flared and he jammed a finger in Reza's direction. "One more time, Sergeant. One more fucking time and that's your ass."

Reza saluted sharply, essentially turning what should have been a rendering of honors into a giant fuck you the way only a senior NCO could. "Yes, sir. I won't let you down."

"Get out!" Marshall broke down and finally screamed.

And he'd never once asked about Wisniak.

Reza shut the door quietly behind him, as the operations folks all around him pretended they hadn't heard every word.

The day just wouldn't quit. For once, though, Teague wasn't cracking any jokes as he plopped down in the chair across from Reza's desk and propped his feet up. He pulled a bag of sunflower seeds from his cargo pocket and palmed a handful before tossing them in his mouth.

"Get the blood out of your uniform?" Sadly, Teague's question wasn't a joke.

"Dropped it in the trash on my way in to work." Because he hadn't wanted to look at the stains. "I suppose I should have had it disposed of by the medics."

"Probably, but no one is going to check so there's that." Teague spit some of the shells into an empty Gatorade bottle. "Seen Foster today?"

"No. You?"

"We went out drinking last night but I haven't seen him this morning."

Normally a sergeant and a captain wouldn't hang out together but Foster and Teague had been through a particularly nasty battle in 04. Some bonds were stronger than any prohibition the army could decree.

"He's not answering texts or phone calls?" Reza asked.

"Nope. I wanted to see if he'd shown up here before I head to his apartment." Teague didn't sound worried, which went a long way toward easing Reza's mind. Foster was a rock. The kid had never let him down.

"Let me know when you find him." Reza's phone buzzed. *I'm too fucked up to drive. I'll be in after lunch.* He held the phone up. "Speak of the devil and he appears. Foster's alive and kicking and apparently still drunk."

"I'm sure Marshall would love to hear that," Teague said dryly. "I think he gets a hard-on every time he gets to throw a soldier out of the army."

Reza tipped back in his chair, resting his hands on the top of his head. "You've known Marshall a long time, right?"

"Sadly, I have to claim that fuckstick as a member of my officer basic corps class. Why?"

"Did he ever…" Hell. How exactly did one ask if Marshall… "Did he ever get in trouble?"

"He got told to chill out a couple of times by the instructors. He was big on being part of the team and man, if you weren't on his team, watch out. He was fucking intense." Teague glanced over his shoulder toward the door. "Still is. He's worse now because he's a commander. He's such a sanctimonious prick." Teague spit more seeds into the bottle.

"There's something you're not telling me."

"I can't, man. This is one of those things that I really wish I could get your thoughts on the whole thing."

"Wait. There's a scandal involving Captain Asshole and you didn't tell me?"

Reza shook his head. "This is actually serious."

"So am I. I've been waiting for this day."

"Why?"

"You ever get the sense that someone is just not right in the head?" Teague wasn't joking. Reza straightened. "So what's it going to take to get you to tell me what's going on?"

"Can't, dude."

"Beer? Alcohol? A bottle of Johnny Walker Black?"

Reza shot him a deadpan look. "I'm pretty sure what you're doing right now is called enabling the alcoholic."

"Which it would be if you were an alcoholic," Teague said, waggling his Gatorade bottle at Reza. "You're a recovering alcoholic."

Except for the night Sloban died. He took a deep breath. "Sure. Look, just keep an eye on things around here and let me know if you hear anything funny."

"You know I'm in a better position to deal with this stuff than you are, right?" Teague said, suddenly serious.

"How's that?"

"Officer. Enlisted. The chain of command is going to be

a hell of a lot more reticent to send me up the river than they will you. Especially with your history."

Reza ran his tongue over his teeth, the truth of Teague's words hitting below the belt. "This isn't about me." And yet it was, because Reza had set up conditions that put Wisniak on the outside of the circle of trust.

"You know I'm right. What the hell is going on?"

"Shut the door." Reza sighed and leaned forward. "Wisniak told Captain Lindberg that he was being hazed by a bunch of Marshall's guys. With Marshall's permission."

Teague frowned. "That shit happens all the time."

"This got out of hand and Wisniak is pressing charges now."

"Define out of hand. What, like assault charges?" Teague's expression hardened as Reza nodded.

"Yeah. The investigators are talking to Wisniak today."

Teague sank back into his chair with a heavy sigh. Slowly a grin spread across his face.

"This isn't actually funny," Reza said quietly.

"I know. But I've got to tell you, I've waited a long, long time for Jimmy Marshall to get what's coming to him." He popped a sunflower seed in his mouth. "That probably makes me a bad person, doesn't it?"

Reza rocked back in his own chair. "I wouldn't tempt karma like that if I were you," he said after a while.

Chapter Seventeen

A quiet knock on Emily's door interrupted her first five minutes of alone time that day. It wasn't even lunchtime and she'd been going full bore since she'd dragged her corpse into the office a couple of hours ago. Five days had gone by since the shooting. Five days since her life had turned upside down, and she'd been trying to find her way out of a mountain of paperwork.

Five days since she'd started second-guessing every packet that came across her desk.

But when she glanced up, her day took a rapid detour away from dragging tail. Reza filled the doorway, his broad shoulders spanning the narrow passage. He leaned against the doorjamb, looking far too relaxed.

She was barely functioning on less than four hours of sleep this morning. For several moments he stood in the doorway, simply watching. She'd wanted to call him. Oh but she'd wanted to call him. Instead, she'd thrown herself into work, trying to spend more time with each packet. Trying desperately not to make the same mistake twice.

"Hi." His throat moved as he swallowed.

"Hi." She picked up a pen in front of her as her chest

tightened. Emily's lungs had a difficult time filling. "Last time you were here, things didn't go so well," she said softly.

His lips curled in a faint smile. "Yeah, well, bad things can't happen like that two visits in a row." He frowned. "Can they?"

"No." She glanced at her computer screen, then locked it, so she could pay attention to the big man filling up her doorway. Oh, but those shoulders . . . "What can I do for you?"

He looked pained. "Wisniak. How is he?"

Emily watched him carefully as she folded her hands in front of her on the desk. "He's going to be okay."

He took a single step into her office and closed the door behind him.

"Reza," she breathed, his name a recognition of what they'd shared the other night. In the midmorning light, his skin gleamed like polished copper. There was no trace of the beard that had marked his jaw the other morning. No trace of the rumpled, snoring man who'd held her in his arms when they'd both finally succumbed to sleep and a need for something more than just a casual sexual release.

The tight lines around his mouth relaxed, just a little but it was enough. Enough to spark memories of the other night curled up on his couch, kissing, touching, tasting. Experiencing something outside of the normal she'd tried to define for herself.

He crossed the small space and sat in front of her desk, leaning forward to rest his elbows on his knees.

The urge to round her desk and crawl into his lap pressed against her. She wanted, oh how she wanted . . . but she had to be a professional here. Her boss might not care what she did outside the office, but she shouldn't be flaunting it right in front of him. But everything that had happened between them was twisted up now around Sloban's death, drawing them closer to a place that neither of them was supposed to be.

There was something on his mind. Something worrying him. Something he would not say.

She came around her desk and slid into the chair next to him. Not quite in his lap where she wanted to be, but close enough. "My boss figured us out," she whispered.

A thousand unsaid things flickered across his face but he said nothing for the longest moment. "And?"

"And he doesn't care. So long as it stays out of the office."

His words were rough, his voice thick. His hands settled on her shoulders. "Normally no one would know that you spent the night at my place. The army only goes after stuff like that when it's tied into some other crime." He smiled and it did not reach his dark eyes. "And neither of us killed Sloban," he said sadly. He nudged her chin up. "Emily, what's wrong?"

His dark eyes searched hers and she fought the urge to look away. She felt him penetrate the defenses she'd carefully erected since leaving home, probing deep behind her walls. Breaking down her excuses and her shields until all he saw was her, naked and raw and unbound.

Slowly his eyes warmed with emotion. "Talk to me," he whispered.

"I just haven't slept well since...since the shooting." She refused to anesthetize what had happened with a clean, sterile word like "incident." A small act of defiance.

"It'll take some time," he said.

"I know that. It's my job to know that." But she slipped into his embrace, feeling his arms slide around her. "I've been worried about you," she whispered.

"I've been fine," he said against her hair. "Busy."

Silence hung between them for a long moment. She glanced up at his face to see a thousand emotions flickering back at her.

"I was wondering what you were doing tonight?" he asked.

"Why? Exciting plans for a Monday night?"

"Because it has occurred to me that I haven't had a chance to take you out on a real date. And I know we've both got a shit ton of chaos at work and all but I wanted to break away and see if you'd join me." He leaned down, brushing his lips against her cheek.

She covered her mouth with her hand and laughed. Resting against him, her head against his heart, she laughed until tears leaked out from her eyes. "I've got a hail and farewell tonight," she said. "You could meet me there?"

He met her gaze. "I'd like that."

Emily didn't want to go to the hail and farewell at *Talarico's.* Not by a long shot. Her shoulders were tight, her neck stiff. She tried to act like everything was normal. Colonel Zavisca had also behaved as if there was nothing wrong, but had avoided making eye contact with her at the evening sync meeting.

She felt like a pariah even though no one had said a word about the shooting. She brushed her hair out of her eyes and looked at the Tuscan-style restaurant overlooking Belton Lake.

Gripping her purse, she climbed out of her car and headed in to the festivities. It felt like she was walking into a funeral. Her own.

Talarico's was busy, but then again it was a Monday evening and she suspected more than one group of soldiers was scattered around the wide-open space. Emily didn't feel like being sociable. It was enough that she was seen. She was planning on escaping as soon as she could. She skirted the room and headed out to the bar on the outside deck and ordered a glass of moscato. She turned toward the lake and watched the sun sink lower in the sky, hoping Reza would hurry.

Because she didn't feel like being alone.

"You look like you'd rather be conducting a proctology exam."

She turned, a faint smile on her lips at the sound of Reza's voice. "Hi."

He was a ray of bright light in the darkness of the evening sky. His skin glistened in the fading light in stark contrast to the light blue button-down shirt he wore.

Reza was a welcome sight. An anchor that she had to fight the urge to wrap her arms around and hold on to. She glanced down at the beer mug in his hand then back up at his face. There was a rough shadow along his jaw and her hand twitched with the desire to run her fingers along it. His gaze was warm and dark, his eyes rich and dark.

"I take it that's a no on the proctology exam?" he said, his voice low and warm.

She smiled. "I'll pass, thanks."

"How long do you have to stay?"

"Until I'm seen. I was planning on sneaking out in about forty-five minutes." She swallowed a sip of her wine. "You made it."

"Couldn't leave you alone." He cleared his throat and set his drink down. She reached for it, taking a sip. Relief washed over her as the water slid down her throat.

She braced her hip against the wall and studied him, swirling the remains of the wine in her own glass. "What are we doing, Reza?" she whispered finally.

Reza shifted and looked down at his hands. "I don't know." An honest answer.

"I can live with that," she said softly.

"You can?" Reza looked at her sharply, her skin cast in golden shadows in the sunset.

He'd meant to check on her once more after the morning, but the entire day had been shot all to hell busy.

Emily shrugged. She looked tired. Strained. "Yes. I can handle whatever it is we're doing."

He fought the urge to brush her hair from her face. "Let me know when you can sneak out of here," he murmured.

"Why?"

"Ever ridden a motorcycle?"

She shook her head. She looked at him from beneath her heavy black lashes. "That sounds terrifying."

"You've already been shot at. How bad can a motorcycle be?" He swallowed a powerful surge of lust then leaned in close, his lips near her ear. "I'll make your first ride a good one."

Her lips parted. A slow flush ran up her cheeks. "How do you do that?"

"Do what?"

"Make something so innocuous sound so erotic?"

He laughed quietly. "Years of practice."

"Really?"

"Not really. I think your mind is just in the gutter."

"I could use a little gutter after last week," she said, turning back to peer into the restaurant. "It looks like they're getting ready to start the farewells. I'll find you when I can sneak out?"

"I'm counting on it."

She took a step toward the dark interior then paused and turned back. "Thank you," she said quietly.

"For what?"

"For checking on me."

He said nothing as she walked back inside. He remained behind, enjoying the quiet. A few couples were outside on the deck talking but by and large, Reza was alone. He watched Emily weave through the crowd to stand near one of the large bay windows.

He cradled the water, determined that he wasn't going

to drink tonight. He was waiting. Waiting for Emily to escape.

Waiting for her to slip away with him, into the darkness where he could hold her and just breathe her in. He wanted to feel her arms wrap around his chest, her legs around his hips as the bike vibrated beneath them.

He needed her. Her strength. Her steadiness.

Her arms around his waist. Just being there.

He wanted her. More, he needed to know that she was okay. He was accustomed to death and Sloban's suicide was keeping him up at night. He needed to know that she was okay.

Because his world was a little better, knowing she was in it.

"You've really never been on a motorcycle?" he asked some time later after they'd both slipped away.

Emily looked dubiously at the bike. It was a Harley Davidson Fat Boy, black with silver and chrome detailing.

"Why is that hard for you to believe?"

"It just is," he murmured. He reached for her, slipping his fingers into the front pocket of her pants and tugging her between his thighs where he rested against the bike. "It'll be fun. You've never ridden until you've ridden with me."

"I've ridden you before."

He coughed and choked on a laugh. "Well played," he said, his voice thick. He sucked on her bottom lip. Just a tiny tug. A hint of things to come. "You ready?"

"Where are you taking me?"

"I'm going to abscond with you to the wilds of central Texas and have my way with you in the mesquite brush."

"That sounds awesome."

Reza said nothing for a long moment. The sadness hiding in the shadows of her eyes really stuck with him and made him want to hold her close and never let her go. "Let's go."

He released her and swung his leg over the bike. "Get on behind me and wrap your arms around my waist." She did as she was instructed. When she clasped her hand over his heart, something caught in his throat. He looked over his shoulder. "Make sure you lean with me."

She pressed against his back, her body tensing. "Okay." A whispered attempt to hide the fear in her voice.

Reza turned the bike over and rolled out of the gravel parking lot. Stones popped beneath his tires as he waited for the road to clear, then he pulled out and headed toward Belton Dam.

The familiar rumble of the bike beneath him was forgotten as Emily's warmth pressed to his back. She still hadn't relaxed against him and he wanted to feel her melt. There was something soothing about having her with him just then, something that made the horrific events of the week seem a little further away.

He turned down the steep decline toward the dam and Emily's arms tightened around his waist. Pulling into a secluded copse of trees near the rushing water, he killed the engine. In the silence of the encroaching darkness, she finally relaxed. Her arms did not release him but her body eased against his.

He turned on the bike, sliding one arm around her waist, and tugged until she rotated around to straddle him. She looked dazed. He gave in to the earlier temptation to brush her hair from her eyes. "Rough week, huh?" he murmured.

"And it's not even over yet." She blinked and glanced around. They were surrounded by low-hanging trees. It was darker here, the only sound the rushing water from the dam a couple hundred yards away. "This is beautiful."

"Figured you'd like it."

Her thighs were draped over his and he shifted to pull her closer until she was pressed fully against him. "We always seem to end up parking somewhere in the woods," she said, twining her arms around his neck.

"You said you wanted to live a little." He brushed her hair away from her throat, exposing the pale line of skin, then leaned closer, pressing his lips to her pulse. It scattered beneath the caress of his lips.

"I guess I did. I never did make out in a car when I was a teenager."

He laughed against her neck, then nipped her pulse. She gasped. "How did you spend your teenage years?" he asked, tracing his tongue over the sensitive spot he'd just bitten.

"Volunteering and debate club." A gasp as she tightened her thighs around his hips and rubbed against him.

"Sounds like a lot of time in the library."

A gentle laugh. "Maybe. Do you have a librarian fetish?"

"Maybe." He nipped her earlobe.

"I can't picture you as a teenager," she said, tipping her neck to give him greater access.

"I was a whole lot angrier and a lot more out of control."

Emily surprised him. She leaned back until she could meet his gaze. She cupped his face in her hands. "I'm sorry, Reza."

There was no pity in her soft words and yet they sparked a familiar anger. "Don't be."

She frowned. "Why do you do that?"

"Do what?"

"Brush off any concern? You're not Superman."

He opened his mouth then snapped it closed. "I know that."

She brushed her thumb against his bottom lip. "I don't think you do."

"Ah, fictional character?"

She shifted, then, leaning back slightly. "I'm serious, Reza."

"So am I." He let his fingers drift up beneath her jacket. The skin at the small of her back was soft and warm. So warm.

She curled into him, melting the ice around his heart just a little. She lay against him quietly. "I can't stop seeing it," she whispered finally.

He tightened his arms around her waist, but then moved to thread the fingers of one hand through her hair. He held her close, breathing in her scent. Wishing he could take away the pain of Sloban's death for her and knowing that wish was futile.

Her fingers were limp against his neck, her breath hot.

"I want to forget." A plaintive cry.

He lifted her face from his neck with his hands. "Time is the only thing that will make it easier," he murmured. "You never really forget."

Regret burned in him. A terrible truth that no matter how hard he tried would not be ignored. Reza closed his eyes and pulled her close once more and wished with everything he had that there was a way for him to erase her pain. But he knew far too well that some memories refused to die no matter how much one attempted to bury them.

But he could help her erase the pain, if only for one moment.

Chapter Eighteen

I never really thought the army would be this hard."

"No one ever thinks handing out flowers and candy to the local nationals is hard."

His voice rumbled through her body. She was leaning back against him now, her feet draped over the handlebars of the Harley. His chest was a solid wall behind her, his arms steel. She felt protected. Safe.

There was little noise around them now. Night had fallen and the woods had grown quieter. She hadn't wept but it had been a close thing. She was a therapist. She should know how to stop seeing a memory flashing over and over in her mind.

Instead, the doctor had become the patient. She enjoyed Reza's form of comfort. Just sitting. Quietly.

She shifted against him and his arms loosened to allow her to find a new position. Then they were back, tight around her once more.

"I'm not naive enough to think that you handed out hearts and candy during the war," she said after a while.

"Most people forget there's a war going on, let alone give any real thought to what war really involves." She loved the feel of his voice, the rumble from deep in his chest. He was a big man. She'd never been attracted to big men. They'd always seemed too much, too overwhelming.

"When I told my parents I was joining the army, they asked me why I wanted to go and do something so stupid. I was too smart to join the army."

"You're not too smart. Contrary to popular belief, we're not all idiot hillbillies with no other prospects in life." He lifted her hair from her neck, exposing her skin to the cool night air.

"Why did you join?"

"To get away from my family," he said. He nuzzled her gently, just below her ear. "My mother died. My dad went to jail. My uncles? That was a whole other story."

She tipped her head. The feel of his lips on her skin was intoxicating, this insight into the boy he'd been more so. "Uncles?"

"Let's just say that there are some members of my family who wanted me to think long and hard about fighting a war against our people." She turned to face him. "My grandfather came here in the fifties with my mother and her brothers from Tehran. My dad married a non-Catholic Persian woman so he obviously was the apostate of the family. That was until I went and joined the war on terror." He nipped her ear. "I left home as soon as I could after my mom died."

"I'm sorry."

"I'm not."

His voice held a strange note and she angled her face to be able to look up at him. "Why not?"

"Would you go running home right now?" he asked, his thumb rubbing gently against the side of her throat.

"No. My family made it abundantly clear that I was to come home immediately, which is the number one reason why I won't go back." She closed her eyes against the pleasure of his touch. She shifted and threaded her fingers through his.

"Your family wouldn't approve of me," he said against her hair.

She squeezed their joined hands tightly. "Their approval doesn't matter to me."

"We both know that's a lie." He rested his cheek against hers, his chin cradled in her neck. "You're a terrible liar."

"Maybe it hurts. Maybe being rejected by your family should hurt. But I know this: I feel more alive with you than I ever have before. And as long as you're willing company..."

Reza straightened and turned her to face him. Her thighs draped over his. In the low moonlight, his features were harsh, unforgiving. He looked like an angel of death.

She could forget that when he was loving her but looking into his face now, she knew she should never put that thought out of her mind again. This man looked comfortable in the darkness. As though he was at home in it.

If she was alone in the woods, fear would likely paralyze her. Reza? Reza looked like he would simply hunker down and wait, at home in the shadows.

"I'm not willing to let you throw away something important just to get a quick screw on the back of my bike."

"Oh, that's what we're going to do out here?" She wriggled against his hips. "I thought we were just going to snuggle."

His dark eyes looked black and narrowed dangerously. The moment hung for what felt like eternity between them.

And then his lips curled into a warm smile.

His little captain kept surprising him. She made jokes when he didn't expect them and looked like she was ready to break at other times. Reza shifted against her, surrounding her with his body and knew a flickering moment of something he'd never felt before: contentment.

"You're such a contradiction," he murmured.

"How's that?"

"Librarian fetish, remember?" he said. His blood felt heavy in his veins. Like he wanted nothing more than to pull her against him and fall into sleep. "You're all buttoned up and tense but now you're talking dirty to me on my bike. It's really hot."

"You were serious about that?"

He lifted one shoulder. "What do you think?"

She twined her arms around his neck and lifted her chin to look up at him. It was such a simple embrace. Simple but powerful. Laced with something more than just sexual attraction.

Something vibrated between their bodies. "Is that me or you?" she asked.

"Me." Reza reluctantly leaned back to pull his phone from his chest pocket. There was an angry text message from none other than Captain "I Don't Text" Marshall. *Wisniak is being held by the military police. They won't arrest him because they say he's suicidal.*

Reza sighed and dialed his commander. He held his index finger over his lips and Emily nodded. "Sir, what's going on with Wisniak?"

How the hell had he found the kid? Wisniak had promised he'd stay in his room until the investigators finished up. Now he was being held by the military police?

"Nice of you to answer your phone." Reza could hear the leading edge of a full-blown tantrum in Marshall's voice. "Apparently, he made some comments about blowing up the theater."

That didn't make a damn bit of sense. Wisniak hadn't been around anyone in the company since Reza had relocated him across post. How the hell had Marshall found him?

"Then why don't they just arrest him?" He had to play it

off like he didn't know anything about where Wisniak had been.

"Because he tried to slit his wrists, apparently."

"Ah fuck." Reza rubbed his eyes with his thumb and forefinger. "All right. I'll head in and pick him up."

"He goes straight to the emergency room for an evaluation so I can brief the battalion commander we're actually doing something with him." There it was. The classic Captain Marshall. No concern about whether or not the trooper had actually tried to slice his wrists. Just, *how could we shape this so the boss doesn't get pissed.*

"Roger, sir." Reza ended the phone call before he said something that would really irritate Marshall. He sighed and looked at Emily. Regret was thick in his voice. "I have to go."

"Is everything okay?" Genuine concern. For once, it didn't piss him off.

"It'll have to be, won't it?" There was no acrimony in his words. Just fatigue that he could feel in his bones. He wanted to tell her what was going on with Wisniak. Maybe he should have. But right then, he didn't want to see the shadows creep back into her eyes. He wanted her to be able to sleep tonight.

He'd call her if he needed to but he hoped that Marshall was wrong.

Emily slid her arms around his waist. Her warmth penetrated his clothes. Made him want to hold on to her with everything he had.

"It's my job," he said softly. "I take care of soldiers."

"Even guys like Wisniak?"

Her words hurt, cutting him with a reminder of his own callousness. He did nothing to staunch the wound. He deserved it. "Especially guys like him. Guess I forgot that for a while."

He tucked his phone back in his pocket and wrapped his arms around her. Brushing her hair out of her eyes, he kissed her gently, struggling to hide the magnitude of feeling that swelled inside him from simply being near her. "I'll take you back to your car," he said softly.

She nodded, slipping off the bike and back on behind him. Her arms wrapped tightly around his waist and he felt her cheek pressed against his back. He closed his eyes for a brief moment before firing the engine.

Everything had been simpler before she came into his life. Now? Everything was twisted and complex. But with her arms around his waist and her thighs gripping his from behind, he knew it was worth it. She was worth it.

Whatever the cost.

He pulled down the gravel drive toward *Talarico's* a little while later and came to a stop near her car. The bar was brightly lit against the night lake and people were scattered in various alcoves surrounding the bar. Emily climbed off and Reza killed his bike, leaving them surrounded by shadows. "Will you be okay?" she asked, smoothing her hair down.

"I'm always okay." A non-answer. For once she didn't press him.

She reached for him, her palm warm against his chilled skin. Her thumb brushed against his cheek, the gesture a comfort. "Let me know if there's anything you need?"

Because he couldn't resist, he tugged her toward him and claimed her lips. It was not a gentle kiss; there was too much storming inside him for it to be anything but fierce. She opened beneath his onslaught and met his passion with her own.

Reluctantly, he nibbled on her bottom lip before releasing her entirely. "Drive safely tonight," he said softly.

She smiled and said nothing, merely stepping back until

she bumped up against her car. He got back on the bike and pulled out, but the last thing he saw was a secret smile on her lips and a promise in her eyes.

Reza straightened and braced for confrontation as he walked into the MP station on Fort Hood. He waited to be buzzed in and then followed the portly young private first class back to the holding area. Reza couldn't help but wonder how this kid would hold up downrange, wearing seventy pounds of gear in a-hundred-and-twenty-plus-degree heat.

He pulled his mind away from the trivial mental gymnastics as they rounded the corner to the holding area.

Wisniak sat in the corner. His shoulders were hunched; his elbows rested on his knees. His eyes were dark. Bleak. There were bandages wrapped around both wrists.

Rage boiled in Reza's blood. If Wisniak had attempted suicide, the cops should have brought him immediately to the hospital instead of holding him here. "I need a copy of the official report," Reza said to the desk sergeant, barely keeping his voice civil.

The heavy PFC slunk out of the room at the sound of an impending battle. The desk sergeant straightened and stood behind a desk fronted with bulletproof glass, and his expression flickered but he didn't budge. "I need your commander's permission to release that information to you."

Reza slapped his cell phone on the counter with Marshall's phone number visible. "Call him."

He glanced at Wisniak as the sergeant dialed Marshall's number. There was a spot of blood on the bandage on the inside of Wisniak's left wrist. Reza scowled. "Who triaged his wounds?"

The desk sergeant pulled out the police report, holding the phone up to one ear. "His wrists were already bandaged when we detained him."

Wisniak looked up at the sound of Reza's voice. His skin blanched and he turned a sickly shade of green before his lips pressed together in a hard, flat line. He lifted his chin defiantly. Reza lifted one eyebrow at Wisniak's expression and the soldier quickly lowered his gaze back to the floor.

The desk sergeant spoke with Marshall and hung up the phone. Reza held out his hand for the report, saying nothing as he skimmed the pages. Finally he looked up. Wisniak was watching him cautiously. "Let's go," Reza said.

Reza had swapped his bike for his truck on the way to post. Wisniak followed him to it without speaking, then climbed into the passenger's seat. It was only a short ride to the hospital but the closer they got, the more Wisniak physically shrank into his seat.

Reza parked outside the emergency room, grateful that it didn't seem too busy.

"I don't want to be here," Wisniak said. His voice was hoarse, as though he'd been screaming.

"You don't get much of a choice after you threaten to blow up one of the theaters," Reza said, killing the engine.

"I didn't."

Reza shifted and pinned the kid with a hard look. "So you're telling me the military police have started arresting people for shits and giggles now?"

"I didn't do that, Sarn't Ike." There was an urgency in his voice that quickly faded. "Not that I expect you to believe me."

"Then explain it to me, Wisniak, because right now I've got Captain Marshall calling me, telling me you've been arrested, I've got a police report of a text-messaged threat, and I've got you sitting in the police station with bandages on your wrists. So right now, your claim of innocence isn't holding a lot of water with me." Reza sucked in a deep breath and eased back the boiling rage in his voice. "You've got one chance to set the record straight."

Wisniak looked at him, his eyes wide with shock. His mouth moved for a moment before sound actually came out. "Song set me up."

Reza said nothing. Mike Song was one of Marshall's boys, part of Marshall's so-called A-Team, a crew that he'd brought with him from his previous unit once he'd taken command. "Wisniak, I saw the picture of the text message," Reza said, wanting to shake Wisniak so badly for trying to lie to him once more.

Wisniak balked and looked at Reza like he had a dick growing out of his forehead. "You're not very tech savvy, are you, Sarn't Ike? All he did was take a screen shot of a contact that said my name. There's nothing to prove the message was from my number. He faked the pic and sent it to Captain Marshall."

Reza considered Wisniak's argument. It wasn't outside the realm of possibility, especially since one could manually create contacts on phones. "Why would Song do that?"

Wisniak looked away and sat silently for a long minute. "It really sucks not having a combat patch." There was shame in his voice. "It sucks not being a good enough soldier."

Reza frowned, rubbing his hand over his mouth thoughtfully as he listened to Wisniak's words and thought about what to say. His own prejudice rang loudly in his ears.

Finally Wisniak looked back at him. "All I ever wanted to be was not a fuck-up." He blinked rapidly then squeezed his eyes shut. "Song said he was going to make sure I was run out of the army because I was a waste of time. That I didn't deserve the honor of wearing our uniform." He looked back at Reza, his eyes filled with the loss of something much more fragile than the most precious glass. "He's right."

"You tried to kill yourself tonight, didn't you?" Reza finally said softly.

Wisniak looked down at his wrists. "I even fucked that up."

Reza swallowed a hard lump in his throat as a memory collided with his present reality. This was not the first time he'd sat with someone wearing bandages on their wrists.

He was at a loss for words. He searched for something to bridge the gap between him and the wounded young soldier next to him.

He settled on the truth.

"We all take a knee sometimes," Reza said softly, his voice rough.

Wisniak eyed him warily. "You never do."

Reza pressed his lips together into a flat line. "You didn't see me six months ago."

"What happened six months ago?"

Chapter Nineteen

Reza took a deep breath. Fear gripped his throat as shame twisted in his belly.

It was hell to admit to someone that you were an addict. One fist clenched in his lap as he rubbed his hand over his mouth, thinking long and hard before he answered. Very few people in the battalion knew that Reza had gone to rehab. Even the army didn't officially know he'd gone because he'd been on convalescence leave at the time.

But maybe this kid needed to know that Reza had spoken the truth: everyone had a breaking point. He held his breath until his lungs burned and begged for release.

And then he spoke, his voice raw, his words harsh.

"I spent a week in rehab." Wisniak's eyes widened but he wisely said nothing. Reza might have broken if he'd dared breathe a word. "I drink. A lot. It got out of hand on a mission a few months ago." That was all he could manage of the truth. He looked at Wisniak. "So don't think we've all got our shit together because we don't. None of us do." He swallowed hard. "We're going into the emergency room and we're going to have a doc look at your wrists and another doc look at your head. And you're going to need to take some time to figure out what is going to make you happy. Not me, not your dad, not some mythical hero you think you want to be. You. Because this is your life. No one else's."

Wisniak's eyes were wide as saucers. He blinked rapidly then nodded.

There was nothing more to say. Reza led him into the ER and checked him in. Because of the cuts on Wisniak's wrists, they bypassed the normally hellish wait and were taken right back. Once it was verified that there was no physical risk of Wisniak dying, they began the wait for the on-call doctor. Around midnight, the on-call doc still wasn't answering his calls, so the hospital began trying to get hold of the head psych doc.

They waited. There was no small talk but the silence was no longer filled with acrimony and harsh judgment. No, Reza had taken on another role the moment he'd shared his weakness with Wisniak. He refused to consider that Wisniak now looked at him like some kind of fucked-up hero. Reza didn't deserve to be put on a pedestal.

More likely it was the first time someone had been nice to Wisniak. Reza felt the sour taste in his mouth echoing back at him over how badly he'd treated Wisniak and all the other troopers Reza had felt were unworthy of being called soldiers.

Guilt and shame danced at the back of Reza's neck, a dreadful duo that made him crave the oblivion of alcohol just to escape the wretchedness that threatened to consume him. One more person knew that Reza had fallen down on the job. One more person could now look at him every single fucking day and wonder if he'd had one or two or six beers before lunch. One more person might stand a little too close to see if he'd taken a pull off the flask before first formation.

Admitting his weakness shamed him. It had been the

right thing to do but still, he felt like a failure. Like a broken thing on top of a trash heap.

An old washed-out infantry sergeant who could no longer cut it. Some wrung-out GI who would be relegated to sitting around, swapping war stories while young men went off to actual war.

Reza suddenly felt far older than his years. Infinitely older.

He wanted to go to sleep and not get up for a week. Maybe then he'd feel something akin to normal. Maybe everything would turn out to be a bad dream and he'd wake up and everything would start over. Sloban would still be alive and he'd think to ask how his former soldier was doing. Wisniak would not have taken a dull blade to his wrists and Reza could ask if he needed help instead of condemning him like everyone else had.

He rubbed his hands over his face. He wouldn't have met Emily, though.

He considered the sweetness of her laugh, her terror as he'd taken her through the shoot house. The way her eyes had darkened the first time she'd seen the memorials he'd carved into his skin after each deployment.

There was a quiet knock on the waiting room doorjamb.

Reza looked up into a familiar face.

Emily stood in the doorway.

She hadn't had time to pull on more than old sweatpants and a long-sleeved t-shirt when the call came in. She'd been half asleep, drifting into slumber with the memory of Reza's kiss on her lips, worry for the man weighing on her heart.

She'd known immediately who waited for her at the hospital. Part of her had hoped that she was wrong, that it wasn't Wisniak.

Emily didn't bother to ask where the on-call doctor was.

She spent five minutes with one soldier, a skinny kid from someplace called Benedict, Arkansas, before she had him admitted. He was high from smoking synthetic marijuana and believed that ants were crawling on his skin. Lacerations covered his arms and legs. He'd need to spend time in Intensive Care before they could admit him to Psych.

The second kid had puked up a fifth of Jim Beam and was, according to him, feeling significantly better. No, he'd just been screwing around when he'd told the guys he felt like he'd be better off dead. Yes, ma'am, he'd be fine.

She couldn't hold him against his will. No matter how much the staff sergeant who sat with him demanded she did. She wrote up a profile that recommended he be kept under unit watch for the next 48 hours, which prompted the staff sergeant to get loud enough that Reza came into the exam room a moment before the security guards. The sergeant wisely shut his mouth when he saw Reza glaring at him from the door.

And then it was time for Wisniak. She pulled Reza into an empty room. "So what's the story?" she asked, skimming the triage notes. Strictly professional, regardless of what was between them.

"He's admitted he tried to kill himself," Reza said, mirroring her stance and keeping his distance. "But he says he was set up with the bomb threat."

He looked exhausted but the last thing Emily could do in the middle of the emergency room was offer any sort of physical comfort. She was the doc. He was the supervisor.

Nothing more. At least not right then.

"He's pretty upset. I think if he's right and some of the guys did set him up, they probably saved his life." Reza's voice was rough. Broken.

"Okay. I'm going to talk to him. You'll have to wait outside." Reza's smile was flat. "I know the routine."

It took her more than an hour to get Wisniak to admit to still thinking about hurting himself. But when he did, she did everything she could to reassure him that he was going to be okay.

He shook his head sadly. "Ma'am, I appreciate everything you've done, but I doubt it. I always feel this way."

Emily paused from writing her notes and looked up. "It feels like that now but you don't have to feel this way. We're going to figure this out."

Wisniak nodded and said nothing as she stuck her head outside and motioned for Reza to step into the room. "We're going to admit him," she said softly. "My assessment is that until we get him stabilized, he poses a risk to himself."

Reza nodded and said nothing. He looked dead on his feet but still he stood ramrod stiff and straight. She had no doubt that if he'd needed to react to an emergency right now, he could have done so.

Thankfully, the rest of the night didn't call for anything so extreme.

It was another two hours before Wisniak was escorted upstairs, leaving Reza with instructions to have someone bring a change of clothes and some very basic hygiene items within the next day or so.

The sky was still pitch black when Emily finally walked out of the emergency room to the parking lot where she'd left her car. Reza waited for her, leaning against his truck in the cool morning air. She wondered when he'd swapped his bike for his truck and figured it didn't really matter.

"You look exhausted," he said softly as she approached.

"You flatterer," she said with a tired smile. "But you're right. Double shifts are often rough." She paused. "Come home with me?" It was less than a question, more than an order. There was something needy inside her, something that wanted to be held and comforted.

She didn't want to be alone but more, she didn't want Reza to be alone. He looked edgy tonight. Raw.

He reached for the keys in his front pocket, but not before she noticed his hand was trembling. "I'm not really fit company tonight, Emily."

"You've said that before." She took a single step closer to him. Close enough that the heat of his body radiated into hers. Close enough that she could snag his hand and cradle it between hers. She didn't care that they were in the hospital parking lot. That anyone could see them as the parking lot lights hummed overhead. "And I don't care."

He raised both eyebrows at her quiet words. He nodded then, after an impossibly long moment, and tugged his hand away from hers.

She drove out of the parking lot, anxious that he might not actually follow her.

But as she drove out of the main gate and away from Fort Hood, she breathed a silent sigh of relief that the headlights from his big truck stayed right behind her the entire way.

It probably wasn't a good idea but then again, nothing with Emily seemed to be. He followed her away from the middle-income homes of Killeen, past Harker Heights and out toward the new development in Nolanville.

He was still marveling at the woman who'd captured his interest when he stepped across her threshold and into her home. It was exactly how he expected her to live. Books were stacked around the living room. Overfull bookshelves filled a small study. An empty wineglass sat on a coaster on the coffee table.

"You drink alone?" he asked.

She lifted one shoulder as she dropped her keys into a small dish on a table in the foyer. "Not against the rules." She toed off her shoes and crossed the scant distance between them in bare feet.

The door closed behind him as her arms came around his waist. He pulled her close and rested his cheek against the top of her head. "I'm so tired," she whispered. Her warm breath penetrated the thin fabric of his t-shirt.

He said nothing. He felt the fatigue in his bones. The need for a drink was even stronger.

She tipped her face up, brushing her lips against his. There was something deeply comforting here, something he was selfish enough to crave.

He followed her to her bedroom, noticing all the things he hadn't noticed before. The comforter was deep tan laced with gold. One half of the bed was neat, the other slightly rumpled, as though she only slept on one half of it. Her furniture was solid. Expensive, not particle board like something a kid in the barracks would buy.

He felt her eyes on him as he toed off his own shoes, then pulled off his t-shirt. She slipped out of most of her own clothing, leaving on the t-shirt and panties. He ached for her but tonight, it felt like the most natural thing in the world to simply slide into her bed, feel her body soft and warm nestled against him. Her hair was cool against his shoulder when she rested her cheek against his heart. Her legs twined with his, smooth where his were rough.

He drifted for a while as her fingers traced the names on his upper arm. For once, a woman's attention on his tattoos didn't make him go cold. He hadn't etched those names and places into his skin for a woman's attention. There was a reason he wore long-sleeved shirts most of the time.

He did it for himself. To honor the men he'd served with. The men he'd failed. But as her fingers traced over al Najaf and Fallujah and Ramadi, he was oddly comforted by her soft touch. For once the scars on his soul didn't burn, didn't drive him to raid her kitchen for a drink in a vain attempt to deaden the pain that he knew he'd never escape.

His body settled into the idea that he was wrapped in a woman's embrace and for once, there was nothing sexual about it. Reza didn't sleep with women. Not like this. And yet, it felt like the most natural thing in the world to lie with her as her breathing deepened. Her fingers traced the letters on his arm until she shifted and her palm came to rest on the black sickle that covered his heart. Her hand was warm and soft over the exposed, ragged wounds tonight. As he drifted into a restless sleep, he turned his face toward Emily and rested his cheek against the top of her head.

The cool kiss of her hair against his skin took him down into sleep.

Emily came awake to the sensation that something was wrong. She opened her eyes to see a very tense Reza, asleep in the center of her bed. Instantly alert, she leaned up at the sound of his mumbled words. His mouth moved but the words were incoherent. The emotion behind them was not.

His fists spasmed as he argued with whatever demon hunted his sleep. She'd never seen this side of the big man. He was always so fierce, so strong. She nudged his shoulder gently, a thousand stories racing through her mind of women who'd tried to wake up lovers from nightmares. Fear skittered down the center of her spine as his eyes flew open.

A pregnant moment hung between them. He scowled, his expression harsh and unforgiving. She held her breath, bracing for his anger, but then he blinked slowly, his expression softening even as a flush crept up his dark skin.

"Did I hurt you?" The first words out of his mouth were thick. Rough.

"No." She wanted to ask him if he wanted to talk about it but the words were frozen in her throat.

He turned toward her and opened his arms. She slipped against him, her body surrounded by his, her skin absorbing his heat. He smoothed her hair down and rested his cheek against her head. The gesture soothed the ragged fear that had clung to her like a wet cloak since she'd woken him.

He shared her bed but that did not mean he was willing or even able to let her, as he'd put it the first time they'd slept together, go poking at his demons.

The barrier bothered her on a personal level and had nothing to do with her profession. She wanted this man, desired him like she'd desired no other since . . . ever. She'd never desired her ex this way.

Her eyes fluttered closed as sleep pulled her back down, the rhythmic feel of Reza's breathing surrounding her. And as she slid down into sleep, she chased the idea that maybe someday he would start unpacking all the baggage that weighed on his sleep. If not with her, with someone else.

She was not naïve enough to think she could be strong enough to save him. But Reza was worth saving. Worth fighting for.

If he was talking to someone, to anyone, she would be happy. Knowing he was getting help, knowing he was unpacking the weight in his rucksack.

It was worth it, for now, just to know he was safe.

Chapter Twenty

Emily glanced up as Olivia slipped into her office Wednesday morning. "Someday, you're going to have to teach me your secret. How do you always look so polished?"

Olivia worked at the hospital legal office and always managed to look dressed to kill, regardless of whether she wore the Army combat uniform or her Dress Blues. Her dark hair gleamed in the mid-afternoon light and her makeup was always flawless, no matter how close to the temperature of the sun it was in Texas. "It's part of the job. Convincing the jury or the judge to listen to me is much easier if they're not critiquing my hair or makeup." Olivia sank into the chair across from Emily's desk.

"Back to the matter at hand," Emily said with a smile. "What's up?"

Her friend's expression shuttered closed. "It's about the shooting last week."

"Figures," Emily said dryly, her emotions still tender and raw from everything over the last week. For the first time since she'd known her, Olivia looked uncomfortable. "Olivia?"

"Em, there's a formal investigation being launched. Against the company leadership. Against Reza and his commander."

Her throat went dry. Had he known? Why hadn't he told her?

Olivia shook her head, her hair reflecting the light overhead. "I'm on the team. And the commander wants someone from his staff that he trusts to look into...the mental health aspect of this death."

Emily felt all the blood drain from her body. She sank back into her chair. "What is he looking for?"

"Whether there has been any undue influence regarding the medical care soldiers are getting." Olivia offered a sympathetic smile. "I wanted you to hear it from me first."

Emily searched for something, anything, to say but words escaped her.

"The entire chain of command is being investigated, Em," Olivia said quietly. "You might want to stay away from him until this whole thing shakes out. This could go badly."

"What do you mean, badly? We've got company commanders scheming to put soldiers out of the army before they can get the behavioral health care they need. How much worse could it go?" She couldn't keep her composure. Everything she'd believed in about her new life seemed like a lie.

"You could get caught up in it. Be brought in because of undue influence through your relationship with Reza."

Her blood was cold in her veins. Olivia's hand on her forearm was unexpected and warm.

Emily glanced down at the gesture of friendship and it was suddenly the only thing that felt real. She felt hollow and empty. Unmoored.

Like everything she'd believed in was a lie.

Reza was being investigated along with his commander.

"You need to keep this to yourself," Olivia said quietly.

"Who am I going to tell?" Emily said, not restraining the sarcasm in her voice. Reza. Reza was being investigated.

"Regardless. Em, this is echelons above your pay grade."

Emily smiled but it felt as cold as her hands. "I'm fine. I won't discuss it." She tried to warm her eyes. She failed. "I'll keep it to myself. Thank you . . . for letting me know."

"Sure." Olivia stood, lifting her bag onto her shoulder. "Are you sure you're okay?"

Emily shrugged. "Kind of have to be, don't I?"

"Em . . ."

"I'm fine. Really."

"You can talk to me, you know." Emily looked up at her friend. "You know, if it starts to get to you?"

This time, Emily's smile came from the heart. Her chest expanded with it. "I know. Thanks for looking out for me."

"We'll try to move this along as quickly as we can, okay?"

She said nothing as Olivia left. The silence echoed in her office. Her fingers shook.

And fear crept like ice up her spine.

Reza sat in his truck outside headquarters and took a deep breath, trying to steady his hands without reaching for the fresh pint in his glove box at oh dark thirty on a Wednesday morning. A week since Sloban had killed himself. A week since Reza's world at home had been shattered by the same violence he lived with downrange.

Five days since his last drink.

He didn't know why he kept it so close. A smarter man might have removed all the temptation. He hated thinking of himself as weak.

But the pint was there and every time he didn't take a drink, he felt like he'd won another round.

He'd already dragged his dead ass onto post the morning after pulling an all-nighter with Emily in the ER. Now he just had to summon the energy to go into the office. He didn't want to deal with Captain Marshall's bullshit.

He slammed his head back against the seat rest, frustrated and tired. Maybe he needed to take some leave. He was starting to lose his mind. He should head down to Mexico and completely lose his shit for a few days. Come back rested. Relaxed.

Sober.

He snorted and grabbed his keys out of the ignition. He didn't know the meaning of the word. Locking the truck behind him, he headed into the office before formation to get a head start on some of the day's paperwork. He still needed to finalize all the paperwork he'd need for Sloban's memorial.

Some soldiers didn't believe soldiers who killed themselves deserved a memorial. Reza wasn't about to entertain that shit.

Sloban deserved a memorial.

He should have known better than to think the day was going to be anything but a disaster. Why had he thought Marshall would just sign the paperwork and leave Reza to do his job?

Instead, Marshall's reaction punched him square in the gut.

"Fuck no."

Reza's skin went cold. It was too early in the morning for this shit. "Sir?" Reza asked through clenched teeth.

"I'm not doing it. I'm not doing a memorial ceremony for some coward who kills himself."

The hair on the back of his neck prickled. And now he knew why some soldiers were grumbling about suicides. It was coming straight from the top. Reza chose his words carefully. "Sloban was a good kid, sir. He was a warrior."

Marshall's all-American smile twisted into a sneer. "He was a coward. He didn't deserve the honor of wearing our uniform."

"He did three tours. All of them in heavy fighting." Inside

him, the beast was lashing at its bonds, struggling to break free and slam Marshall's head into the desk to wipe that sneer off his face. "He wasn't a coward."

"I don't care. I'm not signing that fucking paperwork."

Reza ground his teeth and balled the paperwork up in his fist. Marshall glanced down at the crumpled memorandum.

"Watch it, Sergeant. I might mistake that as a threat."

Reza threw the paperwork at his chest and barely managed to keep his temper in check. "Take it however the fuck you want."

He left the office before he gave in to the temptation to do bodily harm to Marshall.

He said nothing to Foster as he passed him on the way to formation. Teague tried to make him laugh with some stupid story from his latest adventure in trying to piss off his boss.

Rage pulsed through his veins. He needed to cool off. To calm down.

He needed a goddamned drink.

He counted to one hundred as the flag went up, then turned the platoons over to their respective platoon sergeants before he took off, heading out of the parking lot. Needing to put a few miles of asphalt between himself and Captain Marshall. Maybe if he ran the three miles from First Cav to the Cavalry Regiment's headquarters and back again, he'd be able to make it through the morning's staff meeting without punching his commander.

He was a coward.

Cold fury detonated inside him as he sprinted down the main avenue. Sloban wasn't a coward. They'd broken him. They'd done this to him. The commanders who failed to listen when a soldier said he was hurting, commanders who needed boots on the ground.

Fuck that. Sloban had gotten a raw deal. Reza hadn't known how bad it was.

It was his goddamned fault that Sloban was dead. He could have helped him if he'd been sober.

He turned down Battalion Avenue and headed toward the Regimental headquarters, deciding to do the run after all. He wove through the bodies and the mass formations running down Battalion. He tried to focus on the rhythm, on the beats of his feet hitting the pavement. Instead, his mind kept circling back to Marshall's words.

To the abject desolation in Sloban's eyes the moment he pulled the trigger.

He ran. The images flashed through his brain and still he ran. His feet hit the pavement. Left. Right. Left. Right. Until his breathing fell into rhythm with his steps.

Left. Right. Left. Right.

He ran until the sun came up over the Corps headquarters and the sweat ran into his eyes. Until his mind emptied and his lungs burned.

He stopped just before he collapsed. Hands braced on his thighs, he knew he needed to straighten up and walk it off. Instead, he bent over and sucked oxygen into his starved lungs.

He straightened after a long moment. And looked dead on at the Cav Memorial. The granite gleamed in the morning sunlight. Names were carved into the polished stone.

The grief flooded back. Sloban's name would never be on that memorial. He'd died by his own hand, killed by the enemy a year after he'd left theater. Because Sloban's enemy was no less deadly than the mortars and the rockets and the deep buried IEDs in the sands of Iraq.

He looked up at the sound of shoes crunching over dried grass.

Teague walked up, his chest pumping hard.

Shame and grief and a thousand unsaid things washed over him when he realized that Teague had been behind him the whole time. Teague said nothing as he approached. He simply stood next to him, shoulder to shoulder, facing the memorial that held so many friends' names.

"Marshall won't do a memorial for Sloban," Reza finally said.

Teague said nothing for a long moment. "Then we do one anyway."

"I can't get the chapel without the commander's signature."

Teague spat into the grass. "Then we do it in the motor pool. We do it at the hatch of our old Bradley."

Reza nodded slowly. "Sloban would like that." He cleared his throat roughly. Hiding the fact that his voice had cracked.

"I'll take care of everything." Teague gripped his shoulder.

Reza said nothing. He didn't have to. They had a plan now to honor one of their own. They simply stood in silence for another long moment.

And after a time had passed, the knot in his chest eased up. Not much. But a little. Enough that he could breathe again.

For now.

Reza couldn't remember the last time he'd slept, truly slept. None of that mattered, though, because he had work to do. Sloban's memorial was going to be today. Reza wasn't even remotely close to ready but he had to be. Evan Loehr had left him a voice mail, needing to speak to him about Wisniak first thing. Of course, Evan probably didn't know that Wisniak had been admitted two nights ago. There was no reason for Evan to have known—Wisniak wasn't in his company. Looked like Reza would probably be the first one to tell him. A great way to start off a morning. He stopped for coffee, needing the caffeine if he was going to survive the rest of the day.

Evan was the investigating officer because he outranked Marshall. Still, it was a sticky thing to investigate someone in your own unit. But Reza trusted Loehr to do the right thing. The man didn't know how to do the wrong thing.

Reza snorted. He supposed that was why Loehr was such a good match for Claire. They kept each other on their toes.

A short time later, he walked into the battalion headquarters and headed down the hall toward the conference room. Evan was already there, drinking from a stainless steel mug branded with the Reaper design. He glanced up when Reza walked in.

"Hey, Sarn't Ike."

"Sir."

They'd served together on the mission in Colorado and on that last rotation to Iraq. Evan had been part of the team that had been responsible for putting together legal reviews on some of the actions Reza and his boys had then carried out. It was nice knowing there was a team somewhere blessing off on the targeted operations that in theory were helping to keep his boys—and in theory at least the Iraqis—safer.

"Anyway, you know why you're here." Best not to pull punches.

Reza pulled up a chair and leaned both elbows on the table. "Yeah. Wisniak and the allegations he's made." Reza took a sip from his coffee. "Have you heard he was admitted to the psych ward again?"

Evan scribbled a note. "Nope, that's first heard."

"He attempted to kill himself but there's a twist." Reza pulled out his phone and showed Evan the screen shot that Captain Marshall had sent him last night. "Wisniak thinks he was set up." He explained how Wisniak thought the text messages had been faked while Evan scribbled quickly.

"You know I can't use any of this officially? It's all hearsay."

"I know, but you need to question Song about his cell

phone and you might want to talk to Captain Marshall about his boys. It's crossed the line if they're assaulting people."

Evan scrubbed his hand over his jaw. "Marshall is a grade-A fuckstick," he said grimly.

"Tell me something I don't know." Reza sighed. "I question, though, whether he knows the full extent of what's going on with his boys."

Evan frowned. "Why do you say that?"

Reza leaned back from the table. "We always say the commanders are responsible for everything their formation does or doesn't do, but honestly, how can they possibly know everything? I'm the last one to defend Marshall but I've seen good commanders get rung up for shit they just didn't know."

"Wisniak told his shrink that he informed Marshall and then the harassment got worse."

"But what did he tell Marshall? Did he lay it all out or did he say something vague like 'I feel like the guys are fucking with me'?" Reza paused. "It makes a difference, especially for guys like Marshall, who act only on facts."

Evan continued writing quickly. "Good point, actually. I'll have to interview Marshall again to find out just what Wisniak told him." He looked up.

"What do you think?" Reza asked cautiously.

"I think Marshall's boys are out of control and he's not doing anything to rein them in, either because he doesn't know, refuses to see, or simply can no longer control a gang of marauding asshats that he was a part of. I'll know more once I talk to Marshall."

Reza leaned forward and took a pull off his coffee, staring off into space. "Do you ever think we're not fighting the good fight anymore?"

Evan tossed his pen onto the table and leaned back. "Every day I question what I'm doing, brother. Every day." Evan studied him quietly for a moment. "You thinking of hanging it up?"

Reza lifted a shoulder and dropped it. "Not much out there by way of jobs for a washed-out infantryman unless I want to go mercenary. I kind of like that whole food on the table thing."

"You don't give yourself enough credit. You know where I think you'd be great?" Reza lifted both eyebrows, waiting. "Middle school gym teacher."

Reza choked on his coffee, coughing roughly. "Where the fuck did you come up with that good idea fairy?"

Evan grinned. "You've got the kind of personality that people look up to. Think of the difference you could make in a little kid's life before they end up all fucked up by their parents."

"Yeah, 'cause I'm such a great fucking mentor." The tattoos on his arms ached with failure.

"Just saying. It's a lot like what you do now except you'd be teaching kids how to hit a ball or make a basket instead of kicking in doors. You know, if you were serious about getting out."

Reza frowned. "Yeah, well, thanks; but there aren't a whole lot of soccer moms who would be comfortable with a man like me teaching their kids to play ball."

"You'd be surprised. People look at the uniform and see the shiny hero, not the mud, blood, and tears that go along with it sometimes."

Reza said nothing as he stood. The idea of him wearing bad shorts and a whistle to work was beyond insane. He'd go crazy without the constant stress and strain of army life. It might take everything he had some days to get up and go to work but it was all he knew, all he'd ever done.

His upper arm itched and he rubbed it absently. The idea of hanging up his career in the middle of the war felt like . . . treason. Worse, cowardice. What kind of soldier would he be if he cut and run while his boys headed back into combat without him? He'd survived so long and so much crazy shit, going back downrange felt like the only way to thank the fates that had kept him alive for so long.

It felt like a sin not to prepare soldiers the best way he knew how.

He crossed the quad toward his company operations office, not really wanting to deal with Marshall. Then again, there was never a good time to deal with Marshall but today was going to be particularly bad when Marshall found out about the memorial. And he would find out.

Reza had passed the point of caring. He walked into his office and turned on his computer. Temptation beckoned to him from his desk drawer. He held the bottle in his hands, twisting the cap off and on until his hands no longer shook as he logged onto his e-mail and skimmed for anything important.

He could do this. On. Off. On. Off.

Three e-mails but the most important one was from Giles asking about Wisniak. He fired off the update and included that he'd finished his interview with Evan. He didn't expect a response from Sergeant Major Giles and he received none.

Reza was getting ready to face the most aggravating part of his duty day when Teague walked in. Reza was instantly on edge. Teague hadn't shaved and looked like he'd been up a hell of a lot longer than Reza. "What happened?"

"Nothing. Foster and I were up commiserating last night.

"You look like you were doing a lot more than commiserating. What was the occasion?"

"Two years since the firefight where we lost Deek and Bo."

Reza sat back in his chair, his heart twisting with the memories the names inspired. Lieutenant Deek Merreck and Sergeant Dave Bonamie. "They were good dudes."

Teague scoffed quietly. "Does anyone ever say, 'man, they were such fuckheads'?"

Reza didn't laugh. He wasn't sure he'd be able to hold up for another trip down memory lane. He was keeping things together by a strand of five-fifty cord and hundred-mile-an-hour tape as it was. "No, I suppose not."

They sat together in silence for a long time. There were no words that could put the myriad of feelings churning inside him to voice. There was no need, either.

The silence of shared experience said enough.

After a long while, Reza glanced at his watch.

"Ready for the memorial ceremony?" he said, looking at Teague. They'd pulled it together in record time—less than 24 hours. It would be small but the people that mattered to Sloban in life would be there to commemorate his death.

It was the right thing to do.

It still sucked.

"Are we ever ready for those?" Teague asked quietly.

"No," Reza said softly. "I suppose not."

"Specialist Sloban?" Reza's voice did not break as he called the roll. A small crowd of soldiers from across the Reaper brigade surrounded the ramp of the Bradley.

These were men who remembered Sloban from before he'd begun his descent into drugs. There were still a few of them around and willing to brave the shit storm of disobeying an order.

Reza couldn't have been more proud.

He owed Teague a beer after this. Marshall was likely to have kittens if he knew that they were having a ceremony for Sloban but Reza didn't rightly care.

"Specialist Neal Sloban." His voice rang out across the silent crowd. Heads were bowed. More than one battle-hardened infantryman wiped his eyes.

Silence greeted Reza's call once more.

A third time, his voice rang out.

"Specialist Neal H. Sloban."

Reza turned and saluted Teague. "Sir, Specialist Sloban out of ranks."

His voice cracked. Teague returned Reza's salute then motioned for him to come up onto the ramp. The ceremony was less formal than one conducted by a chaplain. By rights, Captain Marshall, not Teague, should have officiated.

Sadly, Marshall wasn't alone among those who were of the mind that suicide was an act of cowardice that did not deserve to be memorialized.

Reza counted himself lucky that he served with men of character, even if he was not such a man himself. He rubbed his hands against his sides as he climbed the ramp. Facing the crowd, he recognized men from his old platoon. Familiar faces like Shane Garrison and his pain in the ass sidekick Vic Carponti. Teague and Foster stood at the edge of the crowd. Foster didn't look like he was holding up too well. He was either hung over or still drunk and Teague—while he was putting on a good show—didn't look like he was doing much better.

But this was important. The most important thing Reza would do today.

"We're here today because one of us has fallen." His voice cracked and he cleared his throat roughly. "We lost a brother by his own hand." Reza paused. "And that pisses me off."

All eyes lifted as one.

"Sloban was a good kid. A brave warrior. But those of us who knew him best failed him. None of us knew how badly he was hurting. None of us took the time to make sure he was okay. We failed him." He rubbed his hand over his mouth. "We're not supposed to be here right now. Some of our leaders think we should pretend those who die by their own hand do not deserve the honor of a memorial cer-emony. But we're here because we know better." He swallowed a lump blocking his throat. More than once. "We're here because we know that all of us have come home different. Maybe not as broken as Sloban was. But different. Changed." He paused. "I'm tired of losing our brothers to an enemy we can't see. I'm tired of saying good-bye to friends who made it through the war only to come home and face a different battle alone." His eyes filled and he blinked the tears back. There were nodding heads in the crowd and still he kept going. Unwilling to break down in front of the boys. "I want you to look at the man next to you." Awkward shifts in the crowd but no one moved. "Do it. Look the warrior next to you in the eye. Tell him you've got his back." At the edge of the crowd, he saw Teague rest his hand on Foster's shoulder. "I don't want to do this anymore," he said. His voice barely carried over the small group. "We can't rest. We can't stop. We've got to do better." He paused. "Our soldiers deserve better."

Reza stepped off the ramp. A hand clapped him on the shoulder. A gesture of sympathy. He swallowed roughly as Teague called for anyone who wanted to speak. A few soldiers stepped up, sharing their favorite memories of Sloban before the war had done something to the fun kid they'd all known.

"What the fuck is going on here?" Someone jabbed him hard in the shoulder.

Reza turned slowly, yanking on his emotions. Marshall. Who else?

Reza wasn't in the mood to deal with his commander. Not at all.

"What's it look like?" Reza said, offering a salute that was ignored. He dropped his hand.

"I thought I said no memorial ceremony." Marshall looked ready to explode.

"No, you said you wouldn't do a memorial ceremony. We decided to do one anyway." Reza felt someone come to stand behind him. He hoped it wasn't Teague. In his present condition, Teague looked ready to battle and Marshall was a likely candidate for an ass whooping.

"This borders on mutiny," Marshall growled.

"Do you know how to spell mutiny?" This from Teague behind him.

Great.

Reza flexed his hands and widened his stance.

"Go fuck yourself, Teague," Marshall said. "If you were a real infantryman, you'd have already commanded instead of hiding out on the staff."

"Maybe there are limits to how many hairy asses I'll kiss to make major. Feel free to continue for the both of us, though," Teague said. There was no humor in his voice.

"You're in charge of this ceremony?" Marshall said to Reza.

Reza lifted his chin and said nothing.

"You're fucking pathetic, Iaconelli," Marshall spat. "Sloban died because of you and you're going to stand here and get all weepy and teary-eyed?" Marshall dragged one finger beneath his eye. "You're a goddamned disgrace to the NCO Corps."

Reza didn't think.

His fist connected with Marshall's jaw before he'd even realized he'd moved. Marshall caught him with a vicious left hook and the brawl was on. Teague tackled Marshall and even though Marshall had a good thirty pounds on him, Teague was willing to fight dirty. Reza got a couple of good shots in on Marshall before someone dragged him off.

Garrison. He should have known the fucking Boy Scout would break up the fight.

"Fucking stop, Ike." Garrison shoved him back as Carponti yanked Marshall off. "Calm your ass down before you get court-martialed."

"You messed up your hair," Carponti said to Marshall. But despite the smart-ass comment, Carponti looked pissed and ready to fight. Reza took a single step backward.

Marshall wiped his lip then spat onto the concrete before he tried to take one last shot at Teague, who blew him a kiss. Foster knocked Teague back a step. "Cut the shit. Sir."

Garrison broke the crowd up, effectively ending the memorial ceremony. Reza tried to melt into the crowd, not really interested in hearing Garrison's lecture.

"You need to fucking stop, Ike."

Reza hung his head, clenching his fists at his sides. Garrison had always been a Boy Scout. Maybe that's why he grated on Reza's last nerve.

"I'm not really in the mood to listen to your preaching, Garrison."

"I'm pretty sure I don't give a shit." Garrison stepped in front of him, forcing Reza to either take a step back or stand his ground.

He stood his ground.

"You need to stop drinking. You need to pull your shit together. Sergeant Major can't protect you forever and you might have just cashed in your last favor with this little fiasco."

"I'm really not interested in your opinion. And for the record, I'm not drinking. So stick that in your pipe and smoke it."

"Do you realize what you just did? You gave that asshole a way to throw your ass out of the army. You're a hell of a good infantryman. You've got more combat time than most of the leaders in this entire brigade. But none of that is going to mean jack shit if you get yourself court-martialed over some stupid captain running his mouth." Garrison did something Reza didn't expect. He gripped Reza's shoulder.

It took everything Reza had not to pull away.

"I've heard all of this before. I've got things under control," Reza said.

"Punching your company commander is your idea of control? How much did you have to drink before you came to work today, Ike?" Reza frowned, but Garrison continued. "There are a lot of people who would move heaven and earth to protect you but you're out of favors this time. You have to get sober."

He yanked away. "Fuck you, Garrison. I told you, I'm fucking sober."

He heard the echo of another conversation. Another friend, worried about him.

Reza took a step backward, shaking his head. "I'm not drinking but shit, but I might as well."

Garrison refused to relent. "Maybe you're not but you're still not one hundred percent. There are too many people who care about you for you to keep doing stupid stuff like this." Garrison walked off, leaving Reza alone in the motor pool.

Hitting Marshall had felt good, damn good, and long overdue. But regret throbbed in his veins now that the adrenaline from the fight had worn off.

Garrison was right.

He'd just given Marshall a way to end his career.

He'd managed to stay sober. Mostly. And he'd fucked up.

His phone vibrated in his pocket. Sarn't Major Giles needed him in his office.

The bitter irony rose up to choke him.

What was the point in staying sober when all he did was fuck things up anyway?

Chapter Twenty-One

Goddamn it, Iaconelli, I'm fucking through with you."

"Sergeant Major." Colonel Horace's voice had been calm. Dead calm.

There had been no emotion in his eyes at all when he'd handed Reza the paperwork advising him of his rights.

Reza twisted the cap off the bottle and slammed back another drink. So this was what falling off the wagon felt like. Again. Shame threatened to choke him each time Reza swallowed another hard bite of liquor. Officers tended to frown on assault. He grimaced down at the bottle held loosely in one hand, then stared at the form on his beat-up coffee table.

He hadn't gone in to work. He'd thought about going out. Thought about calling up Teague and Foster and going out to wreck the town. But he was sober enough not to want to drag them down with him.

He kicked his feet up on the table and tossed back another pull from the bottle.

"I'm not going to make any decisions tonight, Sergeant Iaconelli."

Fuck, the memories were in fine form tonight. He'd heard

those words before. A different officer. The same disappointment. Three of his soldiers had died on the Thunder Run to Baghdad almost six years ago. The mission where he'd run out of ammo and water and waited for Claire to come and bail his happy ass out of a hot spot. The first of many rescues.

His commander had threatened to relieve him then, too. In the middle of the fight for Baghdad, Reza had been read his rights.

Man, Claire would kill him if she saw him tonight. He'd thought he could beat the alcohol all by himself. Tonight, when Colonel Horace had handed him his paperwork, he realized he was a fool for even trying. He fucked up fewer things when he was drunk.

Things didn't hurt as bad when he was drinking.

If he closed his eyes, the green haze of looking out through his night vision goggles danced across his vision. Countless faces looked back at him.

He took another drink. Maybe rehab wasn't such a bad idea if he was seeing shit while he was awake. Nightmares were one thing. Hallucinations? Yeah, that wasn't fucking cool.

He held up the bottle. The clear liquid glittered from the single light in the kitchen. Two thirds of the half-gallon were already gone.

Fuck. Why couldn't he just go to sleep and wake up Monday morning and face his fucking sentence? Office call first thing Monday morning. Because the brigade commander wasn't going to make a decision while he was still furious.

Someone beat on the door.

He took a long drink, wondering if he'd locked the door behind him or not. Teague would just walk in.

The knocking came again, louder this time.

He closed his eyes, seeing the field of eerie green darkness. He opened them right back up again at the sound of more knocking.

"Fuck," he mumbled, staggering to the door. He wrenched it open. It hadn't been locked.

Emily stood on the other side.

He was always surprised by how different she looked in civilian clothes. A simple black long-sleeved t-shirt hugged her curves. Dark jeans that made him want to peel them down her hips. She looked elegant and put together.

She looked pissed off and ready to fight. A small frown gathered between her eyebrows as she took him in.

He held on to the door to keep from swaying.

"Obviously, you're having a crappy night," she said by way of greeting. She didn't come in.

"I'm not fit company tonight."

"I think we've had this conversation before. The one where you're drunk and I'm an idiot for being here." She folded her arms over her chest. "I'd like to skip it if it's all the same to you. Right now, I'd like to make sure you don't die in a pool of your own vomit."

"I thought you were supposed to be looking for romance. Telling the hero you hope he doesn't die in a pool of his own vomit isn't exactly romantic."

"Yeah, well, romance isn't always hearts and flowers. Sometimes, it's hard work." She looked pissed, he decided, not just mildly irritated.

"So we're having a romance?" He leaned against the door, something warm unfurling inside of him at the sight of her. Maybe he wouldn't have to spend tonight alone after all.

"I don't know what this is, Reza," she said, her voice wavering. "But I'm worried about you."

There it was. That tiny note of concern that broke a little piece of his heart. "You shouldn't waste your time. I've been drinking since before you were born."

"Now you're just being an ass. I'm not that much younger than you are." She shifted and folded her arms over her chest. "Can I come in?"

"No."

She flinched at that single word. He hurt her. Good. He couldn't deal with her tonight, no matter how well intentioned she might be.

He closed his eyes, willing her to turn around and walk away and let him drown his sorrows by himself. It was all he was good at.

He'd tried to do the right thing. He'd tried to make sure one of their boys was honored the right way.

Turned out, no one cared about doing the right thing. He still didn't want her here. He wanted to get drunk and pass out and piss away his last weekend of his military career. It was over.

Because if she stayed, she might see the worst of him. The side of him he'd hidden away from everyone he'd ever cared about. There was a reason he'd never gotten attached but now this stubborn woman who'd run from the good life to join the army threatened to get behind the barriers he'd held in place through sheer orneriness.

And what an inglorious end his career had come to. No more war. No more retirement.

Just a whimper at the end.

Emily took a single step toward him, closing the distance between them. She lifted her hand, placing it over his heart. Her skin was warm, strong. She was tougher than she looked. He realized that now.

"Too bad," she said softly. She lifted her chin, pressing her lips to the corner of his mouth. "I'm not leaving you alone."

He had no intention of letting her in. She saw that clearly from the moment he'd opened the door.

Emily considered her options as she stood in his doorway, her palm burning where she touched him. She knew about addiction.

Right now, none of that mattered. What mattered was Reza was hurting. She'd never seen him as broken as he looked right now. He was a man who radiated strength, who was power and confidence.

And tonight, she caught a glimpse of the man he tried so hard to hide from her. More and more of the pieces fell into place, revealing a complicated man who hid so much more from the world than she'd ever realized.

All the pamphlets, all the research said she was supposed to force him to choose: his addiction or her. She was supposed to walk away and leave him, cutting him out of her life if necessary.

She knew about cutting people out of her life. She'd done so before and had no qualms about doing it. But the sudden thought of her life without Reza?

They weren't going to have that conversation tonight. Not if she could help it.

And what if he chose the bottle instead? What if he wasn't willing to give up the vice he turned to every time the world went to hell around him?

She couldn't live like that. And she couldn't stand there and watch him slowly kill himself either.

Her throat tightened. No, her life would no longer be the same if Reza Iaconelli wasn't in it. But drunk or not, she couldn't leave him alone tonight. Maybe that said more about her own personal weakness than it did about his.

Reza was worth fighting for.

"Let me in?" She hesitated. "Please."

Reza sighed hard, lifting his hands to scrub his eyes with the bottle still gripped in his hand. "Fuck it."

He turned and staggered back to the couch, sinking down

into it and kicking his feet up on the coffee table, bottle cradled between his thighs.

Emily followed him in, closing and locking the door. He held the bottle out toward her. She shook her head. She wasn't there for shots. She settled on water and curled into the other end of the couch.

Silence was heavy and thick between them. Beneath his unspoken anger, his pain was a palpable thing.

"So what happened?" she finally asked.

"Beat up my company commander yesterday. Got my ass handed to me last night by my brigade commander. Pissed off the one sarn't major who still believed in me by disobeying a lawful order from a commissioned officer." He raised the bottle. "Typical day at the office."

"Why would the sergeant major be mad about that?"

Reza said nothing, refusing to look at her as he took another pull from the bottle. "You're fucking adorable, you know that? You say sergeant major. Like the full word. Everyone else who has been in the army for more than a day says 'sarn't major.' Not you."

"And your point is?"

He leaned forward in a rush of energy, slamming the bottle on the coffee table before he twisted and faced her. "My point is that you have no idea what life is like in the brigade combat teams. The commanders and the sarn't majors are the be all and end all. If Sarn't Major Giles told me to pick up his dry cleaning, I'd do it. If he told me to take his daughter to the prom, I'd do it. And enlisted men don't disobey orders. And we damn sure don't beat the hell out of the men giving them."

"These people aren't God, Reza."

He sneered angrily. "You don't understand the power a brigade commander or a sarn't major wields. They can save your life or ruin it. All with a word. One order. One directive." He snatched the bottle back up from the coffee table and sank back into his corner of the couch.

"Why do I think you're not talking about Colonel Horace?" she whispered, fear slithering up her spine.

"Maybe I am."

"And maybe you're not. What did Captain Marshall do to make you hit him?"

Silence greeted her question. It hung between them, heavy and filled with a thousand unspoken words.

It was a long time before Reza spoke.

"Marshall is just like his boss. Just a kiss-ass officer trying to make his own report card look good so he can get promoted and turn around and have someone kiss his ass. It's how it works."

"There are good officers out there. I've met some of them."

Reza snorted. "You know who the good guys are? Guys like Teague. He's a smart-ass who will tell you straight up that a plan is stupid. He won't get promoted because of it. He can't get a company to command because he hasn't kissed the right ass. He went on the line for us yesterday so we could have the memorial for Sloban." He pointed toward her with the bottle. "You think you know how the army works. You only know how you *think* it works."

"I know how it's *supposed* to work," she whispered.

"And it doesn't work anything like that." Another pull from the bottle. He said nothing for a long moment. An impossible silence hung between them as a thousand emotions rushed across his face.

"I fucked up, Emily. Sloban is dead. Wisniak is in the hospital. Marshall is under investigation." He took a long pull off the bottle. "My career is over. Maybe it should be."

Emily scooted across the couch, sitting by his side. He kept his face covered. He didn't acknowledge that she now sat shoulder to shoulder with him.

"They're throwing me out of the army," he whispered.

When he looked at her, his eyes were red and heavy lidded, his face flushed.

He hadn't meant to say that. And the vodka had lost its appeal.

Her hand slid up his back and stopped on his shoulder. She rested her cheek against him. No questions. No nagging. He expected them. But she said nothing.

She simply sat with him.

And in doing just that one simple act, she broke him.

"Ah fuck, Emily. Why couldn't you just go?"

"I wouldn't be much of a friend then, would I?"

He shifted to look at her. There was worry on her face. Worry, but no judgment. "Is that what this is, then?"

"Maybe we should stop asking what this is and just accept that I'm here right now. Despite you being an ass." She smiled weakly.

He wanted to reach for her but his bones were frozen. His body refused to obey the want pulsing through him. Because he knew he was going to screw this up, too. It was only a question of how much he was going to hurt her. "Maybe that's more than anyone has ever done for me."

She nuzzled her cheek against his palm. "That's really sad, Reza."

He shook his head. "Not really." A slight frown but she didn't pull away. "I'm not cut out for the role of significant other."

"So you keep saying," she said. "But you were doing well enough. Until tonight, anyway."

"By getting half lit and pouring out my soul?"

"Consider it a bonding experience," she said lightly.

The words he needed were there, just there. Everything. The violence of his father. His fear until he was big enough to take the man on. The pain of the beating when he realized he had to be bigger and stronger to beat the monster inside his dad. He wanted to tell her how the war had made him a man, a man he thought would do the right thing. The nightmares. The death.

A man who turned away from others' demons because his own were too fucking much to deal with. Wisniak deserved his support. Instead, Reza had stood silently by while the younger man broke. He'd never really thought about things from Wisniak's point of view. That the kid had wanted so badly to be a soldier, to not think of himself as a fuckup anymore.

Reza knew that kid. Because he'd been that kid, once upon a time.

And Reza had done nothing, *nothing*, to help him.

Blame and shame and guilt and fear twisted a furious, wild riot inside him.

And the words were stuck in his throat.

He wanted to lay it all out there for her, all the crazy, all the rage and the hate and the madness that threatened to smother him. But it was too much to ask of one person.

He looked away from the compassion in Emily's eyes. It was too bright. He was selfish enough to want to keep her near him so that maybe, just maybe, he could sleep. Which was a completely bullshit fantasy. There wasn't some magic formula that would keep the nightmares at bay. Hell, there wasn't enough alcohol or pills that could keep the nightmares at bay.

"You should go." He scrubbed his hands over his face. "I'm not some special project for you to save."

A sharp intake of breath. A direct hit. "I'm not here because of some noble desire to save you from yourself. I'm here because you're hurting and I care about you. There's nothing more than that."

"Why? So you can see the big sarn't break down? So you can have me as some kind of case study in fucked-up GIs?"

She flinched beneath his anger and the shame squeezed a little tighter on his throat. "That's uncalled for."

"That's exactly what this is!" He shoved away from the couch, staggering to his feet. "I'm not some fucking conquering hero. I'm a goddamned infantryman who is only good at three things in this world: drinking, fucking, and killing. I'm no good at anything else, so if you're looking to save me and break me out at dinner parties as your personal hero, you've got the wrong man."

She opened her mouth to speak but he cut her off. "Don't stand there and tell me this isn't some bizarre fetish about a man in uniform. That maybe you can be a personal hero to the man you claim to care about. I'm not a friend. I'm a fucking project for you."

"If this is the real you, I've been missing out," she said softly, her words a mask of hurt.

"What you see is what you get. I've never hidden that."

"Like you hide your tattoos?" She lifted her chin, defiant, just like the first day he'd met her. "Don't go half asshole. Go all the way to full-blown asshole."

"You don't get it. I don't want someone to save me."

"I'm not here to save you, you ass!" She shot off the couch and stepped right to him. "I'm not here to be your shrink or your fucking head doctor. I'm here because I care about you, you idiot."

"And so what if you do?" He sank down to the coffee table, staring at the empty hands in front of him.

She shocked the ever-loving shit out of him by kneeling in front of him. "When I first met you, I thought you were a powerful man. Intimidating. And you are. But you're more than you give yourself credit for."

"I didn't see Sloban heading for the wall."

"No one can see that."

"Everyone could see that." He jabbed his thumb into his chest. "Except me. I fucking failed him."

"So getting drunk is a great way to atone for that?"

"Fuck you, Emily." He shot to his feet again. "You don't know anything about me."

"You're right. Because you're really good at keeping things light and fun, aren't you? No deep soul searching. Not our boy." She stepped into his space. "Did you ever think that maybe you drink so much because you've been trying so long to be so strong for everyone else, you forgot to take care of yourself?"

Reza opened his mouth to argue but Emily cut him off. "I know about your history. I know what you've been struggling with." She placed her hand over his heart. Right over his mother's name. "I'm here anyway. You said I can't see the real you but you're wrong. This isn't the real you. This isn't the man I care about. But if it's all you can see, I can't fix that for you." She took a single step backward, her heart lodged in her throat.

"Enjoy your bender, Reza. Call me when you want to have an adult conversation."

Chapter Twenty-Two

It had been a week since her fight with Reza. A week she'd tried valiantly to stay busy and ignore the gaping wound somewhere in the vicinity of her heart.

It hurt that he'd walked away so easily from what she thought had been growing between them. She'd avoided the gym, changing her routine to avoid any chance of running into him. But still, when she'd gone for a run out by Engineer Lake, the disappointment that he hadn't been there had stung. It wasn't like she expected him there but a tiny piece of her heart had hoped.

Hoped that he would make the next phone call. That he cared enough to try again.

But her phone had stayed silent and she had thrown herself into work, doing her best to ignore the pain. To try and move on.

It was like Reza Iaconelli had fallen off the planet.

She'd faced the reality that night as she walked out of his life. The cold, dark reality that she'd fallen in love with a man who had a serious alcohol problem. She couldn't enable that.

And it broke her heart not knowing how he was.

She knew the man she'd seen that night was only the façade he put on for the world. Oh, he was big and powerful and intimidating but the man she'd seen that night had been something so much more. So much stronger and yet so much more broken. He was fighting a losing battle.

And he'd been determined to fight it alone.

And it *hurt*.

It hurt that she hadn't been enough for him. That he hadn't let her in. Hadn't trusted her enough to let her stand with him when he'd stood with her.

That he'd pushed her out of his life and that she was left worrying without any answers.

She could get the answers she needed. But it would involve violating every ethical principle she had.

After a week, the need to know pushed even that concern aside.

She'd made up her mind that morning to check his medical records to make sure he was okay. She wasn't going to read them beyond ensuring he had not checked into a hospital or worse. Her skin chilled from the barest hint of the thought.

But she had to know.

She'd simply never done anything like this. It was violating a dozen policy letters, probably the law and everything she was supposed to hold sacred. But the worry ate at her. Tore at her heart until all she could see was the twisted grief on Reza's face.

She just wanted to make sure he hadn't been admitted to the hospital. That he was okay.

It would be enough to assuage the incessant worry. She could move on after that.

She could let him go.

She walked into her office and closed the door behind her. Her hands shook as she opened her laptop and logged on. She held her breath while she logged in and searched for Reza.

Her heart clenched in her chest. No recent hospital visits. That was good. She hoped.

She logged off his information and closed her eyes, wishing her heart didn't feel like it was breaking in her chest.

Reza braced for the worst. He half expected Sarn't Major Giles to take his ID card and rip the rank off his uniform.

But it was so much worse than he expected. The week had ticked by with aching slowness. Each day that there was no phone call summoning him to the colonel's office, the dread had tightened further and further around his heart.

Sarn't Major didn't yell. Didn't scream. He just left Reza standing outside his office at parade rest for more than an hour while he was in with Colonel Horace, discussing Reza's fate.

There were worse feelings in the world, Reza supposed. Getting blown up. Having the shit scared out of you when a rocket missed your truck. But there wasn't much that topped the feeling of sweat trickling down your spine as you waited to find out how your career would end.

The hands on the clock over the secretary's desk ticked by with aching slowness. It felt like dog years just standing there. His shoulders ached but he dared not move because the way his luck had been running, he'd probably move just as Giles opened the door.

He'd made a choice. A hard choice in the shattered glass of a broken vodka bottle.

He didn't think it was going to matter. He'd gone down this road before.

But he had to try.

He could never make up for the hurt he'd caused Emily. He couldn't take that back or make it go away.

He had nothing left. He'd run the one good thing he had out of his life. He'd thought it was the army. He'd thought it was the men he led.

He was wrong.

He'd never felt the aching, burning emptiness like he felt without Emily in his life.

His career was over and none of that mattered.

He'd lost her. He'd driven her out of his life, pushing her until she'd left.

He'd tried to tell himself that was what he wanted. He'd tried to convince himself that he was better off alone, that people were better off if they didn't get too close to him.

But there was a hole inside him now. A chasm.

He could never ask her forgiveness. He didn't deserve that.

But he could clean himself up for good. He could do that. And maybe, someday in the far distant future, he could be man enough to beat back the demons that haunted him.

It was a lifetime before the door opened. Sarn't Major Giles stuck his head out. "Report to the brigade commander."

Reza breathed deeply then knocked on the door loudly. At Colonel Horace's command "Enter!" Reza walked into the office. He stopped three paces from the colonel's desk and saluted.

"Sarn't First Class Iaconelli reporting as ordered, sir."

Colonel Horace returned his salute but did not tell him to stand at ease, leaving Reza rigid at the position of attention.

"Sarn't Ike, you have a problem."

Reza swallowed, remembering the last time he'd been in this office. It had been another commander, another incident. Then, he'd walked out of the office unscathed, his pride mostly intact. "Yes, sir, I do."

Now? Now Reza wasn't so sure.

"I'm not going to read you your rights again, Ike." Horace

looked up at him over the rim of his glasses. "Everything right now is off the record."

Reza resisted the urge to glance at the sergeant major, who stood to one side, arms folded across his chest, one finger curled around a fat, unlit cigar.

"Roger, sir."

"You put on a memorial ceremony, did you not?"

"I did, sir."

"For Specialist Sloban?"

"Yes, sir."

"And you did this, knowing it was the policy of this brigade not to honor those who die by their own hand?" Horace's voice was mild.

"Yes, sir."

"Why?" Horace removed his glasses and set them on the desk. "I encourage you to think carefully how you answer, Sarn't Ike."

"Sir, I've known Sloban since he was a private. He deployed twice with me, once with Bandit Company. He came back wrong this last deployment. Something changed and none of us caught it until it was too late." He cleared his throat. "I didn't catch it. Sloban served with honor, sir. He's a casualty of this war just as much as if he'd died by the enemy's weapon. Sir."

Horace said nothing for a long moment. "Did you get into a physical altercation with your company commander at the memorial ceremony?"

Off the record? He could only hope Horace was telling the truth. "Roger, sir."

"Are you aware that there is an investigation into the command climate in your battalion? That there is a soldier who is currently in the mental health ward who initiated that investigation?"

"I am, sir." Wisniak was staying in the hospital because

of a complication from the cuts on his arms. The kid was going to be okay.

Reza had visited him every day since he'd been admitted.

"What is the command climate in your battalion, Sarn't Iaconelli?"

Deep breath. "Sir, we used to pride ourselves on the strength of our teams. But somewhere along the way, we crossed the line from building strong teams to picking on those weaker than us. We should have been protecting guys like Wisniak and Sloban. Instead, we ostracized them."

"You're including yourself in this." There was amazement in Horace's voice.

"I am, sir."

"Why not just blame the commander?"

"Because I have been part of the problem, Sir."

"Ike, you're painting a damning picture of the environment down there. You're not doing yourself any favors." Sergeant Major Giles's words were a harsh reality.

"Sarn't Major, maybe we need to do something different." One last chance to make a difference.

Colonel Horace glanced up at Sergeant Major Giles. Giles nodded once sharply.

Reza took a deep breath. "Sir, I've been drinking for as long as I can remember." He cleared his throat roughly. "I'm not handling it as well as I need to be. I'm not going to ask for my career, sir. But I'm going to ask to go to inpatient treatment before you put me out of the army." A deep breath, to dislodge the knot in his throat. "I want to get clean. Really clean." Reza swallowed.

Horace folded his arms over his chest. Silence hung in the room. Reza kept his head and eyes locked on a spot over Horace's head. His lungs burned. His throat was tight.

The silence was crushing.

"I can do that." Horace's chair creaked as he leaned

forward. "This is the last chance you will get, Sergeant Iaconelli. Get sober, get your temper under control. Figure out how to unpack all the shit you're carrying around with you that drives you to drink. Because if you can't, your career will come to an inglorious end. I need boys like you in the fight but I cannot and will not allow you to continue on your current path. I will not protect you from yourself. Do I make myself clear?"

"Rog—" he cleared his throat. "Roger, sir."

"Dismissed."

Reza sat in the sergeant major's office, staring at a sheet of paper. In the harsh fluorescent light, it consumed his entire field of vision. A bright, gleaming hope on the steel gray of his desk.

He left for rehab tomorrow. Saturday was the first step on his path to sobriety. Real sobriety.

Granted it was supposedly some swanky place on Lake Austin so it wasn't like he was going to prison.

Except that he'd rather be deployed and getting blown up than go sit in a circle and talk about his feelings. He scrubbed his hand over his face with a frustrated sigh.

But if that's what it took, he was going to do it.

There was a tendril of hope unfurling in his stomach that had little to do with rehab, but it didn't matter. Nothing blocked out the sadness and the sorrow from his fight with Emily.

He wasn't a blackout drinker. It would have taken a hell of a lot more than a few shots of vodka that night to make him forget what he'd done.

He remembered every vivid detail of their fight.

Part of him was glad she'd used her backbone and left. She didn't deserve to have to put up with his shit. Reza was not a nice person; he wasn't even a good man.

Because he did fucked-up shit like throw good people out of his life.

"Fuck," he muttered.

It was a long time before Giles closed the door behind him.

Giles sat and kicked his feet up on his desk and chewed thoughtfully on his cigar. "Captain Loehr turned in his recommendations to the boss."

Reza met his sergeant major's eyes. "And?"

"Let's just say that things are going to change significantly by the time you get back from rehab."

A stone in Reza's throat. "Define change?"

"There will probably be several new folks in leadership positions by the time you get back." Giles scowled at him.

It was a rare thing for Reza to see the sergeant major at a loss for words but for a long moment, Giles just sat there, chewing on the end of his cigar. "So when are you leaving?"

"Tomorrow morning, Sarn't Major." He didn't need to ask where Giles meant. It felt tattooed on Reza's forehead. Rehab.

He pushed aside the twisted nerves.

Giles said nothing for a long moment. "This is going be a good thing for you."

Reza shifted uncomfortably. "You're not going to bare your soul to me, are you, Sarn't Major? 'Cause I've seen you bare enough in the shower and you're not really my type."

"Fuck you, Ike." But there was a glint in Giles's eyes that made Reza think he'd almost gotten a grin out of him. "Look, get your ass in there, clean yourself up, and I'll get you out of the headquarters and back in a line platoon."

Reza looked up sharply. A chance to lead men again. A chance to stay. To be part of the team. The chaos, the noise: that was all part of his normal.

A normal he'd been trying to drown every single time he'd come home from the war.

A normal he wasn't sure he wanted anymore. He sucked in a shaking breath.

The war was simpler than this. Just the war. Rough and gritty and dirty. Covered in mud, dirt ground into his pores.

He looked down at his hands. *Blessed be the Lord my strength, which teaches my hands to war, my fingers to fight.*

He closed his eyes briefly and saw his hands cradling Emily's face, shaping her hips. Regret was a sour taste in his mouth and blocked his throat.

He met Giles's eyes. "Can we talk about that when I get sober, Sarn't Major?"

Giles said nothing for a long moment. "Don't go getting clean and turning into a tree-hugging hippie on me. I need you to teach these kids how to shoot a motherfucker in the face."

"Never, Sarn't Major." Reza stood to go.

"Ike..."

He paused and looked back. "Yeah, Sarn't Major?"

"Nothing. Get yourself fixed. I need you back in the fight."

"Roger that."

He stepped into the ops office. He wanted to ask Evan about the investigation.

He didn't expect to see Claire in his office instead.

Her hair was pulled back tight, her face leaner than he remembered. She looked tired but good. She looked up at him, her eyes glinting dangerously. She rocked back in Evan's chair, folding her arms over her chest.

She looked like she'd just come in from the field. She was wearing her body armor and her hair was plastered to her head. Claire was a consummate warrior and he wondered how someone like Captain America Evan Loehr had managed to tame her.

He wondered where Evan was and why Claire was sitting at his desk.

"So. Rehab again." Oh, but she was looking for a fight. Reza was not in the mood.

"Thanks for telling the entire office."

"There's no one here but us." She rounded the desk, her hands braced on her hips. She was the only woman he knew that could probably kick his ass. "When is it going to end, Reza?"

"Claire, I love you but this time, my life is none of your damn business. I have other shit to worry about than you being pissed at me."

She chewed on her bottom lip for a moment before she turned away, surprising the hell out of Reza. "Fine."

He'd been around long enough to know that Claire not arguing was a portent of bad things to come. "Come on, Claire. Don't be mad."

She turned around. "I'm not mad, Reza." Her voice broke. "You're my best friend. I'm terrified that I'm going to lose you."

He pulled her into his arms in an awkward embrace because of her body armor. "I'm not going anywhere," he said. "I promise."

"I'm really tired of you making her cry." Evan walked into the office. "This shit needs to stop, Reza."

"It's going to," Reza said. He had to try.

Because he couldn't quit. He wouldn't. Evan nodded and with one last glance at Claire, Reza left. He'd hurt her, but then again what else was new?

He held up his hand. Took in the still-healing knuckles, the pink flesh mixed with brown. His skin color had never been an issue for him in the military. His hands had waged war. Caressed women and cradled drinks. The three things he'd told Emily he was good at. His hand shook and he balled it into a fist.

He still had to get through the rest of the day and then set conditions to be out of the office for a month. The company had to keep running while he was gone.

But his thoughts were racing, churning and twisting.

He had a thousand things to do. He wanted to see her but he had no right.

He needed to get clean first. Maybe when he got home, he could go. See if she could forgive him for being an asshole.

That would take a hell of a lot more courage than he currently had.

His hands shook, the hunger clawing at his belly.

To hell with it. Reza was going for a run.

Emily ran because she couldn't concentrate. The clinic was unusually empty today so she took advantage of the clear calendar to head to the gym.

She started toward the treadmill but the idea lost its appeal somewhere near the free weights. Heading for the door, she popped her ear buds in and headed for the trail.

It was hot and sticky. She didn't care. The sun had already started baking the thick brush as she found her stride. She lost herself in the rhythm, the music pounding in her ears, the feel of her feet pounding the earth. The tension in her shoulders disappeared after the first mile as civilization drifted away, leaving her alone with her music and her thoughts.

Rounding a corner, her rhythm was shattered.

Reza was there. On the same trail. Running toward her. Her stomach shattered, her stride faltered.

He met her gaze. Her breath caught in her throat. He was missing his customary long-sleeved shirt. He was missing any shirt.

The man was running on a trail in nothing but loose black shorts that left very little to the imagination. His body gleamed with sweat. The reaper over his chest rose and fell with each hard breath.

He came to a stop a short distance away. An impassable chasm.

The sun bore down on them. In the distance, traffic rolled down East Range Road.

It was Reza who broke the silence.

"How much farther were you planning on going?" he asked.

A truce. Common ground. Okay, she could do that. For now. Just to see where this might lead them.

"Couple more miles."

He rubbed his forearm across his forehead. There was darkness in his eyes. Wicked fear and uncertainty and a myriad of things she couldn't name. "Can I run with you?"

She frowned slightly. There was no apology there, nothing more than a tentative gesture. She could walk away. Probably should, all things considered.

Somehow, none of that seemed important right now.

At that moment, the most important thing in the world to her was that he was there.

That he was okay.

"Sure."

He fell into step beside her and their strides quickly matched. It was strange running with someone else, especially when that someone else was Reza. And since she hadn't seen him in more than a week, her blood was pounding for an entirely different reason.

She was curious. It did nothing to decrease the hurt from their argument but she still felt compelled by this man in a way that she shouldn't allow. And still, she basked in the familiar warmth of just being around him. A sense of protection, of things being right.

Things couldn't be right if he didn't make some important changes. She knew that. She'd always known that.

And her heart had broken when she realized that he was not going to pick up that phone.

His silence had broken her heart.

Her stride faltered.

Reza gripped her arm to keep her from stumbling. She caught herself and kept running. Up a small hill, down an old tank trail. She ran until she emptied herself and focused only on the rhythm of her heart.

Until she was aware of nothing but the beating of her heart and the strength and heat of the man next to her.

She finally stopped at a place that sent her blood pounding with renewed intensity. Engineer Lake, where she'd broken the rules and loved the man next to her in broad daylight.

He stretched his arms over his head as she walked off their run. Silence, comfortable and warm and filled with a thousand words unsaid, hung between them.

Finally, Reza broke the hush.

"I'm an alcoholic, you know."

She swallowed and shifted, unsure of what to do with her hands. They hung limp by her sides as she simply stood. And listened.

"I don't drink downrange. At least, not very often." He snorted quietly. "Too damn hard to get liquor anyway. And it's hell on the nerves trying to have a beer when the base gets blown up."

She said nothing.

"I was six the first time my father put my mother in the hospital," he said quietly. "I was twelve before a judge ordered him to rehab before he killed my mother with his drinking." He breathed deeply. "He killed her anyway." His breath shuddered. "I don't remember the first time I drank. But I remember the first time I got drunk."

She watched him quietly, letting him speak. Unsure of what she would say. Of what she could say. She knew his father had beaten his mother.

She hadn't known it had defined everything about his young life.

Her heart broke in her chest for the boy he'd been.

"It wasn't the war that fucked with my head but that's a big part of it. I was wild way before I joined the army." He swiped his arm across his forehead. "I've always thought I had everything under control."

"Until you didn't."

He nodded grimly. "Until I didn't." He stepped into her space. She didn't step away. He lifted his hands. Hesitated. Then rested them on her shoulders. The reaper on his chest flexed and twisted as he moved.

"I'm sorry I hurt you," he whispered.

Chapter Twenty-Three

She turned away, slipping out of his grip easily. She walked to the water's edge.

Reza said nothing. He looked down at his hands again. Empty. More used to holding a rifle than a woman.

"I left home because I wanted something to believe in. There's no deep emotional trauma in my life, no dark secrets. Just a scumbag ex and a best friend who turned out not to be." Emily turned to face him.

"Which is exactly why you shouldn't be with me. You should be with some normal, well-adjusted man who can take care of you, love you." He swallowed. "Make a family with you." He met her gaze. "I'm not that man, Emily. I said it badly the other night but it's true."

"So you're breaking things off because I'm not screwed up enough?"

A sharp, bitter laugh. "That's one way of putting it."

She shook her head, biting her lips. Her eyes filled with sadness. "So what now?"

Reza dropped his gaze. His hands clenched by his sides. "I'm going to rehab, Emily." A tortured whisper. An admission ripped from his darkest fears. War was easier than coming home. So much simpler.

"Why?"

He held out his arms. The names and the places tattooed into his skin spoke for him. He lifted his gaze to hers. "Because I don't know what I'm doing anymore. The war is . . . simple. You go over there, you patrol. You hope to come home. But here at home? I don't know what I'm doing. I'm lost. I don't know how to take care of soldiers' lives, not like this." He glanced away before forcing himself to look at her once more.

A smarter woman would have left him alone. Would have kept on running away—toward her home and the remnants of her career.

He sighed hard. "I'm in a lot of trouble. I have been since before I met you."

"I know." She caught his hand between both of hers. "I won't be with you unless you want to get better, though. I can't enable you."

He shook his head. "Sometimes I have my first drink before ten a.m. I feel normal when I drink." He refused to meet her gaze.

"Deployments must be hell, huh?"

"You have no idea." He laughed bitterly. "I'm baring my soul to you and you're making jokes."

"Just stating the obvious. I've seen you drinking, Reza. If you're trying to run me off because you have a problem, I've got news for you. We're all a little screwed up. And last time I checked, no one expected you to be perfect."

"No, just sober. Which I have a hell of a time pulling off."

"Do you want to be sober?" she asked softly, tracing her thumb against the palm of his hand.

He met her gaze once more. "I don't know how."

"You've done it downrange."

"But there is a shitload of adrenaline and stuff to do to keep me busy. After I get through the DTs, that is."

"I did a paper on the detox process. It's awful."

"Nothing quite like feeling like you're losing your mind. Wondering if the spiders crawling up your skin are real or not." He scoffed quietly. "Makes for a really interesting first thirty days in-country, that's for sure."

"How many times have you deployed?"

"Six. Five times to Iraq, once to Afghanistan."

"Did you detox each time?"

"Yeah." Shame colored his eyes now, twisted in the harsh line of his lips. "I want to be a better man." He looked up at her. "I never wanted to hurt you, Emily."

Silence was thick and sticky between them, clinging to their skin.

It was Emily who moved.

"You held me when I needed to be held. You've been there for me more than anyone else in my entire life and I've only known you a short while. If that's what you call using someone, I'd hate to see what happens when you really care for someone." She stepped into his space, lifting her hands to his cheeks. "The day I met you, you were so determined, so strong." He tried to look away but she held him. Met his gaze with a fierceness of her own. "You've been taking care of soldiers at war for so long, maybe it's time someone took care of you."

"I don't want to be taken care of," he whispered. "That's not how I'm wired."

"Then how about letting someone stand with you?" Her thumb caressed his cheek. "I don't want to be your doctor. I don't want to be the only adult in this relationship." She lifted her mouth to his, brushing her lips against his. "But I'll stand with you, if you'll let me."

"Why?"

"Because I believe in you. Screwed up and angry, you're still the best man I know."

He scoffed quietly. "You don't know many good men."

"I've met a lot of men this year. Men who are supposed to be leaders but who are bullies instead." A caress. "You're a better man than all of them."

He shook his head. "I'm just a washed-up GI."

"Well, when you wash something, it comes out clean." She smiled gently and Reza shook his head with a smile that felt real.

"That was really corny."

"Yeah, I know. But it made you smile."

Words escaped him. His throat went dry. Emotion squeezed air from his lungs.

He crushed her to him and as long as he lived, he would forever remember the feel of her arms sliding around his waist and holding him. Just holding him.

Standing with him.

Epilogue

He had no idea how to do this. Reza sat in the back of the van that was bringing him home from the rehab center. Thirty days he'd been gone. Thirty days he'd learned how to be sober. Not for a day or a week.

For a lifetime.

It was easy, in the sterile environment of the clinic. There was no stress. No phone calls in the middle of the night. No sergeant major stepping on his neck.

But all of that was over now.

All of that changed the minute the van stopped in front of the headquarters and let him out.

There was a terrible taste in his mouth. A dryness that no matter how much water he drank, he couldn't moisten.

Emily had promised to be there to pick him up.

And he was terrified.

Terrified that he would fail. Terrified that he would hurt her again.

Terrified that he wasn't man enough to beat this addiction.

That he wasn't man enough to be worthy of the faith she had in him.

The sun was sinking into the Central Texas hills and

still he sat in the back of the van, unable to take that first step.

He couldn't remember the last time he'd been as nervous as he was sitting in the back of the van, staring at his hands, waiting for her.

It felt like an eternity before she pulled into the head-quarters parking lot. It was a Saturday. She stepped out of the car in jeans and a plain white t-shirt.

Her hair was down, framing her face in soft chestnut. There was a wariness in her eyes, a smile on her lips.

Her eyes warmed as she approached the van. He slung his backpack over his shoulder and slid across the old bench seat.

He stood there, paralyzed as she came closer. Close enough to touch.

He reached up, cupping her cheek, embarrassed that his hand shook. "You came."

Reza blinked rapidly and clenched his fists, brushing her cheek with his knuckles. Steadier. At least a little bit.

"Of course I did."

She took a step closer, sliding her arms around his waist, molding her body to his. He could smell the soft sunshine smell of her hair. Felt its silk against his cheek. He hesitated, not trusting himself to move, to take that last step and hold her in his arms.

It was stepping into something bigger than himself that wasn't the war. It was a step toward healing the wounds that a lifetime of fighting had left on his soul.

Finally, he closed his arms around her. Pulling her close until there was nothing between them. No space, no dis-tance. Nothing but time and too many clothes.

"You came," he whispered again.

She leaned up, her eyes filled with shimmering tears as she met his. "Oh ye of little faith," she whispered.

They stood that way for a long moment. Until the van pulled away and they were alone in the parking lot as the sun sank below the hill country.

"Are you hungry?" she asked after a long silence.

He nodded, unwilling to let her go. Terrified that she would disappear. "Missed lunch."

"You're in luck. I made spaghetti. It's one of my signature dishes."

He tipped his chin, adjusting his backpack as it started to drop down his shoulder. "You have signature dishes?"

"There are several that I am really, really good at making." She slipped the pack off his shoulder. His blood warmed from her touch. "We should get you home."

Home. Such a foreign concept. He'd had so many places to lay his head. He never really thought of any of them as home before.

She lifted her face to his. "How hungry are you?" she whispered against his lips.

"Starved," he murmured before claiming her mouth.

He crushed her with his urgency. Pulled her against him until their bodies were fitted together. Until she breathed for him and him for her. Her fingers fisted in the short hair on his head, her body arching into his.

It was Emily who pulled back. "Home?"

His lips quivered. "Home."

They talked of inconsequential things on the short ride to her place. He would tell her about rehab some other time, but he would talk to her.

He'd spent too much time shutting out people who cared.

He wouldn't shut her out. Not again. Not ever.

They made it home before he pulled her to him. Before he kissed her like a dying man and held her like she was the only thing anchoring him to this world.

Because she was.

He stripped her clothes from her body, needing her far more than the air he breathed. They fumbled with belts and boots until they were both naked in the middle of her living room floor. Until he paused, just there, and looked down at her.

Her hair spread out beneath her. Her lips were swollen and flushed. But it was her eyes that whispered the truth he'd been afraid to see. Her lips that formed the words he'd never heard.

He slid deep and slow, her whispered words a breath against his ear. "I love you, Reza."

He moved inside her, his answering words lost in her hair, in the intense wave of emotion that overwhelmed him. It was more than passion, more than simple pleasure.

It was a joining.

He shattered with her, tumbling into the abyss that for once was not filled with darkness and terror and regret.

She lost herself in the paradise of his arms, his whispered words capturing her heart.

His big strong arms, marked with the names of lives he'd lost, places he'd bled, held her gently. And it was his whisper, quiet on the stillness of her home, that snared her heart forever.

"I love you, Emily," he said, cradling her face in his hands. A kiss against her lips, their bodies joined. "I love you." Surprise in his voice.

She kissed him. And held him. Vowing that she would stand with him. Always.

"I'm afraid."

Her arms tightened around his waist. "I know."

He didn't give voice to the fear that she might not have been standing there when he got off the bus. That everything would turn out to be another haunting dream, tormenting him with things he could not have. He kissed her gently, pouring a thousand unsaid words into that kiss. He wrapped his arms tight around her and held her against his chest, breathing in the scent of her hair.

"The docs said this wasn't going to be easy." Fear choked his words.

"It won't be." Her arms tightened around his waist. "But you won't be alone." She pressed her lips to his.

"I won't let you down," he said against her mouth.

It was that promise that took him through the long days and longer nights. A promise. But it was more than her promise that kept his strength. It was his own promise to be a better man, to be a stronger man. A promise to be a man who was worthy of her love.

It was a promise worth going through hell to keep.

Dear Reader,

This book was difficult for me to write. Suicide is an epidemic facing our force, and try though we might, we are no closer to stopping it or understanding it than we were before the wars started.

This book is not meant as an indictment of our men and women in uniform or the military that we serve or the thousands of leaders who do the right thing every day and try to take care of their soldiers.

If you know someone who is hurting, if you suspect someone is having a hard time, ask them. Don't be afraid. Speak up. Ask the question. Because you never know what someone else is going through.

And you might just make a difference.

Sincerely,
Jessica Scott

Captain Ben Teague hates the administrative BS of company command, until a legal case puts him up against Major Olivia Hale. She is as by the book as a lawyer gets, but there's something simmering beneath that icy reserve—and Ben just can't resist turning up the heat...

Please see the next page for a preview of

It's Always Been You.

Prologue

Northern Baghdad

FOB War Eagle 2005

Is this hell? Because it feels like hell." Second Lieutenant Ben Teague swiped his sleeve across his forehead and accomplished absolutely nothing. Sweat still dripped steadily down his forehead as he walked the perimeter of their tiny combat outpost with his platoon sergeant.

"Don't start complaining about the air conditioner again." Next to him, SFC Escoberra scowled at him.

Ben smirked and patted Sarn't Escoberra on his shoulder. It was so easy to get his platoon sergeant irritated. "I was not going to mention the a/c. What makes you think I'd do such a thing?"

"Fuck off, LT." Escoberra looked down the alley toward the city that hated them. It was a shit position, as shit positions went. Nothing quite like being alone and unafraid on the battlefield.

"Easy there, big fella. Didn't mean to get your PTSD all riled up."

Escoberra snarled and Ben grinned. "You're in a lovely mood. Don't tell me you're cranky about this lovely little mission, too?"

"Don't start, LT."

"What? We can barely defend our position, we don't have enough ammo, and we're not serving any purpose other than to hold some piece of real estate down. The commander can't even give me a good reason for us to be out here."

Beside him, Escoberra sighed heavily and lifted his weapon, checking the field of fire. "LT, you need to quit pissing and moaning about this. The men are going to hear you."

Ben sobered and snapped his mouth closed. His platoon sergeant was right. It wasn't good to let the boys hear the leadership arguing about the mission. "Let's change the subject to something less depressing. How's the family?"

Escoberra's eyes crinkled at the edges. "My wife seems to think our almost twelve-year-old daughter needs a personal trainer."

Ben coughed, trying to hide a laugh. "Yeah, 'cause that's all you need is to think about your daughter getting smoking hot while you're deployed."

"Not funny. I'm not ready for her to grow up yet and she's not even mine," Escoberra said quietly. "I love that little kid. I swear to God if some raging hard-on hurts her..."

"No boy is going to dare come around with you there."

"That's the problem. I'm not there," Escoberra said. "I'm stuck here."

Ben adjusted the strap on his weapon then toed the concertina wire strung across a low concrete barrier. "Does her dad ever come into the picture?"

"Nah. He's out of the picture. I'm not complaining, though. She might not be mine by blood but she's family by every other way that matters." Escoberra glanced down the road. "And speaking of the commander, guess who's coming to the family dinner for a site visit later tonight?"

Ben rubbed his eyes beneath his sunglasses and let out a hard sigh of frustration. "I don't want to deal with the fucking commander. I'd rather deal with my mother."

Escoberra snorted. "What's wrong with your mother now?"

"The Almighty Colonel Diane Teague called the battalion commander and tried to get me moved to go take an executive officer job. Fuck that, man. I don't want to count pens and toilet paper." Ben wiped his gloved hand over his forehead, looking out over the edge of the barrier on the roof. Their single building stronghold wasn't exactly an impenetrable fortress but at least it provided a nice view of the city. When things were getting blown all to hell around them.

"She's just trying to look out for your career."

"My mom needs to worry about her part of the war and let me worry about mine." Grit scraped over his skin. "Fuck, man, moms are supposed to bake cookies and kiss your booboo when it hurts. Mine eats napalm and pisses razor wire."

"You never struck me as the kind of guy who had mommy issues," Escoberra said.

"Screw you, man. I don't. I was just saying I'd rather deal with her than the commander. The commander is a pain in my ass that can get me killed as opposed to just a pain in the ass. See the difference?" Ben spat into the dirt, not actually wanting to delve into talking about his mother. He shouldn't have brought it up. "We need to get ready to head out on patrol. Maybe I can avoid the commander if I'm too busy getting shot at."

"Play nice, LT. I'm tired of the first sergeant running a wire brush over my ass because of you constantly fighting with the commander. You're a lieutenant, he's your boss. You don't get to tell him how you really feel about things," Escoberra said. His words were mild but beneath the calm was a temper. Ben knew this firsthand, and as much as he liked screwing with Escoberra, he also knew his limits.

He wasn't entirely sure that Escoberra wouldn't take his head off if given the right provocation. "Think of it as an exfoliation treatment," Ben said after a while.

After an impossible silence, Escoberra finally glanced at him, then looked back out toward the endless, dusty city. It was too quiet out there. "The sun is getting to you. You should drink water."

Ben bit his bottom lip where it had split sometime during their last firefight. It opened again with the movement and warm, coppery blood coated his tongue. He spat into the dirt. "It's a hundred and twenty-six degrees. Of course the sun is getting to me." He adjusted his body armor, itching to go out on patrol and *do* something. "Tell me again why we're hanging out here?"

"Waiting for the bad guys to drive right by." Escoberra pointed at a white pickup that zipped by the end of the road, then stopped. Two faces peered out at them.

Ben's stomach flipped beneath his ribs. His heart started racing in his chest. "You're really fucking scary sometimes with that warrior intuition shit you've got going on."

Escoberra palmed the butt stock of his weapon. "Call it in. Get air support en route. This could get ugly."

But Ben didn't get the chance. A brilliant flash of heat seared across his skin a second before the boom knocked him on his ass.

And then all hell broke loose.

Chapter One

Fort Hood, 2009

Four years later

Captain Ben Teague prayed to the caffeine gods and waited for the espresso machine to dispense the morning sacrifice. He'd never really considered why an infantry battalion had an espresso machine in the middle of the battalion operations office but right then, he wanted to kiss the man who'd had the foresight to buy it and keep it well-stocked with beans.

Somehow, he didn't think that Sergeant Major Cox would appreciate the gesture.

It was four-thirty in the morning on a Monday and someone had had the good idea to call an alert. Which meant that instead of getting to sleep like a normal person, Ben and everyone else in this clusterfuck of a battalion had dragged their carcasses on post at the ass crack of dawn.

Ben was liable to stab someone if he didn't get coffee stat.

Funny, he'd actually thought he was going to finally get some sleep when he'd actually nodded off. But as usual, it had all been a tease. The phone had yanked him out of that fog between sleep and waking. Damn it, he was getting caffeine before the morning briefing.

He kicked his New Kids on the Block trucker hat higher up on his head and counted to ten while the espresso machine ground the beans, then dispensed the precious liquid.

The warning light flashed red and the steady stream of espresso dripped to a halt. Ben wanted to cry.

"It needs water, sir."

"Thank you, Captain Obvious." Ben shot Sergeant Dean Foster a baleful look then jerked his thumb toward the espresso machine, saying nothing further. He wasn't in the mood to deal with Foster's smart-ass comments this morning. Not when Ben's sense of irony was still hung over from the night before.

"Did someone wake up on the wrong side of the bed?" Foster asked, taking the lid off the reservoir. "Do you need a hug?"

"No jokes before caffeine. Off with you, minion." Ben narrowed his eyes then waved his hands. "Now to figure out why the hell we're here at this ungodly hour," Ben muttered.

Not that it mattered. Ben had long ago given up trying to change things. And to think, once upon a time, he'd thought he could make a difference.

What a miserable joke.

"Teague, I don't give a flying fuck how much you were abused as a child, if you don't get that goddamned hat off in my building…"

"Good morning to you, too, sunshine," Ben said to the battalion sergeant major. Any day he could get the sergeant major's goat was a good day. It was one of life's few pleasures.

"Teague, one of these days…"

Someday, that would backfire on him. Until then, though… "We'll go take a long hot shower together and you can tell me your childhood traumas?"

Sarn't Major swung at him but Teague ducked. His hat wasn't so lucky. Cox grabbed it and tore the thin white mesh in half. Sarn't Major Cox was five and a half feet tall and about as wide, and none of it was fat.

"Oh come on!" Ben threw his arms up in mock disgust. "It took me at least four hours of surfing the Internet to find that hat."

Cox held up a single finger then balled his hand into a fist around Ben's hat. Cox balled up the hat and threw it at Ben's chest. "We've got brothers and sisters who died in this uniform. How about you start treating it with some fucking honor?" he growled as he stormed by. "Get your sorry ass in the conference room. You've got a meeting with the boss in twenty minutes."

Ben ground his teeth looking down at the rank on his gray uniform. Honor?

Ben knew all about it. It didn't get you anywhere.

Foster walked back in, carefully carrying the water. "Mission accomplished?"

"Yep. Right on target. And I even did it before coffee." Ben sighed. "What's going on?"

Foster shrugged. "No clue but there's a line of dudes outside the battalion commander's office right now."

Ben frowned. "Huh?"

"'Bout fifteen dudes lined up in the hallway." Foster said, jerking his thumb over his shoulder.

"No shit?"

Ben walked out of the office and turned down the hall toward the conference room. Foster wasn't kidding. There were sergeants and officers from every company in the battalion. Ben couldn't remember the last time he'd seen a line like this outside the boss's office.

Ben stopped short, his breath caught in his throat. Escoberra stood near the front. His arms were folded at parade rest, his palms resting at the small of his back. He stood solid and unmoving. Ben stood there, frozen. Escoberra shifted. For a moment their eyes locked and for a the briefest flicker, Ben saw the warrior he'd admired and looked up to when he'd been a scrappy, smart-assed lieutenant. Before he'd failed to defend a man he'd have followed to hell and back again.

Escoberra was still a warrior. It was Ben who had changed. Ben who had let the time and the bad memories drive him away from a man who'd been as close to a father figure as Ben could have asked for.

There were shadows in his former platoon sergeant's eyes now. Deep and dark.

Ben took a deep breath. A single step toward a man he admired and looked up to. Heat crawled up the back of Ben's neck. He wanted to speak, to say something to the man who'd saved his ass more times than he could remember.

"Escoberra!" The sergeant major's voice rang out. Escoberra ground his teeth and looked away, before he snapped to the position of attention and disappeared into the sergeant major's office.

It took everything Ben had to stand there while Escoberra walked away. He wanted to ask how the family was. How he was doing since the last deployment.

But Ben let him go. Because to say anything would be to acknowledge that the man in that hallway had changed. Ben didn't know if it was the war, if it was some fucked-up trauma, but the war had changed him, changed them all.

And Ben no longer knew the man in that hallway. Shame burned on his neck, the weight of his failure heavy around his shoulders.

Ben broke into a wide grin as he walked into the conference room and saw an old familiar face. "Holy shitballs!"

Captain Sean Nichols looked up from his BlackBerry, his

dark expression going from guarded to grinning the moment he recognized Ben. "Holy shit, you're not in jail?"

"Very funny." Ben gripped his old friend's hand and pulled him into a one-armed man hug. "Some things never change. What are you doing here?"

"Looking for a job, apparently," Sean said.

Ben frowned. "Huh?"

"Supposedly there's some command positions opening up soon." Nichols ran his hand over the back of his neck. "I'm supposed to interview today but there's some massive shitstorm going on."

"Yeah, I saw that. Where have you been?"

"Iraq, Afghanistan, and back again." Sean nodded toward the other officers in the room. There was a big dude in one corner who looked like a professional wrestler, talking with one of the first sergeants. "These all your guys?"

"Nope. Never seen any of them before," Ben said.

The battalion commander, Lieutenant Colonel Gilliad, walked in, followed by Sarn't Major Cox and a small brunette major Ben had never seen before. She walked stiff and straight, and her hair was pulled back sharply from her face. Her right sleeve was missing a combat patch. Ben found himself wondering how she had been in the army long enough to be a major but had somehow managed to miss the war.

He didn't look away as she scanned the room, her eyes cool and appraising.

Ben wasn't fooled. He'd seen that look far too many times.

She was a woman on a mission. Just what they needed: a lawyer on crusade. Ben didn't do crusades.

They all snapped to attention as the commander walked to the center of the room.

"Gentlemen, welcome to Death Dealer Battalion. Congratulations. Every one of you in this room will take command in less than a month," Gilliad said.

Silence hung in the heavens for half a moment. No one moved. No one spoke.

Ben breathed in deep and slow, keeping the ragged edge of his emotions in check. "Uh, sir, I think there's a mistake."

Gilliad pinned him with a hard look. Next to him, the major looked down at her paperwork, shaking her head, disapproval written on her pretty face.

"Teague, I'll see you in my office." Gilliad turned back to the other captains. "Bello, you and First Sarn't Delgado have Diablo Company. Martini, you and First Sarn't Tellhouse have Assassin Company. Teague, your first sergeant will be here before the week is out. You're taking Bandit Company. Navarro, you and First Sarn't Sagarian are taking Headquarters Company. Nichols, you and First Sarn't Morgan are taking Chaos Company."

"Sir—"

"Let the commander finish, Captain Teague," Sarn't Major Cox warned quietly.

Ben ground his teeth and fought the anxiety twisting in his guts.

Gilliad cleared his throat. "Every company command team in this battalion has been relieved of their duties effective immediately. You all are the new team. Major Hale is going to help with transition on the legal side of the house. We have our hands full, gentlemen, and I expect you to clean house and get this unit back to fully mission ready."

Ben blew out a low whistle. He'd never heard of something like this. Not in his entire life as a military brat or his own career. One commander, maybe two in rapid succession, but an entire battalion worth of company leadership fired on the spot?

And Gilliad expected Ben to be one of the new commanders? Not in this lifetime.

Gilliad continued. "The forward support company leadership is changing out as well. That new command team will be on the ground shortly as soon as the support battalion figures out who that will be." He glanced over at the small major. "Major Hale has my guidance. Your number one priority for the next forty-five days is getting rid of the shitbag soldiers running this unit into the ground. I want the druggies gone. I want the dealers and the gangbangers gone. I want the fucking criminals out of my army. Am I clear?"

A murmured *hooah* went through the gathered men.

Ben couldn't speak.

His lungs had stopped working.

Command.

He didn't want this. He couldn't do it.

There had to be a mistake. The boss could find someone else.

He had to.

Because to command, you still had to believe what you did mattered. He released a shuddering breath.

And Ben hadn't believed that in a long, long time.

Major Olivia Hale watched the captain at the edge of the room. His back was stiff and straight and he radiated unspent fury. She wondered at the tired lines beneath his eyes, the hard set of his jaw.

He was so furious at being told he was taking command. The rest of the men had stiffened with awareness. Excitement. Command was the greatest reward for an officer's hard work—a chance to lead soldiers and make a difference. Olivia would command in a heartbeat if she could. Successful commanders made their units better places.

Why didn't this dark and angry captain want the job?

She lifted her chin. Whether or not the pissed-off captain took the job wasn't her problem. Her job was to help clean up this unit. She'd been asked personally to assist by the division commander—she'd been on his staff many moons ago when she'd been a brand-new shiny lieutenant and she'd loved working for him. He'd been decisive. He'd been a mentor.

She hadn't been able to say no when he'd asked her to help this battalion.

"Gentlemen, I need time with each of you to go over the current status of your legal situations." She pointed to the stacks of folders in front of her. "I've got each company's information here. Please take your files and look them over before you come see me."

Gilliad nodded once in her direction. "Olivia is the best at what she does. We are going to clean this battalion up."

The angry captain shifted and she saw his nametag. Teague.

"Motherfucker," he muttered, loud enough for the entire room to hear.

"Teague!" Sarn't Major Cox exploded but LTC Gilliad held up his hand.

"In my office. Now, Captain."

Teague shoved off the wall and stalked out of the conference room, followed closely by the battalion commander.

She watched him go, her gaze hanging on the man struggling with such fierce resentment at being given a great honor. What kind of man interrupted his battalion commander?

What kind of man was so angry at the chance to be a leader?

She pushed her thoughts away. He was not her problem. She focused on the men in front of her as they stopped by the conference room table.

A tall, lean captain with dark hair and green eyes stopped near the table. "Sean Nichols, ma'am. Do we have any discretion in these cases?"

"What kind of discretion are you talking about, Captain Nichols?"

"In general. Do we get to say this kid did a dumb thing and he deserves a second chance?"

There was nothing Olivia could say. She knew there was a difference between the right answer and the legal answer, and even the army answer. "That's going to be a conversation between you and the battalion commander."

The tall captain nodded once and left, and after another moment, Olivia was alone in the conference room with the sergeant major.

She didn't quite know what to think of Sergeant Major Cox. He was her height but stocky and he looked mean as hell. She definitely wasn't used to his kind outside of the hospital headquarters where she used to work.

"Things are going to get rough around here, ma'am," he said after a long silence. His voice sounded like gravel and rocks.

"I'm not sure I understand what you mean."

"You start taking away people's livelihoods and things start getting tense. So while I have no doubt that the new command teams can handle things, just watch yourself around here. Don't hesitate to let me know if you're having problems with any soldier."

"Thank you for the warning," she said, not wanting to alienate the command sergeant major. "I've seen the misconduct you have down in this battalion, Sergeant Major. The quantity doesn't even come close to some of the terrible things I've seen."

"I hope you're right." Cox rubbed his hand over his mouth. "One more thing. You see that?"

He pointed toward a black cowboy hat with gold cord wrapped around the base that he'd carried in with him. "Yes?"

"Get one. You can't be assigned here without it."

She smiled flatly. "I'll add it to my to-do list."

She couldn't care less about the silly hat, but she just smiled and nodded and headed to her next meeting.

She was here to do a job, not buy a hat and the swagger that went along with it.

Fall in Love with Forever Romance

LAST CHANCE FAMILY
by Hope Ramsay

Mike Taggart may be a high roller in Las Vegas, but is he ready to take a gamble on love in Last Chance? Fans of Debbie Macomber, Robyn Carr, and Sherryl Woods will love this sassy and heartwarming story from *USA Today* bestselling author Hope Ramsay.

SUGAR'S TWICE AS SWEET
by Marina Adair

Fans of Jill Shalvis, Rachel Gibson, and Carly Phillips will enjoy this sexy and sweet romance about a woman who's renovating her beloved grandmother's house—even though she doesn't know a nut from a bolt—and the bad boy who can't resist helping her... even as she steals his heart!

Fall in Love with Forever Romance

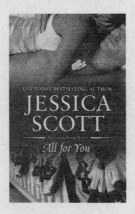

ALL FOR YOU
by Jessica Scott

Fans of JoAnn Ross and Brenda Novak will love this poignant and emotional military romance about a battle-scarred warrior who fears combat is the only escape from the demons that haunt him, and the woman determined to show him that the power of love can overcome anything.

DELIGHTFUL
by Adrianne Lee

Pie shop manager Andrea Lovette always picks the bad boys, and no one is badder than TV producer Ice Erickksen. Andrea knows she needs to find a good family man, so why does this bad boy still seem like such a good idea? Fans of Robyn Carr and Sherryl Woods will eat this one up!

Fall in Love with Forever Romance

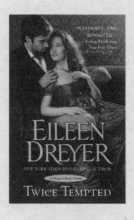

TWICE TEMPTED
by Eileen Dreyer

As two sisters each discover love, *New York Times* bestselling author Eileen Dreyer delivers twice the fun in her newest of the Drake's Rakes Regency series, which will appeal to fans of Mary Balogh and Eloisa James.

A BRIDE FOR
THE SEASON
by Jennifer Delamere

Can a wallflower and a rake find happily ever after in each other's arms? Jennifer Delamere's Love's Grace trilogy comes to a stunning conclusion.